BOOK ONE OF THE STARBLOOD TRILOGY

STARBLOOD

Carmilla Voiez

Starblood

This book is sold subject to the condition that it shall not, by way of trade or otherwise, be lent, re-sold, duplicated, hired out, or otherwise circulated without the publisher's prior written consent in any form of binding or cover other than that in which it is published and without similar condition including this condition being imposed on the subsequent purchaser.

©Text Copyright 2011 Carmilla Voiez

This is a work of fiction. All characters and events portrayed in this novel are fictitious and are products of the author's imagination and any resemblance to actual events, or locales or persons, living or dead are entirely coincidental.

Cover by: Paul Grover
Edited by: Richard Findley,
Vanessa Knipe, and That Editor Chick

Starblood was my debut novel in 2011 and is set in 2005. It is an angry book that I wrote during the breakdown of my second marriage. Writing it was a large part of my healing, and I hope reading these pages will help you heal as well. At the very least, know that you are not alone in your pain.

I dedicate Starblood to my wonderful daughters, and the readers and publishers who have believed in me and allowed me to grow, including Rick, Nicola, Sarah, and Karmin. Thank you to my beta readers: Ricky, Ann, Vanessa, and Susan whose encouragement and guidance mean more to me than they may ever know.

Recommended Reading Order

Starblood
Psychonaut
The Death and Resurrection Show

Trigger Warnings

The Starblood Trilogy deals with potentially distressing topics including mental illness, depression, self-harm, suicide, murder, sexual assault, castration, rape, incest, drug references. Please be aware that this list may not be exhaustive.

STARBLOOD

CHAPTER ONE

SATORI STANDS in the centre of his bedroom. His fragile looking, angular body is lost in the forest of writing that expands around him— a web of ancient knowledge. His fingers and the lace cuffs of his shirt are stained from the charcoal he uses to scribble symbols. Markings cover every surface: the bare floorboards, ceiling, and walls. Even his wardrobe and door are covered in intricate black sigils.

He unbuttons his shirt, swearing as he leaves fingerprints on the cotton. After tossing the garment on his bed, he unzips his jeans and forces the denim down his legs to the floor. Standing naked, he smells himself. There is no trace of her scent on his body and realising this feels like losing her all over again.

He pulls silver rings from his fingers, removes the hoops from his left ear and the silver stud from his pointed nose. His jewellery jingles like tiny bells as he lets it fall, scattering like distant stars across the midnight duvet. On his pillow, dozens of photographs lie like fallen leaves; some are intact, but most are torn or defaced. Her face holds his thoughts for a moment: pale, perfect, and framed by a mass of ebony curls.

He shakes his head to clear her image. After this is over, he will make her love him again. A wolfish grin grows across his face at the thought of Star on her knees, begging him to take her back. He licks his lips. His face feels hot, his body cold, but despite his impatience, his desire to complete the ritual and achieve his goal, he waits. He sucks air through his nostrils and collects his thoughts— he must not rush; he must keep control of himself and his desires.

He draws the same glyphs on his body, starting with his toes and the soles of his feet then moving upward with practised dexterity. Charcoal drags against his skin, which blossoms pink below each mark. The growing tattoo obscures his features while the tips of his fingers prickle with energy.

Although he knows what he needs to say, he reads the passage again, draws two circles on the floor, and steps into one of them. With the fingers of his right hand, he traces a pentagram in the air before him and recites the words, pronouncing each syllable with care.

'… This is my will,' he says finally.

Lifting a silver dagger above his head, he concentrates. An excited grin spreads across his graffiti-covered face and with tremendous force, he plunges the knife downward, severing the air in front of him. Through the tear, he glimpses swirls of darkness: Chaos. He calls to Furfur, creator of love between man and woman, to share with him his demon's power, so he can win Star back.

A long, slender leg steps through the gap, followed by a lily-white body. The interloper is female, naked, and hairless.

'I am Satori.' His voice quivers with fear and excitement. He coughs and tries to speak with more authority. 'I have brought you—'

'Brought me? I think not. I saw the door and came to meet the fool who caused it to open.' Her emerald eyes are full of contempt.

Satori's confidence withers. Malice thickens the air like gelatine, and the demon's aura chills the room. Although, he suspects it is fear rather than the cold that makes his body shake and his bones rattle. Staring at her in silence, he realises he has made an error. *What went wrong?* Instead of Furfur, contained and compelled to do his bidding, ready to elevate him back into the arms of his beloved, he is faced with something else, something threatening. He raises his dagger above him again, ready to expel her before it is too late.

She knocks the dagger away with the back of her hand. 'I am

your guest not your minion, and you will not dismiss me.'

Satori falls to the floor, nursing his wrist. Thousands of drawings swim before his eyes as she steps into view, pale feet smudging his glyphs.

He watches, transfixed, as her white toes sharpen into points and black ectoplasm spreads over them and the sides of her feet until they meet at the back to form a shiny slipper. Her heels rise, and her feet arch as stiletto heels stretch beneath the soles. Spellbound, he watches the same process in action across every part of her body. A leather corset grows over her chest and stomach, and with each moment, the material becomes more defined like a rapid rewinding of decomposition; five red trimmed straps emerge from the black leather, each with a silver buckle at the centre. Lace panties spread over her crotch, obscuring the shock of red hair. Over the underwear, a shiny black mini skirt forms, skimming her thighs. Her face is painted; her crimson lips match the shade of her luxurious hair; her closed eyes sprout thick, black lashes; above these, perfect eyebrows arch toward her delicate nose. When she opens her eyes again, Satori's body responds to her beauty.

She laughs. 'I am not yours, magician.' Cold, green eyes sweep around the room, her body flexes and tightens, and a frown creases her forehead and chin. 'Open the door.'

'Who are you?' His voice carries no authority, and he's surprised that she answers.

'Lilith.' She strides toward the door as if she has already forgotten he is there.

'No! I have to send you back.' It is a moot point, but he feels better for making it. He must not let her see his powerlessness.

She turns to him. Crouched on the floor, he feels her judgement. He tries to stand, but under the power of her scorn, his limbs are like liquid. She moves like quicksilver. He has never seen a body, human or feline, move as gracefully or effortlessly. Fear strengthens his resolve; he takes a deep breath and tries to rise. The mocking smile on her face makes his stomach twist and tighten. He feels anger at her dismissal of his power, yet his penis aches for her, rebelling against his will.

'These symbols,' she says, 'will not hold me.'

She opens her hand and places her palm against the door. The charcoal shapes move and twist across the painted wood. They detach themselves with a final tug and swirl and dance through the air before racing toward Satori and buzzing around his face like mosquitoes. Confused, he bats them away with his arms then calms himself, clears his mind, and wills the airborne glyphs away. When he opens his eyes again, the swarm and Lilith are gone.

CHAPTER TWO

HEELS CLICK against stone as Lilith strides along the city street. Long legs carry her swiftly past vacated office buildings and busy eateries. Aromas of burnt cooking oil and chicken invade her nostrils. Customers stare at her as she marches past windows. *Let them look*. Her voluptuous pout is drawn in scarlet, and the trace of a sneer tugs the corners of her lips downward. The pillar-box red hair and beautiful face lend her the appearance of a comic book superhero, while her near-nudity suggests high-class prostitute.

Cars crawl past and glazed eyes stare through half-open windows as she heads out of town, head held high, returning no more than the briefest glance. Each car keeps moving, matching her pace for a while before accelerating away.

She quickens her steps, eager to leave the dark room and weeping boy far behind. The evening has left a strange hollowness inside her chest. He acted as though she was not what he wanted. His whispered pleas for forgiveness still burrow through her mind, and that name repeated over and over again— Star.

The busy restaurants and bars are behind her now. Darkened factories and warehouses line the street: remnants of Victorian wealth. The only light comes from a full moon, which stares down with silent longing. She is almost there.

At first, she doesn't register the heavy footsteps keeping time with her own. She is lost in dreams of adventure and freedom. As she rounds a corner, a dark shape darts into shadow. Alert, she recognises the slap of leather on tarmac as the stranger speeds up. She varies her speed, but the pursuer keeps pace. She turns again and heads along a narrow alleyway, shoes crushing glass as they descend. The stranger is close; his odour of fresh and stale sweat mixes with the scent of his sex, advertising his arousal. The closeness of him fills her head. Her pulse quickens, and her saliva tastes like metal. It is hard to formulate a plan while picking her way between broken concrete blocks and steel girders, staggering when her heels slip over the uneven ground. The pain of an ankle twisting makes her swear. She glances back into the darkness.

The footsteps gain ground until she can feel his breath in her hair.

He whispers insults as though they are terms of endearment. 'You're so beautiful, bitch. Fucking whore, worthless slut, we're gonna have some fun.'

Her legs and arms feel heavy, as though they belong to someone else. She pushes forward despite her aching limbs.

His menace taints the air. 'I know you want me. I can smell your filthy cunt from here, my love. I'll make you scream for more, then I'll gut you like a fish.'

Breathing deeply, she sucks strength from dust-filled oxygen. The flat edge of a cold blade presses against her throat. She freezes when the hunter pushes himself into her back, and the rough denim of his jeans rubs against her buttocks. His hand fumbles between her thighs, pawing at the underwear beneath her skirt. The metal strap of his watch scratches her legs. Her pulse hammers against the tooth of the knife. He growls in her ear and reverses his hold. The thumb and forefinger of his left hand now squeeze her throat as his knife tears at her panties. The lace tangles itself around the knife, falling away like broken cobwebs. He lifts the knife and holds it, almost tenderly, against her breast then plunges the fingers of his left hand inside her.

The shock of the sudden invasion makes her gasp. She can feel his rough fingers searching within her. Her eyes close and she imagines tearing his hand from his body. Metal pierces her skin as she struggles. A thread of crimson trickles down her chest, and she sees the cold blade flash inside her mind. She lifts her face to the moon and smiles.

The fingers no longer squirm inside her. The man withdraws them, lifting them to his face and snorting the scent of her. He trembles and sucks his fingers like a hungry baby. His ragged breath in her ears, she raises her left arm and touches the fist in which his knife is clasped. He seems frightened by her icy fingers and pulls away. She spins around on her stiletto heels to face him— a small man with greasy, greying hair, smoothed over his misshapen skull. His arms and legs are brittle twigs, his blue eyes weak and moist.

'You're going to die. I'm going to fuck you in every hole I gouge out of you,' he stammers.

He recoils from her smile. Knife clutched in his right hand and the fingers of the left pressed against his nose, he watches her. She towers above his pock-marked face, lifts her arms, and places a hand on either side of his jaw. It requires no effort to lift him. His feeble kicks are too weak to leave bruises. His hands fall to his sides, and he stares at her in terrified silence. Holding his clammy face between her palms, she thrusts her tongue into his mouth, squeezing his skull just enough to let him taste her strength without losing consciousness, then she releases him and grabs the knife from his hand.

She toys with the knife— a good knife, heavy. His eyes widen as she lunges and slices the air between them. The stink of his fear taints the air. Her smile broadens, and she reaches for the sweat-soaked cotton of his shirt and slashes through it, revealing his chest, then places her fingers over his stammering heart.

Tears flow freely down the man's cheeks. She places the knife handle between her thighs and squeezes with her powerful muscles until her steel phallus bobs eagerly.

'Suck my cock,' she orders.

He resists and Lilith has to force him onto his knees amongst the rubble and glass. She wraps her fingers around his hair and pushes his face into position. He gurgles as blood coats the blade.

Falling backward, he pleads with her to show mercy. His broken tongue spits promises he will not keep.She ignores his words and roughly spreads his legs then plunges through the denim. Exquisite screams of agony echo through the alleyway as she makes her virgin hole and fucks him until he stops twitching.

CHAPTER THREE

SATORI CROUCHES in a sea of magical symbols. His sweat has made the marks run into each other, both across his body and beneath it, and he resembles a creature rising from a pool of tar.

Working his stiff muscles, he stands and crosses the room to his bed. Dozens of faces stare up at him, their expressions confused, hurt, and blank— Star, the woman who left him six weeks before. He presses his lips to each sweet mouth and tears spill as he whispers apology after apology.

I am a fool. What did I hope for? The anger he felt when she told him she was leaving still crouches in his chest ready to pounce. Tears blur his vision as he sinks back on his duvet, losing consciousness amid the worn and battered images of his ex-girlfriend.

After a fitful sleep, Satori wakes to his nightmare. He grabs all his magical books—modern paperbacks and older, clothbound volumes—forty-two in total. Then, paying no attention to size or age, treating all as equals, he fans them out into a wide circle. The jumbled works become a mystical ring, a zodiac of arcane knowledge. He retrieves the discarded dagger from a corner and sits in the centre of the circle. Athame in his hand, he closes his eyes to dowse for the right book. He tries to focus on the question *how can I stop her?* but his mind is full of the demon.

When he closes his eyes, he sees her body bound by that magical outfit, her hair moving around her face, and those eyes burning like fireflies while her pointed tongue licks soft, full lips. His mouth feels dry and his jaw aches. Lilith arouses him, and he hates himself for it. *It's just been a long time*, he tells himself, shaking her image from his mind. *A long time… weeks!*

A seed of hope, the tiniest thought that he might win Star back, was all Satori had needed. Hope is what brought him to this point; hope and an overwhelming desire to receive her love again or, at least, an answer to his constant question, w*hy did you leave?* The first two weeks after she left, he watched her home and followed her. She never met another man.

Star, you are my world. The others before you are dust. He wishes he could do the same with his memories of her, tear the thoughts from his mind. She called him schizophrenic. Laughing at the word, he surveys the chaos of his room. *Schizo-fucking-phrenic? If only.*

The jewelled hilt of his knife refracts daylight across the bedroom walls as he twists the blade through the air. He holds out his other hand and watches the colours play across his pale skin. Inside him, his heart continues to pump, but his blood burns like acid. *Will I ever be free of this?*

He tosses the blade away again and picks up the first book. The dust jacket is black, and a green tree dominates the front cover. He scans each page, willing an answer to appear— four, five, six books are read and thrown behind him. Hours pass and Satori's desperation grows as does the cairn-shaped mound. So many ceremonies, but only one to dismiss such a powerful demon. It requires Lilith's presence in his magical space, and he doubts his ability to trick or force her to return to this room. He must think harder. *There must be a way. There is always a way.*

'This is my will,' he says, mocking himself.

The telephone rings four times then silence. Footsteps approach his room. He runs to his door, barring it.

'Phone call for you, Steve,' his mother calls through the wooden barrier. 'It's Sarah.'

Star? What does she want? Why now? His body tingles in response to her name. 'Okay, I'll take it up here,' he shouts, lifting the receiver. 'Star?'

'Hi, Steve,' she answers. 'How are you?'

The melody of her voice fills his head. He presses his hand

against the wall and closes his eyes. 'Fine, thanks. What do you want?'

'I'm sorry. I shouldn't have…' her voice drifts into silence.

Satori replies before she can put the phone down again. 'It's okay. I'm just surprised to hear from you. You kinda made it obvious you didn't want to see me again.' A tear tickles his cheek. He brushes it away, keeping his voice steady.

'I had a vision, about you,' she says. 'That's why I phoned. I was worried. However, you're fine, so I'll go.'

'No! Wait!' he says. 'Please, come over.'

CHAPTER FOUR

'STEVE, WHAT have you done?' Sarah sits on Satori's bed. Her eyes scan the room once more.

He hasn't bothered opening his curtains, but even in the gloom she can see his frantic work. Marvelling at the intricacy of the designs, she despairs at this new evidence of his deranged mind. At her feet she sees a crumpled photo and bends to pick it up, but Satori is too fast and snatches it away before she can flip it over. She frowns at him. There is no point in fighting him for the picture. She already knows whose face fills its glossy surface.

Last night, sitting in her living room with Raven and Donna, she felt a sudden coldness creep over her. Instead of her flat, she was here in this room. Satori was naked and there had been all these markings…

He does not meet her stare. Instead, he gazes at his feet as he scuffs out charcoal marks with the heel of his shoe.

'Please, call me Satori,' he says.

Sarah laughs. *Satori! You pretentious bastard.* She wonders why she came, why she allows him to draw her back. *If only I wasn't so enamoured with these people— Steve and Raven— they pull me under. Why am I so attracted to them? Fuck it! I'm not your Star any longer. I'm Sarah: practical, logical, sane Sarah.*

That is why the vision was so cruel. Not only because, once again, his image filled her head, but because she knows where it comes from, that hidden, secret part— the vortex deep inside her mind that she has struggled to ignore for so many years.

'Names are important,' Satori replies, looking at her. 'Satori is a powerful name, and I need all the power I can muster.'

'Okay, okay,' she says, shaking her head. She is shocked by the weariness in his eyes. They were always so bright and alert when they were together. Instinct demands she embrace him. She stops herself just in time. 'What have you done? In my dream, I… I saw a knife and a woman. Now I see all this chaos. What I saw was real, wasn't it?'

'I made a terrible mistake,' he admits. 'I thought… I thought I could control it, but it's gone.'

'I don't understand. You're always talking in riddles. Just tell me. What was it? What did I see?' *And how did I see it?* She knows how, but she will continue to deny it, even to herself.

'I wanted to invoke a demon, a lesser one, and channel some of its power. Maybe I could… well… change things… you know. It shouldn't be like this.' Pausing, his eyes search hers for validation. When he speaks again, he tries a different approach. 'I followed all the instructions. These marks you keep staring at, they're for protection. It should have worked. I don't know what went wrong.'

Without a word, she stands up and tramples across his magic, desperate to reach the door and escape his madness before she loses herself in it again. Her hand hovers at the door handle until she relents and turns to face him.

'Okay, so you're weirder than I thought.'

Pain twists his mouth.

For the briefest moment, it gives her pleasure before the guilt bullies its way back in. 'No, I'm sorry Steve… Satori. Fuck! So, you tried a spell, a big one and it went wrong.' She cannot believe she is having this conversation and yet the words keep pouring out of her.

He nods. 'Something else came through. The woman, well demon— more powerful than I was expecting. She was beautiful and terrible. I couldn't contain her.'

She doesn't know how much longer she can stand here listening to this. The vortex inside bubbles and hisses while her hand reaches for the cold metal of the door handle.

He should see someone. This conversation is just feeding his psychosis, and yet a deeply buried part of her is intrigued: that evil, unclean cocoon in the core of her mind— the part she always tries to suppress, the part which had the vision. She almost had it under control until last night. Chewing her knuckles, she thinks. *Why do I keep seeing it: the tear and the darkness beyond; it calls to me.*

'And what does that mean, precisely?'

'I don't know. She terrifies me. I must find some way to stop her. These books… they're useless.'

'Then we need to find better books,' Sarah says, not willing to let fear take over.

'We?' He shrugs and brightens a little. 'Okay,' he agrees. 'We'll find better books and we'll stop her… together.'

We? Did I say that? She bites her lip. *There must be a way out of this.* She notices his sudden transformation and is wary. Even covered in black smudges Satori is beautiful. At twenty-four, he is the perfect Goth archetype with a body so slender it is difficult to imagine him eating. He wears androgyny as though it were a style he created, his skin white even without makeup, and his hair— black and straight— shines like raven feathers as it falls around his narrow shoulders. And yet he is strong, very strong. Her thighs feel hot and weak. She grips the handle and pushes it down until she hears it click.

He looks up at her from the bed and she feels herself melting. *Why am I doing this? Is he the perfect boyfriend? Sure, he's clever and sensitive and he loves with an all-consuming fire, but he is obsessive and weird, and when I'm with him… I'm weird, too.*

They stare at each other in silence. The graffiti-filled room gapes between them like a wound. *One, two, three…* the silence shreds Sarah's nerves. *I have to say something, but what? Goodbye seems too cold, too final.*

'Any idea where we should start?' she asks. In that moment, silence's spell is broken, and she plunges into a strange and un-welcome adventure.

'Paul,' he replies. 'I'll get my coat.'

'Shower first,' she insists. 'You look terrible.'

She wants to remind him that this does not mean they are back together, but he leaves the room before she can form the right words. She digs her thumb and fingernail into her forearm, pinching hard. A broken circle of purple and red marks her skin.

They walk together to the bus stop. The pair of them march side by side with their long, black coats flapping in the chill October breeze, their winkle-picker boots tapping a synchronised beat and their pale faces set into looks of intelligent determination. She realises how much she has missed being with him. That he loves her, wants to be with her, makes her feel extraordinary. Everything seems harder without him. Work is more tedious when she isn't replaying their time together in her head, and it takes and inordinate amount of self-control to tolerate Raven's self-involved chatter. The desire to leave, to run away to another town where no one knows her sits uncomfortably beside her desire to lose herself in Satori's arms again. She wants to walk closer to him, link her arm with his, feel the power of their conjoined bodies and share his heat, but she shakes these feelings away.

The bus stop is empty. She reminds herself to avoid looking at the hateful graffiti which covers this side of the wall. *Goths go to hell. Fuck off Freaks. Kill a Goth— go to Heaven*, and far more in the same theme. Relief that there isn't a queue of strangers relaxes her body, and she leans against the shelter wall.

'Are you okay?' Satori asks.

It is the first time in a long time she has heard him ask about her. The knowledge that he cares how she feels softens her resolve. Her head swims as she gazes at his face and sees her reflection in his intelligent grey eyes. His is a face worth painting and she wonders why she never even sketched his portrait. She imagines his eyes as pools of rainwater suspended as if by magic in a face chiselled by Alexander Munro. Only his affectation of growing a tiny beard at the centre of his chin mars the image. She smiles looking at the sprouting dozen pale brown hairs. He tried to dye them black once, she remembers. What a mess he made.

'I'm fine. A bit nervous, I guess. What's Paul like?'

'Brilliant.' Satori's eyes shine. 'He's given me help and advice so many times. I'm sure he'll know what to do, or at least have the books to look it up.'

'I hope you're right.' Falling back into silence, she concentrates on moving a piece of gravel around the pavement with her pointed toe.

Paul lives in a large house on the edge of the city. As they arrive at its gates, Satori presses a button on the telecom and whispers into the microphone. The gates swing open and reveal a vista worthy of any Hammer Horror film— a mock-Tudor building with a sweeping driveway, complete with an avenue of skeletal trees.

'Are you sure?' she asks him.

'Of course,' he assures her.

'Satori, welcome.' The man in the doorway wears a blood red shirt and tight black trousers. His white hair is tied back into a ponytail. Sarah has no idea whether he is old or has lightened his hair. He has one of those ageless faces. He stares at her, waiting for an introduction. Satori's arm sweeps toward her. He clasps her left hand and smiles.

'Paul, this is Star,' he says.

'Ah, *the* Star,' the man says, looking her up and down.

Is he sneering?

He moves to the side with a theatrical bow. 'Enchanted. Please, come in, come in.'

Sarah scowls as they are ushered along a wide hallway with high ceilings and a dominant staircase and into a room on the right. The dancing flames of an open fire light the library. Sarah's skin prickles, and she stands in the doorway shifting her weight from one foot to the other. In contrast to her own irritation, the men seem comfortable here, to the point at which it seems she is already forgotten. She wanders over to the nearest bookcase, scratching her itchy left palm as she walks.

The wall is filled with hundreds of hard-backed volumes. The first bookcase is dedicated to fiction. The works of Bram Stoker, Mary Shelley, Oscar Wilde, and Huysmans stand comfortably shoulder to shoulder with Clive Barker, Graham Masterton, and Steven King. She moves to the next bookcase while Paul and Satori talk. Paul sounds excited.

'Lilith,' Paul says in hushed tones. '… really?'

'She… was,' Steve answers, his confidence growing beneath Paul's admiration. 'But I didn't… She told me she saw the door and came of her own accord. I couldn't control her, and now she's gone. Out there somewhere.'

'And… find it?'

Sarah moves closer, Paul whispers too quietly for her to hear his side of the conversation. They don't look up. They have become the centre of each other's universe for the moment.

'And stop her,' Satori adds.

Paul pauses and rubs his chin with elegant fingers. 'I have a few books that may help you.' He looks across at Sarah and smiles. She shivers.

'Won't you come, too?' Satori asks. 'We'll be stronger to-gether.'

'It is tempting. My god. Lilith, here?' He sighs as he reaches up for a book. 'But no, I'm older than you. I'm a teacher not a soldier. My heart isn't as strong as it used to be. Do you have any idea where it's gone?'

'Not yet,' Steve says, taking the offered book from Paul's hand.

Paul moves to another bookcase. 'Well, that shouldn't be too difficult. We can dowse for it when we're ready. I think I may have a fair idea as to where Lilith has been.'

'What? How?'

Paul smiles. The tension in the room builds, and Sarah has to admire the showmanship. Satori shakes his head.

'A body was found mutilated near the old tobacco factories this morning. The police are clueless. I think it was your demon.'

Sarah's heart beats faster. *Murder?* It feels too real, no longer the stuff of Gothic fairy tales.

Something inside her shifts; she feels it stretching. 'No,' she whispers and forces it back down, dousing the light in her mind. Her heart pounds against her ribs. The internal battle makes her limbs shake. Fear and excitement tear at her stomach with vicious claws. She has to sit down. 'This is nuts,' she whispers.

'What did the police say?' Satori asks.

'Well, of course, they haven't mentioned demons, my dear boy, but it just felt supernatural, both the viciousness of the attack and its sexuality. I doubt a man would do that to another man, and a woman… couldn't.'

'What did she do?' Sarah asks, uncertain as to whether she wants to hear the reply but intrigued despite herself.

'It gouged a hole in the fellow's perineum.' Paul's glare is as sharp as a blade and his lips twist into a sneer.

'I need to go,' Star says.

'Which books should we take?' Satori asks.

'Huh, oh yes, the books. Well, Satori, there are so many to choose from. It's better if you stay here for a few days. We can research together and, of course, I have the practice room. You need to be ready before you face Lilith. If you aren't prepared, who knows what the demon will do to you.'

'But… Star, what do you think? Can you stay?' Satori asks.

Sarah fights a smile as the pendulum of power swings toward her.

'Oh, um yes, of course, Star. I'd be delighted,' Paul adds with a nod of his head.

'I've got a busy week, Steve,' Sarah replies. He flinches at the name. 'If you do decide to stay, I'll let your mum know where you are.' She glares at Paul as she says this, as if in warning. 'What's your number, Paul, so I can phone if I need to speak to Steve?' *Yes*, she thinks, *I am strong enough to walk away.*

'I have no business with phones. I never use one I'm afraid,' Paul answers.

Sarah faces Satori. 'Call me if you need me. Do you have your mobile with you?'

Satori nods. He looks lost and insecure. She reminds herself that he doesn't need her protection.

'I'll call you if I need to,' she says, eager to be gone. 'Will you be at the club next Saturday? We can talk there.'

'Sure, the club, yeah… probably. I'll call you soon. Will you be okay getting back?'

Sarah leaves the question hanging. Without touching either man or even waving goodbye, she leaves. No one walks her to the door. Only their voices, low and excited, follow her through the hallway.

Sarah calls Satori's landline. No one answers so she leaves a message for Marian to phone her back. Her second call is to Donna, her best friend and flat mate.

'I saw Steve about the… vision,' Sarah says.

'Oh, Sarah,' Donna sighs.

Sarah pauses. She fights the desire to tell her friend about the demon. Donna would not understand. No one would. *I don't.* 'I still love him.' Sarah bites her lip angrily. *How could I have said that?*

'I know. Just be careful. He's no good for you.'

'He's gone to stay with an old man called Paul,' Sarah says. 'He has a huge house out by Snuff Mills. Do you know him?'

'No. What's he like?'

'He's really into magick,' Sarah says thinking back to all the books and his excitement about the demon. 'And I'm pretty sure he's gay.'

'Figures. Raven might know him,' Donna says. 'Shall I ask her?'

'No. Don't tell her anything.' 'What's the matter?' Donna asks.

'Don't you feel it? She wants to control everything and everyone.'

'She couldn't control me even if she tried. I'm making dinner tonight. Bolognese?' There is a pause. When she speaks again, Donna's voice is tender. 'You're worth a thousand of them both.'

Sarah buys a local newspaper, but there is no mention of the murder. She sends a text for a local news update; there is nothing about it there, either. Her sense of unease grows stronger, and she sends a text to Satori to let him know.

CHAPTER FIVE

LILITH STOOD on the dusty earth and looked up at the moon. Giant, white and cold, it hung above her in the silent sky. She opened her mouth and sucked air into her newly formed chest. It chilled her. Stretching her mouth and throat wider, she screeched. Her first sound a soul-splitting wail of anguish. She screamed until all the air had been forced from her body. Her eyes narrowed in a look of accusation.

How dare the moon bow before the sun and cast me away? I am the moon's light. I am the fire, and I will burn as brightly here on Earth as I ever did in the night sky.

Dry soil stretched all around. Its hue, burnt umber beneath her feet, faded to grey beyond her glow. On the colourless horizon, lonely trees stretched their own spindly limbs into the night sky.

Beside her, a male form stirred. He stretched his arms and opened his amber eyes. A beautiful smile lit his face as he saw Lilith standing above him.

'Samael, we are cast out,' she said. 'I will wander, I will learn all there is to know about this brave new world.' She stared at him, trying to remember every detail, knowing he would not come with her. 'What will you do?'

He shook his head and his dark hair shone. She wanted to hold him tight. A tiny part of her wanted to stay in his arms forever.

'I have no wish to wander. I shall build a fiery mansion to rival the discarded light of the moon. Will you stay with me?' He stared up at her, and she felt her resolve soften in response.

'Sometimes, my husband, my brother, sometimes.' Lilith sat beside Samael and traced his chest with her finger. 'You are beautiful.'

'You are too, my love, my light. Don't leave me yet.'

Her eyes trailed across Samael's body, a body newly made, for both were energy alone moments before. Her virgin flesh warmed between her legs. Instinct showed her what to do, how to rejoin with this other. They rejoined again and again, never tiring, and Lilith's screech of fury at the moon's betrayal was soon echoed by a new screech of pleasure and power.

In each other's arms, Samael and Lilith found a form of completion. For a while, the mansion was left unbuilt and the land undiscovered. Instead, they discovered together new forms of pleasure, new ways to burn brighter. They wallowed in the moon's shame as they lit up the night with their desire. From their unions, children were born, demons. Samael charged the demons to build his mansion while he mated with his dark mistress.

Lilith watched as the walls of his fortress were built. 'The walls are so high, dear brother, what do you need to keep out?' *Or keep in? It is a prison not a home. Do you wish to imprison me within its walls?* 'Your mansion is so dark. How will our light penetrate its boundaries?' *My light would perish in that absolute gloom. I need the stars above my head and the moon in my eye.* 'I'll find my own cave, Samael. I will not share yours.' *I shall never chain myself to your side.*

Lilith left Samael seven years after their fall to earth. As she walked away from his strong arms, his shining hair, his eager cock, and his black palace, her steps grew lighter. The moon lit her path to a great river and there she bathed herself until she had left even the scent of that other behind. Burying her nose in the crook of her elbow, she sniffed, warm butter and juniper berries, her odour, not his. The evening was warm, and she did not look for shelter. Beneath a willow tree, she curled up and slept a deep sleep full of sunlight and ripening fruit.

Lilith woke early. A vicious heat licked her toes. Opening her eyes, she saw a golden haze beyond the leafy dome of the willow tree. She pulled her feet into the shade and frowned.

What is that bright light?

Frightened, she sat clutching her knees. The air beyond the

curtain was full of sounds, splashing and chirping, stamping and snorting, a plague of noise that threatened to deafen her. Shaking her head to deny the cacophony, she held her hands over her ears.

Is this how daytime sounds: a thousand voices shouting to be heard? Is this how sunlight looks: a blinding golden light bullying its way through the branches? What have I done, leaving the security of Samael's mansion and coming here alone? I will die here. I will be eaten or burnt, or I will go mad and drown myself in this river. No, the tree will become a pyre and the sun's fire will consume me— the cast down light of the moon, for the sun can abide no adversaries and it will jealously guard its flame.

'Samael, brother, lover, husband— forgive me!' Lilith wept.

Eyes closed, she waited, but death did not come for her. Hours passed before she opened her eyes again and stretched her limbs as far as the shade of the tree allowed. The harsh golden light became a soft blue as the sun fell and daylight was replaced by twilight.

That night, Lilith followed the river as it rushed to join the sea. She reached the Red Sea before dawn and found a deep, dark cave in which to spend the daylight hours. As the eastern sky grew salmon red, she hid herself.

'Why do I cower and hide myself from the sun's light?' she asked. 'Am I not equal to it? Greater perhaps, as I am pure light, the moon's flame. Luna, why do I share your shame, your inequality?'

A voice echoed in her head, a sonorous voice which shook every nerve in her body. It filled her body and mind, and she knew its source. 'You are demon, Lilith, a creature of the night. Daylight is poison to you. Would you prefer it otherwise?'

'I don't know, Father, what do you offer?' she asked. The words seemed hollow and without power compared to the effect of His words. Her cheeks prickled but she refused to cower from the voice.

'A garden and a man, a mate as beautiful as the sun, you will walk in the sun's benevolent light, and you will help him care for the animals.'

'May I see him?'

Laughter shook the cave. Lilith held her ears in terror. Her muscles tensed, urging her to run, but where could she go? The laughter was inside her.

'When the sun sets, become an owl and fly west. You will see the garden.'

Lilith trembled at the back of the cave waiting for the punch of that terrible voice to return. Her back, lacerated by sharp rocks, bled, but she did not register the pain; only relief that the voice had stopped dominated her thoughts. As she grew used to the silence again, other thoughts surfaced: *a man, a beautiful man.*

As evening fell, Lilith crept out of her cave. The sea whispered, and she strained to hear its advice, but the words were too soft. *He told me to become an owl.* She concentrated, imagining feathers growing from her shoulder blades, a beak breaking through her nose and mouth. She concentrated so hard that her mind cramped with the effort but, when she checked, she still had fleshy fingers and toes. Sighing, she sat on the sandy shore and faced the moon. 'I am an owl,' she whispered, stretching her great wings. She ascended and flew westward, dipping and soaring with pleasure at her new freedom while her excited screech filled the night.

Maybe she travelled due west, guided by some internal compass. She was only aware of the cool air between her feathers and the silent laughter bubbling inside her belly. The greater part of her wanted to get lost in the wilderness, soaring and diving forever. Despite her carelessness, she spotted The Garden ahead. There was no denying that this must be the place He created, the jewel in the crown of His great work.

Her throat tightened. Gasping for breath, she fell awkwardly to the ground. Feathers vanished. Skin and hair covered her. Kneeling in the dust, she stared ahead. A high wall surrounded The Garden but, even from this lowly angle, Lilith saw the tips of great trees pierce the sky high above the glistening barrier. Standing up, she tried to brush the dirt from her legs. The dust clung to her; she felt ashamed and looked around for a pool or river. Somewhere she could wash herself and feel worthy of such beauty. Dust surrounded her. She rubbed at the filth with her spit-soaked hand. Stubborn streaks of grey grime replaced the layer of powder.

'Father,' she called, but He did not answer.

Eyes stinging from the tears she refused to shed, she walked toward the towering wall. As she got closer, she noticed a silver gate. A few more steps and she saw two beautiful short and plump human forms, their outward appearance suggested they were children, but Lilith felt their power even from this distance. They were unlike any of the children she had left behind. In their hands they held great flaming swords, guards to the entrance of the garden. Would they let her pass?

Each careful step brought her closer to the gate and she felt drawn to these powerful children. It occurred to her that she might stay there, at the gate with them, and never enter. She could look after them, feed them, tell them stories. She could amuse them, embrace them, even love them. All the feelings she never felt for her own demonic brood filled her now, so that as she reached the gate, she fell to her knees and begged them to let her stay in their presence, to be their friend and mother, to love and protect them.

As the guardians turned away from her, the pure and ethereal rejecting the base and animal, Lilith's spirit plummeted and with it all those soft and nurturing emotions. Without a smile, the cherubs opened the gates and stood aside. Lowering their swords of fire, they averted their heads, refusing to look into the eyes of their would-be mother. Their only acknowledgement of her existence was an uncomfortable shuffling of their tiny feet and a furrowing of their ageless brows. They wanted her gone, but they could not dismiss her. She felt a screech of fury build up inside her but, filled with shame, she swallowed it and stepped through the gate.

Stepping from the wilderness into paradise, Lilith took a deep breath. The air was fragrant with the perfume of flowers that filled her nose and throat, a heady scent. Her eyes were assaulted by a billion shades of green, vibrant reds, aggressive yellows, and startling oranges. Everything was too vivid, so real as to feel artificial. God's glory screamed from every branch of every tree, every blade of grass, and each petal of the thousands of different flowers which grew around her. She took a step forward, teetering on her unsteady legs then fell to the ground.

Lilith opened her eyes. *Was I unconscious for minutes, hours, or days?*

Grass tickled her nose and cheeks and enveloped her in green. Saffron from clouds of pollen decorated her eyelashes, the brothers and sisters of which still floated around her. She didn't rush to look away. Two colours were easier than a billion to absorb. She stared at the green and the yellow and tried to understand them. Looking at her hands, she saw the colour of her own skin— a soft brown stretched over a web of blue.

I have colour, too. I am the hue of the wilderness. These are the pigments of The Garden. Brushing the pollen from her eyes, she dared to raise her face. The sky above her was blue, not dark like the moon-ruled universe with which she was familiar, but a softer shade reminiscent of the colour she glimpsed beneath her skin. Lilith was certain the sun blazed somewhere above her, although her eyes did not search for it, and yet her skin did not blister or burn, just as God had promised. *What does this mean? Am I no longer demon? If so, what am I?*

Footsteps approached, and the plants whispered as something large brushed past them. She rolled over and peered up at the tall man who towered above her; the figure was most definitely male, like Samael and yet nothing like her brother. He gazed down at her and smiled. Lilith's heart pounded in her chest. *Who is this?*

The hand he extended toward her was huge; she could have fit her head inside its palm. His hair was as yellow as the pollen and his eyes as soft as the sky. His skin, although similar to hers, was cleaner, paler, and seemed to glow in the sunlight. Her gaze drifted from his delightful face, taking in his body— it, too, was well made. He looked strong and lean and a generous organ, similar in shape to the one Samael had used for Lilith's pleasure and which she had felt loath to leave behind, hung between this man's legs. *Is this God?* He shone like the sun, and Lilith's eyes watered at the sight of him. Fiery pride and shame battled within her. She pushed herself to her feet. He was taller than her, but she felt almost as strong, almost as great as he. His smile never faltered. His hand still reached toward her.

'Who are you?' he asked. His words were music.

Lilith's body swayed and she struggled to keep her balance. The sweet melody of his question danced around her brain.

'I am Lilith.' Her throat felt dry, and she wondered if he heard it rasp.

'Lilith,' he repeated, rolling the syllables around his mouth with his tongue. 'I am Adam.' Now his hand was at her face, his fingers lifting her hair, investigating her. 'You look like me.'

She looked away from his shimmering skin. 'If only I weren't so filthy. Is there water, here in the garden?'

He nodded and let her hair fall from his fingers. As he strode away, Lilith saw the power of his leg muscles. She ran behind him, trying to keep up with his pace. Beyond the contours of his body, she saw the silver shimmer of water, sprinted past him, and dived into the pool. The water closed around her, and she felt no fear or shame. Breaking the surface again, she blinked water from her eyes and searched for him. He squatted at the edge of the pool stroking the head of an animal as it lapped at the water. The animal stood on four slender legs; its hair was closely cropped and reddish brown, and its huge, brown eyes watched her.

'What animal is that?' she asked.

'A deer.' His voice was soft and full of reverence. 'Isn't she beautiful?'

Lilith nodded. The animal was perfect.

Lilith rests. It is always this way at first, existing on another plane. It takes a while for her to adjust. This world will be fun, though; she can feel it in every nerve ending. The essence of Chaos, which escorted her when she travelled from Binah to Malkuth— Earth— rests in every pore, ready to be unleashed.

Her thoughts turn back to the magician. *Why did she let him live? Such arrogance should be punished.* But there is something about his soft, white body that draws her to him. *Of course, he will be punished, but it will be slow and sweet, and I will savour every moment.*

Stretching her fingers and toes, she smiles to herself. The memory of last night is delicious. The sensuality of the violence excites her. It is a moment worth reliving. Her would-be rapist and murderer slaughtered by his own blade. Although no two experiences can ever be identical, she will have more moments to cherish. Sex and death: her entire universe.

Rising from her reclined position on the bed, she crosses the room and pulls back a strip of newspaper to look out of the grimy window. The street below is busy now. Men and women in colourful costumes are on display beneath her: night-creatures— drug pushers and HIV-positive hookers. They would succumb too easily, half-dead already. She wants to feel again the sadistic pleasure of shock, disbelief, pain, and the refusal to die until the very last moment. If not that then peace, for a while at least, to relive the memories until they lose their shine.

Voices call to her. They do not give her peace and before long, she is itching to go outside and play.

What to wear? Yesterday's corset and mini skirt were perfect for yesterday. But maybe green today? Decision made; she is remodelled by her will. Her hair changes from long pillar-box red to an auburn Cleopatra style bob with a heavy fringe. Her leather bodice is absorbed back into the skin it came from and an emerald silk blouse, open dangerously low, grows like ivy and clings to her breasts and stomach. The hem of her skirt moves downward and a split from knee to pelvis opens along her left thigh. She keeps the green eyes; they remind her of her time in The Garden.

These dark streets are filled with the city's secrets. Visitors pass through looking for sights not listed in *Tourist Information*. Cars cruise by at walking pace. Women move forward and back like the tide, some becoming passengers for a while, others retreating into doorways. Music is everywhere. The heavy beats and fast lyrics of rap and dance music float from open windows. The smell of fried chicken, mutton fat, and spices hang heavy in the air.

With no fixed destination, she moves toward the city centre. People surge out of theatres and into bars to impress their friends or partners with their knowledge and insight. Taxis collect fares, queuing in the shifting light of headlamps and man-made waterfalls.

She chooses a rum bar. A quiet place emitting a warm red glow, *The Lucifernum*, the irony of the name is not lost on her. She settles onto a vinyl bar stool and stretches her legs. The oily, dark-haired bartender hurries toward her.

'Something fiery,' she tells him.

He nods and shuffles away in silence. With reverence, he places a squat glass on the bar. Igniting the gloomy liquid, he smiles as tongues of flame lick hungrily at the air between them. Lilith lifts the glass and downs the drink without extinguishing the fire. She feels his steady stare and nods to him. 'Give me something longer this time,' she says.

Moments later, a tumbler of amber liquid sits on the bar before her. She picks it up and wanders around the room. With its flagstone floor and curved walls, it feels subterranean. The render on the walls looks moist, almost like living tissue. She has to touch it to know it is solid. Hung around the walls are baroque pseudo-Catholic renditions of saints, covered in gilt and rich oils, except that each has its breasts or genitals exposed and a look of sexual ecstasy on its face. Lilith approves. Such art might look good in her humble room.

The bar is empty except for a table of card players intent on their game, and the bartender who watches her in fascination. She sees a dark archway at the far wall and wanders through. A long, dimly lit hallway stretches before her. Striding along it, she passes a child gate on her left. Two sleek Dobermans cower behind it, whimpering. Lowering her face to theirs, she strokes their bony heads. Tails wag, delighted to be accepted. Ahead are three doors; two of which have signs which mark them as toilets. The other displays a metal plate etched with the word PRIVATE. She tries the one marked private, but it is locked. Turning the handle again, she shoves the door, and it swings open.

Stairs lead down. Chords of distemperate classical music waft toward her. She descends. Halfway down the staircase, the wall ends. She peers over an iron banister into the gloom. A ceremony of some kind is being held.

A crowd is gathered, some naked, others dressed in black robes. At one end lies a naked woman, her long hair spread around her. Beneath her pale body is an altar covered in red cloth. Between her teeth and thighs, she holds metal cups upon which candles burn, one black and the other red. Her body is so still that the candles hardly flicker and yet she is obviously breathing. There is no fear in her eyes, but rather a fierce pride as if she is honoured by her role as altar.

Behind this woman stands another. Draped in a red robe and holding a black feather, she faces the other worshippers. Men and women are gathered, mostly women. They are chanting, but their voices are so soft it is hard to catch the sense of the words.

Lilith lingers, hoping to watch the group throw off their cloaks and fall upon each other. Yet their rapturous faces, intent on internal journeys, seem unaware of each other. Each perfectly content in their isolation. Tendrils of distilled power radiate from the worshippers and caress Lilith's body. On an outward breath, she blows air toward the gathering. As her breath reaches them, the group changes. At first, the men and women glance at each other. Some stop chanting and the music peters out. The men's bodies harden, and hands stretch out to touch each other. Men fall upon women and enter them roughly. Women pull at each other's breasts and drink each other's juices. Within moments, one ritual is over, and another has begun.

Delighted by the transformation, Lilith watches until her puppets tire, then she returns to the upper room. Heat and sound fill the bar. The gamblers have been joined by two more. Eyes flicking, tongues rapidly moistening lips, they huddle around a pile of coins and tattered bank notes. Blank faces and stiff postures shield their thoughts and their cards from the scrutiny of fellow players.

Four women slouch together in the corner of the room; they are all young, around the magician's age. On the far left is a blonde girl. Next to her is a tall woman, almost statuesque. Unlike the others, she is not giggling or pointing at the paintings. She sits aloof, sucking her drink through a straw. Physically, she is head and shoulders above the rest. Her build is strong, her black hair thick— a lion's mane.

Lilith's eyes shift right to the next girl. She looks familiar, but Lilith has seen so many faces their features blur into homogeny. The girl's countenance is soft and pretty. Thick, black curls frame her face, her wrists and shoulders look small and delicate: breakable. The third girl is huddled so close to her friend that she is almost invisible. Lilith wonders whether they are lovers. The fourth girl's hair is cut short, in a sharp bob that she wears across her cheeks. There is a scar, just below the girl's eye, and she touches it whenever she laughs.

'How did you find this place, Raven?' the blonde friend asks.

'Your brother told me last night,' the tall girl says, smiling. Lilith understands that smile. 'Star, aren't you going to drink that? What a waste.'

Lilith thinks back over the last twenty-four hours. *Hers is the face from the magician's photographs. This must be his girl.* A smile plays across Lilith's lips. Sipping her drink, she continues to watch the women. The tall one, Raven, keeps glancing across the room. When Lilith smiles, Raven smiles back and shifts in her seat.

Lilith feels the potential for power radiating from the group of girls. Her thoughts touch the blonde girl first: *she is cleverer than she pretends.* The girl makes eye contact. A look of recognition passes between them, but she isn't the source of the power.

Now Raven— *lust and an overwhelming need to be in control.*

Star— *there it is: an energy as yet untapped, ignored. Repressed.* Lilith understands what the magician sees in her.

Lilith finishes her drink and leaves. Outside, her breath makes curls of mist in the chill air. Her lightly covered nipples respond and harden. She laughs, *all flesh is weak.* Despite her involuntary physical reaction, Lilith does not feel uncomfortable as she walks among other bodies that wander or stand outside bars and restaurants. Many of these others are also coatless. She strides through the streets, over cobbles and tarmac alike, along ancient lanes and through modern shopping centres. She is not followed. She returns to her room alone as the sky lightens. It is quiet now. She closes her eyes, allowing her body to rest.

CHAPTER SIX

SATORI RUBS his forehead and looks up from the heavy book. Star's voice crackles and hisses in his head, like a mistuned radio, stuck between channels.

'I don't trust Paul. Be careful,' it warns him.

He nods and tries to reassure her that he is perfectly safe. His power is greater than the older man's, and he will see her soon. The room shifts and floats before his eyes. Closing them, he wonders if coffee might help him concentrate. Unfortunately, getting coffee would involve walking through the house and seeing Paul again.

He wishes Star had stayed. So much knowledge and only Paul to share it with. If Star was here, he could show her some of his power. The research is a revelation. He can bind people by his will. The first time he tried was with a delivery driver. The man was held motionless for three minutes before Satori released him. He sneers thinking back. The power, it's all about the intoxicating power. It works on Paul, too. At least it has stopped the man barging in without knocking. But Paul's strength to resist Satori's will is nothing compared with the power of Lilith, and all of this feels like play.

The more Satori practices, the more he realises he has gone beyond what Paul can teach. Paul's books, however— opening them, absorbing their musty pages and archaic language— he can smell their power. Energy lifts from each paragraph and crackles in the air around him. He doubts their owner has read even a tenth of them. The secrets they hold— power beyond reckoning. He will learn how to defeat Lilith; he is certain of it, but how long will it take? *Will I run out of time?* He could spend an entire lifetime in these books and still leave some pages un-turned.

The room has settled again. His eyes are ready to focus once more. Instantly, Satori forgets the idea of coffee and returns to the book on his lap. He sits cross-legged on the floor. His eyes pore over the words. A noise behind him makes him jump.

'Paul, you scared me.'

'Sorry, Satori. I brought you some water, and I've made lunch. Would you like to eat?'

Satori shakes his head. 'Your library is amazing, but I can't find the answers I need. These books just don't cover battling anything as powerful as Lilith.'

'Well, think about it, Satori. What is Lilith? If it's a demon, it's as powerful as Asmodeus or Satan, but the Kabbalists call it a god. I'm not sure we'll ever find the answer,' Paul says. 'You might as well rest for a while. I'm worried you'll burn out.'

'There is always an answer. We just need help. Maybe to fight a god you need a god. But who? One of the pre-Christian ones? Do you have no ideas at all?'

'I have one.' Paul walks across the room to a black lacquer cabinet. Taking a key from a chain around his neck, he unlocks the door. On a shelf at chest height, Satori sees something covered with black linen. Paul beckons him over. Even covered, Satori can feel the object's power. It frightens him.

'What is it?' he whispers.

Paul pulls the material away, and Satori faces a clay head. Glyphs are carved across the forehead, cheeks, and on either side of the chin. The eye sockets are filled with obsidian, and the mouth, opened in an eternal scream, is stuffed with red clay. Satori lifts his hand toward it.

'Careful,' Paul says.

'What is it?' Satori asks. 'It feels… powerful.'

'It's a Vessel of Balon,' Paul answers, staring at the head. 'And if you break the seal, the demons inside it will tear me apart. It's an oracle of sorts. If I ask it a question, it must tell me the truth.'

'Ask it about Lilith,' Satori says.

'What *precisely* do you want me to ask?'

'Can I destroy her?'

Paul lifts the head and sets it on a low table. He pauses then turns it a few degrees anti-clockwise. His movements are gentle and full of reverence. A thread of sweat trickles down his brow as he concentrates.

'Vessel of Balon, I have fashioned you with my Art and given you life. Now answer in truth. If the sorcerer Satori battles Lilith, can he destroy the demon?'

The room is silent. The glyphs on the head glow red. Its obsidian eyes shine as if lit by an internal fire. Satori's ears strain to hear the answer. Holding his breath, he watches the head. Every hair on his body stands on end. Despite his fascination and desire for knowledge, his body tells him to run from the room and never return.

A trio of cold, powerful voices echo each other. 'No.'

Satori sighs. 'Ask it whether I can get rid of her.'

Paul asks, and the same deep, alien voices reply. 'Yessss.'

'How?' Satori asks. His voice is brighter now.

'The magician Satori must use his instinct. The answer will not be found in one thousand years of research.'

'What kind of answer is that?' Satori yells. He lunges toward the vessel. Paul stops him and holds him fast.

'No, you can't break it,' Paul says, shaking. 'Please, you cannot break the seal.'

Paul's breath tickles his ear. Satori steps back. He needs to think.

'What will you do now?' Paul asks.

Satori shrugs. 'There's never been a magical problem that I've not found a solution for. The vessel told me to follow my instincts, and my instincts tell me I need to keep looking. So, I'll go back to the books until something else pops up, I guess. But at least it means I can ignore all the modern volumes. What have you got older than one thousand years?'

Paul does not answer. He covers the head and locks the cabinet.

'You made that thing?' Satori asks.

Paul nods. 'I often wish I hadn't. It's like the picture of Dorian Gray. It haunts my dreams and plots my downfall.'

'How did you make it?'

'I'll get the book and all the other old books,' Paul tells him. 'After you eat.'

CHAPTER SEVEN

EVERYONE WORE black. No one spoke. *You are the centre of atten-tion, sister.* Music surrounded Freya, voices wailing, trying hard to communicate their pain. Freya did not sing. She watched and she thought. *I know you're there, although your shell is hard and dark and shiny. But I also know you're not. You're still at home, painting your eyes and back-combing your hair. You're still in the park. I hear your screams every time I pass the gates. Most of all, you're inside me. Your rage fills me. Your spit runs from my eyes. Your hatred tastes bitter in my mouth.*

All but one of the heads bowed, a room of whispers. The shell descended, the machinery groaning as if unwilling to accept one so young. Freya shook. A desire to run to the altar and throw herself onto the coffin and into the flames pumped adrenaline around her body. *I cannot take this burden, the only daughter. I cannot be protected, feared for, held forever— a double image on a single face.*

Her brother's fingers reached across her lap and grasped her hand, assuring her she was safe, loved. She bowed her head, and tears fell from her face. Not her sister's spit this time but a spring of regret. *I will miss you.*

Ivan's hand still held hers as they walked outside. The sun hid its face. The sky's funeral garb faded from years of grief. Its cold tears fell on mourners' heads. Mother and Father cried, too. Lorraine, the mother, cried loudest. She could not accept what they did to her baby, her daughter, her life. That beautiful face crushed beneath boots. Her ribs cracked, and her vagina torn. *Why?* Freya loosened the grip on her fist and ran to her mother.

Maternal arms opened to hold her, washing her hair with a mother's tears.

'I love you,' Lorraine whispered.

Is she telling me or you? Maybe both of us.

'Who are you going to see?' Lorraine calls through the kitchen door.

'Just friends,' Freya answers.

'Dad will drive you,' Lorraine insists.

Mother always insists. At fifteen, I've never had a boyfriend. My sister died two years ago. I wish it had been me instead.

'Forget it. I'll stay home. I've just remembered I've got homework to do.'

Freya trudges back up the stairs, wearing one of her sister Tanya's skirts. Tanya's bedroom remains untouched, except by Freya: a shrine to the girl who once was. As she walks, Freya moves her hips in circles like a belly dancer. Satin brushes against her ankles. She feels romantic yet powerful but has no one to test the effect on.

Her eyes linger on her brother's door for a moment. Her heart pounds as she listens to the movements inside. *Does he have a girlfriend?* Her hand hovers near his door handle. One smooth click and she could open the door. She pauses, frozen in time, a statue pointing toward temptation or salvation. She bites her lip then turns away. *He is my brother.*

Throwing herself onto her bed, Freya sighs. Routine crushes her, squeezing the life from her until only a husk remains. She opens her school bag. The smell of old pages escapes into the air. Her electrified hand grasps the book.

On her way home, she passed a bookshop. A book called to her through the window. She wanted it so badly it made her shake.

Checking her purse, she almost walked away. Three pounds would never be enough, but the book dragged her back, its promise like claws tugging her hair. The coins felt like concrete in her purse. *If don't have enough money, I can still enquire.* The shopkeeper smiled and took the book from its stand, his eyes never leaving her. She felt his stare as she grasped the paperback from his hand. Her ragged breath ruffled the yellowed pages.

'Pay me what you have. I'm sure we can make an arrangement to cover the balance. Come back next week,' he said.

'I will pay you every penny.' *Even if it takes longer than a week.* 'Thank you.'

Freya stares at the cover; a beautiful woman with long hair and a snake between her legs laughs at the world. She traces the image's naked curves with her finger. *If I cannot kiss boys, I can at least drink words of love and sex.*

Lying on her bed, thighs squeezed together, she flicks through the pages. She needs to pee, but holds it inside her, luxuriating in the feeling. It adds to the tingle. On almost every page there are line drawings, unusual and exotic people, men with beards, asleep yet ecstatic, mounted by a woman. So many drawings, most, but not all, are sexual. Her mouth feels dry, and her thighs moist. She tries to ignore the burning sensation in her bladder, wanting to stay like this, to feel this heaviness inside of her. She reads the first paragraph. The words are hard to understand. She rereads it, trying to make sense of them. Urgency builds inside her. She really needs that piss. Throwing the book across her mattress, she crosses her legs. Almost too late, she sprints to the bathroom, harnessing her bladder for a few more moments before warm relief and the familiar emptiness returns.

As she walks back to her room, her fingertips brush against the painted wood of her brother's door. She pictures him in his faded jeans and white t-shirt, bare-footed, his nose buried in a book while his iPod whispers music into his ears, lost in his own world.

The doorbell rings. Mum shouts up the stairs. Ivan does not hear so Freya opens his door. He is exactly as she pictured him, and he looks up at her as she enters. A smile breaks across his face. She mouths words at him. He removes his headphones and tilts his head.

'Satori's at the door,' Freya tells him.

'Thanks, sis,' he says, closing his book and winding the wires of his personal stereo. He puts both on his desk then kisses Freya on her forehead. 'See you later. Don't do anything I wouldn't do.'

It's a traditional farewell, but she has no idea what he would or wouldn't do, he never tells her. *I wish he would.* Even if she knew the boundaries he was setting, she could not escape her prison to fulfil them. She watches him leave. He takes the air with him, and for a moment, Freya feels lost in a vacuum; her sense of balance and gravity are confused; which way is up and which down? She grips the smooth surface of the door until the edges of it press into her flesh.

Gradually, her orientation, her knowledge of the physics of this world, pushes back into her mind. She walks unsteadily across the room and glances at the book on Ivan's desk, but it does not hold her interest. She thinks of her own, waiting for her on her pillow as she unwinds the wires of her brother's iPod and listens to the music: heavy guitar and melodic voices. Shaking her head, she carefully winds the wires around her wrist. *Will he notice any difference?* Part of her hopes he will. She wants him to challenge her, argue with her, curse her. *Why did I tidy them at all?*

On her way back to the bedroom door, she reaches into the linen basket and grabs an unwashed t-shirt. Draped carelessly across her bed, nestling in the musky cotton, she picks up her book and reads.

CHAPTER EIGHT

'I DON'T trust Paul. Be careful.' Sarah screws up her eyes and imagines Satori hears her warning. He has been silent for days, no messages, no calls. His mobile is always switched off.

Sarah finds it impossible to concentrate. Sitting at her desk, hooked up to the telephone, she feels like a machine. She hopes no one will review her calls today. *Smile when you're speaking. The client will hear you smile.* Her frown deepens. Blinking, she logs off the network and hurries to the bathroom. It isn't her break time, and chances are she will be summoned to the office for leaving her workstation without permission, but she needs a moment to close her eyes and stretch her legs.

Fragments of colleagues' answers to unheard questions buzz past her as she scurries across the busy room.

'Yes, that's right…'

'Yes.'

'Our most popular tariff…'

'… with unlimited texts…'

'No, there's no tie in after the initial…'

'Yes,' 'Yes,' 'So that's,' 'Yes.'

Voices merge into white noise which fills her head. Running now, she holds her hands over her ears. Just a few more steps and she'll be safely inside a toilet stall. Her stomach churns, and she feels hot. Sweat prickles her neck.

As she passes her boss's office, her manager, Wendy, steps outside. They almost collide, and now Wendy blocks her route to the bathroom.

'It isn't your break. Why are you logged off?' Wendy asks.

Sarah looks at the angry face. She clutches her stomach, bends in two, and vomits all over the woman's designer shoes.

'I… I'm sorry,' Sarah stammers as she pushes past Wendy and opens the bathroom door.

The water is cold and splashing it on her face helps revive her. A strange face with hollow eyes hovers in the bathroom mirror. She stares at it, shaking her head in disbelief. The urge to draw it, pluck it from her head and set it down on paper, makes her fingers twitch, but her bag is still under her desk. Wetting her index finger, she traces the outline on the mirror: an oval shape, black circles like coal where the eyes should be, and its wide mouth, stuffed with a dull red clay or mud. Symbols, like the ones in Steve's room, are carved into the cheeks, forehead, and chin. She can feel its rage and torment, trapped inside its artificial shell— just like her.

It frightens her, and she smears it away, but the face remains in her head. Screwing up her eyes, she tries to think of something else, anything else. Her father's face pushes the mask away. She smiles until she sees the torn paper clutched in his trembling hand. His face is full of disappointment.

'What made you draw these?' he asks her.

Shame burns her cheeks then anger. *They were good. How dare he tear them up?* She does not reply. Standing in front of him, tears stinging her eyes, she bites down on her bottom lip.

The ripped drawings fall to the floor, and his hands are on her shoulders, shaking her then embracing her.

'It's okay. We'll get you some help,' he whispers in her ear.

Sarah opens her eyes again and stares at her face, distorted by the wet mirror. She licks her lips and tastes blood and vomit. Bending down, she swills out her mouth. *It isn't fair. All I want is to be in control of my own life. Is that too much to ask?*

Satori's familiar face returns to her thoughts. Compared to the mask or her father's disapproving eyes, it is a welcome image and one she embraces.

'I shouldn't have left you there alone,' she says. 'Why don't you text me?'

Blushing, she remembers her garbled conversation with Marian, his mum. Marian did not share her concern, thought Satori could take care of himself; she had sensed the impatience in his mother's voice. *Does she think I'm stalking him?* Sarah wonders how many times her strange yet beautiful boy has stayed away from home. *I guess Marian's used to it.* The time they were together, Satori frequently slept at Sarah's flat. *Where else does he sleep?*

Her empty stomach twists with jealousy. Not only at the thought of Satori sleeping next to another woman, but also at his complete freedom. Whenever Sarah stays away from the flat, Donna worries. Before Donna, Sarah's gaolers were her parents, after Donna maybe a boyfriend, partner, husband. She dreams of a life without obligations; no need to log in and out— a life without walls. Years of studying for an art degree yet she still spends each day advising idiots about the best possible tele-phone tariff. *What do I want?* In the mirror flickers an image: a tiny cottage, surrounded by flowers and trees; ivy climbs its walls. *I'd have no phone. I could paint all day. But who would buy my paintings? Who cares, I'd live simply. I'd get by.* Warmth spreads through her. Could she do it? Live alone, live free. In those odd moments when she does not feel weighted down by life, she imagines her existence is no more than a cocoon from which she will, one day, emerge— transformed.

On other days, she looks ahead and sees only this until the moment she finally slashes her wrists and kisses it all goodbye.

Yes, she envies Satori his freedom, but she still worries about Paul's intentions. Paul seems far too interested in him. *What will he do? No, Satori can take care of himself. That's what being a man means, but there is the other thing— the demon, real or im-agined— what will we do about Lilith?* Only a few days ago she pledged to help Satori defeat Lilith, and yet here they are, al-ready separated by distance and focus. *Am I letting him down?*

'Stop this,' she growls at the mirror. *I'm not letting anyone down but myself. Have I bought into his psychosis again? Satori is a disease. I see his face, smell his skin, and I am lost, drowning in a world of chaos and magic. It isn't my world, it's his, and I don't belong there.* She shakes her head; tears sting her eyes. *But where do I belong? Not here.*

She should go to Satori because standing here in the bathroom is getting her nowhere, then at least she could check he's okay. She dries her face and heads for the door then stops. *Do I want to help or hold him? I left him for a reason, many reasons. It was painful enough the first time. I might not be strong enough to leave again.*

She looks back and stares at her face in the mirror. Fingers yanking her curls, she pinches her cheeks and clenches her teeth. She shakes her head long enough and rapidly enough to leave her lightheaded and dizzy. She must stay at work, concentrate, earn her money, and leave. It is the only way she can be free in this world.

She walks back to her desk. As she reaches it, she hears her phone beep and rushes to her open bag. *Let it be him. Let it be him,* she wills. It is a text from Raven. Logging back onto the network, she puts the mobile back, the text unread. Her phone beeps again, and she rummages through her bag: Raven. She decides that reading the messages and answering is the only way to get some peace.

'Got tickets. You owe me £40. Raven x'

The second text reads, 'Where are u? Answer me dammit.'

'Okay,' she texts back and weeps. Feeling someone standing just behind her, she looks up. It is Wendy.

'I… I'm sorry,' she says again. Her eyes dart down to Wendy's stockinged feet.

'Just go. Come back when you're well enough. We'll talk about it later,' Wendy answers. Not waiting for a reply, the woman marches back to her office.

Sarah gathers her things and trudges to the elevator. Outside, the sun is shining. The air feels warm for October. Gulls swoop and glide overhead. She passes through a cloud of cigarette smoke as she walks to the bus stop. Blinking at the bright sky above her, she wishes she could join the birds.

The bus is almost empty. The few people sitting downstairs

are laden with bags of shopping. A mother reaches for her young son as he yanks a roll of shiny, holly print wrapping paper from a bulging carrier. He jabs at the empty aisle with his prize, humming.

'Michael, give it back,' his mother growls.

'I'm not Michael, Mum. I told you already, I'm Luke Skywalker,' he says, slipping off his chair. A huge grin lights up his face.

'Come here. You'll fall.'

The boy looks up at Sarah and frowns. 'Why's her face all weird?' he hisses at his mum.

The woman shoots a glance at Sarah. 'Shh,' she says, taking the opportunity to pull him back onto his seat.

Sarah blushes and looks out of the window, mobile phone still clutched in her palm. *Maybe I should call him. Make sure he's okay?* His number is still stored on her speed dial.

'Welcome to Mobnet answer service. The mobile you are calling is switched off. Please leave a message after the tone…'

Pressing the disconnect button, she sniffs. *What the fuck is wrong with him? Why can't he think of anyone other than himself? Why do I care?* Frustrated, she throws the phone back into her bag and presses her nose and the palms of her hands against the cold glass. Condensation tickles her skin. Pushing as hard as she can, she imagines the glass melting. *If only I could grow wings and fly away.* The glass remains solid, and her breath obscures the outside world even more. *I hate my life!* She wants to scream the words, but the people around her stifle the sound before it is formed.

The apartment is empty. Sarah switches on the television and turns up the sound. Excited voices fill the room. She takes her mobile phone and places it on the coffee table. One at a time, she pulls open the heavy velvet curtains. Shafts of sunlight hit the dusty air, and, for a moment, Sarah is mesmerised, watching the tiny particles swirl and dance around the room. Picking up her phone, she checks she has a signal then replaces it on the table.

The kitchen is dark, so she switches on the fluorescent strip light which hums and crackles as the tube warms. She fills the kettle and drops a tea bag into a mug. Her favourite mug, the one Donna bought her last year. *You're just jealous because the voices only talk to me.* Today, the slogan makes her smile.

Opening the fridge, she looks through bags of salads, tubs of hummus, and a bowl of lentil salad until she finds a bar of chocolate hiding near the back. She grabs it and a half-empty bottle of milk and pushes the door closed. The fridge exhales as rubber seal hits rubber seal. She replies with a sigh.

Tea in one hand and chocolate bar in the other, she returns to the living room. She puts the confectionery down first and hunts for a coaster. Spotting one beside the television, she grabs it. Peter Murphy pouts from the black-and-white image as she covers him with the hot cup.

Shiny contestants with plastic smiles hover on the screen. She flicks through the channels then switches the television off again. Silence. She reaches for another remote control and switches on the stereo. The music is gentle. It must be Donna's. After checking her phone again, she snaps the chocolate into segments and opens the foil packet. She lets the pieces melt in her mouth as she sips her tea.

The sound of a key in the front door wakes her, and she realises she is still cradling her mug. There is no message from Satori. When she tries to call again, his number remains unavailable. This evening, Donna and Raven move around her like ghosts. She hardly notices them. Questions hang in the air unanswered. When they head for their beds, Donna covers Sarah with a blanket.

The following morning at eleven o'clock she makes herself a pot noodle for lunch. Resisting the temptation to curl up again on the sofa, she fetches her artist's supplies: a wooden box of acrylic paints. Her Muse is hiding; after thirty minutes, she packs it all away again without making a single mark.

Pushing the supplies back under her bed, she pulls out a small, black box. Inside is a packet of razor blades. The steel calls to her. Reaching for a new blade, she smiles. She lifts her skirt, baring her pale thighs, and makes her marks. The steel is cold as it bites into her flesh. Teeth clamped against her bottom lip, she shivers. Her canvas is threaded with red, and pain is her art. Her pulse quickens. The sting cleanses her. All other pain is forgotten, and for a few moments, she is free.

She decides to go back to Paul's house. After pressing the buzzer, she waits for what seems like an eternity. Finally, the gate opens, and she trudges up to the door. Paul blocks the entrance. He is wrapped in a silk dressing gown.

'I was in the shower,' he says.

The ridiculousness of Paul's explanation silences her. His hair is dry, and his body stinks. He repulses her, and the idea of him touching Satori makes her body shake and her stomach burn. Anger bubbles, and a red mist sweeps across her eyes; breathing through clenched teeth, she wills the worst of her anger away until at last she is able to speak.

'Can I see Steve, please?' she asks.

'Of course, he's just… practising. He'll be right down. Would you… like to come inside,' he asks, motioning toward the hallway with a dramatic sweep of his arm.

'Thanks,' she mutters.

Satori descends the large staircase like a debutante. His hand strokes the polished wood banister, and his steps are carefully measured. Sarah does not know whether to laugh at him or cry with relief. She does neither. Impatient for him to reach the bottom, she rushes forward.

'How are you? I tried to phone. Your mobile must be switched off. Have you found anything? Are you ready to come home yet? You look strange. Are you okay?'

'I'm fine,' he answers, but his eyes are glazed. She wonders whether he has slept. 'I've almost got it.' Satori's words sound like yawns. Sarah is worried he might fall over. She reaches for his elbow to support him. He weighs nothing, and Sarah imagines her hand passing straight through his arm. His insubstantiality terrifies her.

'You're not eating,' she says. 'When will you come home?'
He shrugs.

She glares at Paul. 'When will he come home?'

'When he's ready. He needs to be prepared,' Paul answers.

'What's wrong with him?' she asks.

'He's perfectly okay. The magic just takes its toll. He'll go back to being the Satori we know and *love* as soon as it's all over. Now, did you need something? Only, he should get back to work.'

Staring into Satori's eyes, she sees mist rather than granite in their greyness. 'Come and sit down. Talk to me, Steve…Satori. Tell me all that I've missed.'

'He doesn't have time, darling,' Paul answers.

She silences Paul with a cold stare. He looks frightened of her, although she cannot understand why.

'I'll help you,' she whispers in Satori's ear. 'Tell me what to do.'

'Thank you,' Satori answers, his fragile voice barely audible. 'I don't know what you can do yet. Not until…'

'Until what? Tell me.' She feels the familiar bubbling in her mind. *Until I believe.* 'I understand. I want to help you, though. Do you need anything from home?'

Satori shakes his head.

'We've got everything we need, thanks,' Paul answers for him. His low voice growls as though speaking through clenched teeth.

She feels expelled from this place, this time, these people. Hairs on the back of her neck stand on end and her skin prickles. *I shouldn't be here. I'm making a fool of myself. Walk away. Let them have their time together.*

'Just keep your phone on, okay? In case I need you.' *I love you.* Those three words shoulder their way into her thoughts.

She concentrates on each syllable. A smile flickers across Satori's lips, and she wonders if he understands.

'I'm sorry, Star. You need to leave now,' insists Paul.

She fights the desire to leap at Paul's smug face and tear at his skin with her nails. Without saying another word, she leaves, hoping that Satori will remember his phone.

CHAPTER NINE

Satori watches Star leave. *Why can't I speak to her, tell her the research is complex, and I'd be better off with fewer distractions?*

Paul is always there, lavishing attention on him. An altogether more intimate quest threatens to eclipse Satori's search for a way to stop Lilith. Star's departure feels like a final goodbye.

Why can't I just tell her how much I love her— need her? If she asks me, I'll promise to give it all up, marry her, and never look back.

He turns, planning to look for his jacket and turn on his phone, but Paul catches him around his waist before he takes four steps toward the cloakroom. The older man's strong arms hold him firmly but tenderly as his breath gets closer and closer to Satori's throat. He hears Paul's shallow breathing in his ear.

'You're better off without her,' Paul whispers. 'She'll only try to stop you.'

Satori does not answer. The man's sandpaper skin brushes his neck. He closes his eyes and lets his body sway forward and back. The movement disorientates him. He wonders whether he will lose his balance and fall to the floor, or will Paul catch him?

His head is unbearably heavy, and his arms hang like lead weights from his shoulders. Even opening his eyes requires too great an effort. Instead, he allows himself to be guided back upstairs.

In the bedroom, Paul loosens his silk belt and lets his robe fall open. Satori looks at the man's body. His chest is wiry and hairless with nipples so pale that they are barely visible except for the rings hanging from them. Memories of Star's beautiful breasts, small and high with dark pink nipples which point upward when teased, fill his head, and he licks his lips. Paul's boxer shorts tent with excitement.

Hovering by Paul's bedroom door, Satori feels the rapid beating of his own heart. Adrenaline makes his stomach churn. *Fight or flight?* On the other hand, he likes Paul and finds the older man's company stimulating. He does not want to lose the friendship.

Paul moves closer. Like a geisha, he inches toward Satori. *Fight, flight, or fuck?* Any homoerotic fantasies would always be with a man his own age: a beautiful, tentative, Gothic man, a mirror image, with long, black hair, ivory skin, and kohl-rimmed eyes. Not an old, frail man. Not this man. Whispering a few words beneath his breath, he holds the man in stasis. He narrows his eyes and concentrates on Paul's motionless body. Despite his age and claims to a weak heart, Paul looks strong and vibrant.

Time stands still as the men face each other. Like a breath held too long, watching Paul makes Satori's body shake. Something inside him is bursting to be released, burning him, begging him to let go. *Fuck.*

He already knows this moment, this potentiality, is more exciting than the actuality could ever be. This desire is physical, not spiritual and, for just one second, he feels like crying. Then Paul's body draws his attention once more.

Satori's imagination paints pictures on the other man's skin. Symbols burn on the pale flesh then Paul's arms become great tree trunks topped with silver foliage, and faeries dance across his stomach. Pan stretches out to him from Paul's chest. The fawn's lascivious smile invites Satori to join the dance. The images fade, and Paul's body glows as a golden aura traces its path around his form.

He releases Paul, who advances. Satori has no idea whether he wants this. He tries to shrug and smile, but Paul is too close to sense any dismissal.

Satori's lips are pressed by the fleshy mouth of his friend. His tongue is tickled then covered by another tongue. His mouth is full of heat and saliva, and he finds himself hardening, responding in kind to the passion pushing inside him. He grasps Paul's shoulders and pulls him closer. His own tongue explores the other man's mouth, two muscles expanding and contracting, stroking each other, moving blindly. His hands move down Paul's back. His fingers grasp buttocks, and he pulls them toward him, pressing himself against Paul's cock.

Paul guides him to the bed, and Satori no longer judges the man by his age or beauty. He wants to know him, all of him. *What are looks when eyes are too close to focus? What is youth when skin is willing and able to please?*

Paul's scent is intoxicating. All Satori can concentrate on is that smell of sweet musk and a growing need to be inside. His penis aches, wanting to be touched, and Paul's fingers, when they close around it, do not disappoint.

CHAPTER TEN

'THANKS FOR inviting me,' Sarah said. Her eyes shone, and her smile seemed irrepressible.

For a moment, Donna watched her new friend in silence then they hurried along the road again. She wondered why she couldn't find the right words. After all, Sarah was the reason she was going to this party in the first place, the exciting new friend she met a week ago at the train station.

Sarah was twenty years old and in her final year at University. *Why didn't I meet her earlier?* 'It's just a party,' Donna managed at last. 'I don't know whether you'll even like Raven. She's a bit…'

'A bit what?' Sarah stopped walking and stared into Donna's eyes.

For the hundredth time this evening, Donna felt her words melt away. She shook her head and shrugged at Sarah's confusion.

'What?' Sarah pressed.

'W-w-well Raven is very Gothic.' Donna smiled with relief, having successfully finished the sentence then noticed Sarah's frown.

'So? Isn't that why we're going to her party in the first place? Aren't we a bit Gothic, too? At Uni, they call me Ms Le Freak.'

Donna pushed her long fringe out of her eyes and looked again at Sarah. *How could anyone consider this girl a freak?* She looked like Lizzie Siddell and was the most beautiful woman Donna had ever met. She only wished she knew whether Sarah felt anything more than friendship toward her.

'Um, yeah, I suppose so. You'll see when we get there. You can make up your own mind about her, I guess.'

'I can hardly wait. Oh my god, we're so late. Why did I take so long to choose my outfit?' Sarah nudged Donna's elbow and marched ahead.

'Don't worry. It's fine,' Donna said, hurrying to catch up.

'The party's only *from* nine, it'll go on all night.'

'Donna,' a male voice shouted from across the street.

Donna felt cold; she knew that voice. Feigning deafness, she walked faster.

Sarah tugged at her shoulder. 'I think someone's calling you,' she whispered.

Sarah was gone, and Donna felt the pull of her presence far behind. She stopped walking and glanced over her shoulder. Sarah waited on the pavement, ten paces back, eyes fixed on the man who hurried across the street toward her.

Donna walked back toward her friend. With each step, her throat tightened. As those grey eyes met hers, she wanted to flee, but her feet were rooted. She could not leave Sarah alone with him.

'Hi,' the young man said. 'Couldn't you hear me call you, Donna?' His cruel smile seemed to revel in her discomfort.

Donna glanced at Sarah. If she had expected Sarah's skin to crawl in the presence of this creature, she was wrong. Sarah was smiling, pupils wide open, soaking up the vision of this terrifying man. *Why doesn't Sarah look at me like that?* Donna blinked hard. She refused to cry.

'Donna,' he said, nodding. 'And you are?' he asked, gazing at Sarah's open face.

'S-S-Sarah,' she stammered.

'If you're heading to Raven's, I'll walk with you,' he told them.

Neither of the women argued. What could Donna have said, and who would have listened? She knew Sarah was already lost to her. *Why did we walk this way? We should have cut across the park. The attack was years ago, but women, especially Gothic women, still don't walk there.* She wanted to say something, divert Sarah's attention for a while, but what could she say?

Everything she had ever thought to utter to her friend was already said in her eagerness to speak, to listen, to engage Sarah's attention. It was all empty now. Her words had left her, and in their place, a painful lump rested just below her voice box.

Donna tried not to listen as they chatted beside her. Every now and again, a phrase reached her ears, Sarah speaking about art, he about books. Donna tried to define why she disliked him so much. If she could have explained it to Sarah later, her friend might have seen it with her own eyes, felt it crawl on her own skin, but Donna did not know. The feeling was deeper than language, more instinctual. He frightened her.

Raven's flat came into view at last, a discreet door nestling among identical two storey flats in a shabby cul-de-sac. The door hung open, and the thud of industrial beats washed over her last steps. Raven would protect Sarah. Maybe, if Donna asked, Raven would expel him from her home, his scaly tail between his legs. Energised, she hurried up the steps. She knew he let Sarah walk next. She felt him leering at Sarah's back, at the way her buttocks moved as she climbed the steep, uncarpeted stairs.

Donna's stomach tightened. Raven's big, black boots stood firm on the living room floor. Donna rushed to her. She touched Raven's arm, interrupting the conversation. Raven scowled then smiled at her. Her pierced lip moved across perfect teeth, but her eyes remained frosty.

'Donna,' she said. 'Glad you could make it. Oh, and you brought a friend.' Then the words stopped.

Donna looked from Raven to Sarah and the man beyond who seemed to be sniffing Sarah's hair. Raven moved toward them. She raised her hands and grabbed the man's forearms. He smiled at her.

'Satori, my love, you came. Where have you been hiding this past month?' When Satori shrugged, she continued. 'Come with me, my darling. We'll get you something to drink.' With a dismissive wave, Raven led Satori away.

Donna rushed to Sarah and touched her elbow. Her friend's eyes looked unfocused, confused.

'Are you okay?' Donna asked.

Sarah nodded. 'Who is he?'

'That's Satori. He's bad news.'

'He's wonderful,' Sarah whispered.

Donna recoiled. Her fingers felt hot. She brought them to her lips and blew on their tips. *Wonderful?* Shaking her head, she opened two bottles of beer and handed one to her friend.

'Just be careful,' she said.

It was obvious Sarah wasn't listening. She stared at the living room door. Donna sighed and walked through the doorway with Sarah close behind.

CHAPTER ELEVEN

THE WARM water caressed Lilith's skin. She lifted arms then legs out of the surface, scrubbing then inspecting. The smears of grey from the wilderness outside The Garden were gone. Her skin was fresh and soft. It didn't glow like Adam's, but it was beautiful in its own way, and seeing herself, she felt renewed pride. She was well made.

Stepping out of the pool, she towered for a moment above Adam's golden head. He was level with her waist, and as he looked up, turned his face toward her and smiled, she felt her body glow. For a moment, she felt confused, her flames, the fire that burned brightly as she descended from the moon, could not be seen. Her body was not alight. She remembered God had made her human, a child of the sun, not the moon. The power was still there, the overwhelming heat in her groin as she gazed into Adam's eyes. The flames were not visible, but they still burned; they burned for him, for the lover she was promised: a man as beautiful as the sun.

The old instinct which guided her when she first straddled Samael was not needed, but it urged her on, adding fuel to the fire within her. She pushed him onto the soft grass, and the deer snorted and bounded away. He reached for her as she lowered herself onto his belly. When their lips touched, she was transported. The kiss grabbed her soul and launched it into the sky. There, the moon at last merged with her sun while in The Garden, Lilith entered Adam, her tongue reaching inside his welcoming mouth. She closed her eyes and tasted his breath. His hard teeth and soft lips bounced against her own. The fire threatened to consume her. She needed him, all of him. With one eager hand, she grasped his cock and opened herself to his exploration. His gasp of pleasure filled The Garden.

Moving to the rhythm of her heart, Lilith sensed something change. Opening her eyes, she looked at his face. Where there was surrender to the pleasure, she now saw determination. His eyes were clouded, and his jaw jutted in a look of fierce desire. He grabbed her hips and tried to move them to his own rhythm. Frustrated at his efforts, he pushed her from him. Lilith rolled onto the grass. The fire still burned but it was joined by a new heat. Her face prickled with anger and confusion. She kicked his leg; he yelped then growled and kicked her back.

All this happened so quickly that when Lilith was grabbed again, spun around onto her hands and knees, and Adam thrust hard between her legs, she was hardly aware of what had happened, was happening. Adam was fucking her, but where was her pleasure? Why was she filled instead with pain, anger, and humiliation? She struggled to move but he held her firm. She tried to talk but her words were stolen. Her screech shook the trees and, as the echo of it died, she felt Adam shudder and gasp. He released his grip, and she crawled away.

Lilith rests her face against the windowpane. They will not see her. Their eyes, mouths, and hands sense only each other. Her own body grows moist and hot as she watches them caress each other. Hands cling, pull, and grasp. Lust drives them blindly into each other's bodies, again and again.

Lilith places her hand against the glass. Oh, to be in there with them and experience this passion first-hand. Their love-making feels demonic like the way Samael filled her all those years ago when they filled the world with demons to thwart His great work. The magicians' poundings have no purpose other than pleasure and eradication— losing themselves in each other, desperate to forget the world around them, locked inside their own warm, safe place.

The boy is tiring. Or is he crying? He crawls beneath the sheets of the huge bed. The white-haired man plants kisses on his lips, but the boy shakes his head. Letting his lover sleep, the man sits naked on top of the covers, smiling.

He glances up at Lilith and reaches for his glasses. Slowly, as if every muscle in his body has turned to gelatine, he pushes himself up and stumbles bow-legged to the window. Their eyes meet, and he places one hand on the other side of the glass. She smiles at him as he reaches for the window latch with the other. The handle moves but the window doesn't open. Pointing to the lock, he shrugs and motions to Lilith to meet him downstairs.

Sliding off the windowsill, she falls lightly to the ground and lands on her feet with an athletic bounce then crosses the perfect lawn to the front door.

Moments later, she steps inside. The man before her is different from the boy-magician. Sentences beginning and ending with 'your will' and 'humble servant' gush from him.

Her thoughts drift upstairs to the pale body curled up in slumber. Again, she wonders why she feels drawn to him. He is nothing— an awkward, arrogant child. She heads toward the staircase.

'Lilith,' the white-haired man calls to her.

She turns to look at his thin, silk-wrapped frame and weak, obsequious eyes. He is speaking again. The sound annoys her.

'I felt it the moment you stepped from Chaos into Malkuth. The world trembled as your foot touched the ground. We all did. You have an army here, should you want it.'

The words buzz around her ears like ravenous gnats. *An army? What do I want that I might need an army?*

His eyes shine. 'We will change the world in your name. Stay. Lead us into temptation.'

Lilith shakes her head. 'You're a bully, a liar, and a misogynist. You would follow me because you want revolution, freedom, and fire, but if Samael or Asmodeus appeared, you would bow before them and, under their protection, spit at all I am and all of womankind. Why do you desire revolution when this world is already of your making?'

He bows his head, but not before she sees the hatred burning in his eyes.

'You want power and glory,' she says. 'I see through you, into the black heart beating pointlessly in your skinny chest. You are nothing, good for nothing.'

'I am nothing,' he agrees. He kneels before her. 'Please, make me something. Let me serve you. Do you want him? I can call him down. What do you want? I will get it for you.'

Lilith strides into the kitchen. Everything sparkles; it is like magic. Drawing a heavy butcher's knife from a chrome block, she touches the tip and runs a finger along the blade.

'Sharpen this,' she tells the man hovering in the doorway.

He looks at her then sets to work, gathering a wand and leather strap from a drawer. The knife sings as it is sharpened. Closing her eyes, she lets its song fill her.

'Knives. Wonderfully phallic, don't you think?' she says, more to herself than him.

'Yes,' he answers quickly. 'People who carry knives are sexually repressed. It's the act of penetration they crave.' He blushes and turns away. 'I'm sorry… here, it's sharp now.'

She takes the blade from his extended hand. He does not meet her eyes. 'You know what I did. Did you watch? Did it excite you?'

'No… I didn't watch,' he stammers, shaking his head.

'Baron… my guide… told me.'

'Ahh.' Losing interest, she turns on a tap. Water hisses into the sink, beating a frantic rhythm on the aluminium. She turns it off again and looks around the room, but her mind wanders upstairs. Her lips tremble as her smile morphs into laughter. The man stares at her, lips twitching in silent prayer or a mantra. *Is he afraid? Good.* She steps toward him, and he takes a step back then recovers himself.

'I want to help you,' he says. 'We share the same dream: a world full of demons and magic, hedonism and despair.'

'You will help me,' she tells him. She pats the flat edge of the knife against her thigh. The movement attracts his attention, and his jaw drops.

'I'm more valuable alive.' He looks as though he wants to say more, but words fail him.

Another step closer, she can hear his heart beating fast, the rhythm flawed, a beat skips and another echoes.

'No! Please!' he cries. 'Satori, help me!'

His words are silenced by her fist. She smashes open his jaw with her punch. Terrified, he stares at her, his mouth hanging limply. Tearing open her blouse, she reveals the swell of her left breast and pulls his gaping maw to her nipple.

'Worship the terrible mother,' she whispers in his ear. 'For she gives you life and binds you to death.'

He coughs blood on her skin, and she smears it onto his face.

'That's good,' she tells him. 'Drink up. You want to grow up big and strong, don't you?'

He gurgles an unintelligible response.

'Shh, it's okay. Mummy's here.'

She cradles his shoulders with her knife-free hand and guides him to the floor. His mouth flaps silently. His eyes scream for mercy.

She smiles. 'There, that's better. You forgot your manners for a while, but it's okay now, isn't it? You'll be a good boy for Mother.'

His robe has fallen open from the waist, and his genitals are exposed. With her thumb and forefinger, she pinches the head of his cock. His body struggles to move away, but she holds him tight.

'You won't be needing this.' She presses the point of the blade into the base of his penis.

A thread of blood pushes through the hole. Looking at his face again, she drinks in his horror, feeling herself grow wet with the pleasure.

'I'll tell you what. If you make yourself hard for me, you can keep it.' She lets go of him.

His hand grasps his dick, and he frantically moves his fist

back and forth along its flaccid length. The blood gives the skin a pink bloom then a deeper red. He moves faster, but he is still soft. His eyes dart from his unresponsive member to Lilith then back again.

'Oh well,' she says. 'You tried.'

He struggles again. Pushing with his feet, inching across the floor, he tries desperately to get away.

'If you keep moving about, it will hurt.' Her stern face crumples into laughter.

She laughs quietly so only the two of them can hear while lifting his balls and slicing through the loose skin with the knife. Three arcs of the blade, and they are detached. Next, she cuts through the base of his penis. His breath is ragged, and his heart strains to keep beating while his blood soaks her skin and seeps across the floor. Still, he does not scream— or cannot scream, and as she makes the final cut, he passes out.

CHAPTER TWELVE

I WALK through the park. Your park. No-one will attack me. I am under her protection. Freya wears her sister's clothes. Not the ones Tanya wore *that* night. Her mother burned those long along. The long, purple, velvet skirt makes her feel beautiful. She takes off her boots and walks barefoot, the soft material brushing her ankles a contrast to the rough path. She wears the darkness like a cloak and hopes it will hide her when she returns home. Lilith calls her here. This place was in her dreams last night, and the soles of her feet have itched all day. *What will I find?*

She passes the place her sister fell, behind the swings, next to the outer wall. The air feels colder here. She walks across and touches the floor. The blood is long gone. Freya never saw the stain. She wasn't allowed to come here, but friends' hushed whispers were overheard, discussions that always stopped when they saw her and were replaced with sympathetic clichés: 'How are you?' 'I'm so sorry'.

How was I? I was crap. I'm still crap. Life never moved on from the point at which Tanya bled to death, here at this spot.

I've invited death so many times, but it has never come to me. Why were you so special? Why did he answer your call and not mine?

Lilith urges Freya on. The goddess has seen this all before. She wants to show her protégé new things. Freya's body tingles. She hopes. Bare feet carry her across the damp grass. Supple blades bend beneath her and tickle the soft arches of her feet.

She half-walks, half-skips to the old boathouse. It used to be full of rowing boats and pedalos, but the boats abandoned the park years ago. These days, it houses drunks and glue-sniffers. Tonight, it appears to be empty.

Freya's feet take her inside. She feels the sting of glass on her sole and lifts her left foot to check. It is a small piece, a splinter, lodged just beneath the surface. She sits and squeezes the skin around the wound, forcing it out. She spits on her foot and replaces her shoes. Beside her is a piece of flint with a sharp tip. It feels smooth and cool when she picks it up. An image forms in her head, and she scribes it on the painted inner wall: an amulet, a spell, a curse. It feels powerful. It feels good.

She hears giggling and moves away. Beneath a weeping willow, she hides, hugging her knees. Her foot burns. She wants to look at the wound again, but two figures come around the corner, so she stays still. The girl is dressed like Freya. She wears a silver chain belt from which hang a hundred glistening disks. Her forearms are covered in silver bangles. The boy is Freya's brother.

For a moment, Freya thinks the girl is Lilith, her wild queen. She wonders if Ivan has been brought here for her. She almost stands up and runs to him, but she recognises the girl's voice— Raven.

'Show me something,' Raven says.

'What?' Ivan asks.

'Anything. Show me anything.'

Ivan bends over the pond and dips his fingers in the water. 'Watch,' he says.

They all watch. Freya wants to get closer, see better, but dares not move. She holds her breath. *What is he doing? Why is it taking so long? Why did I hide so far away?*

A dark shape breaks the surface of the water and touches Ivan's fingers. Raven gasps. A fish leaps into the air, somersaults over Ivan's head, and re-enters the water without a splash. When it resurfaces, it looks at Ivan for a moment then turns and swims away. Ivan wipes his fingers on his jeans, and Raven wraps her bangled arms around his neck, kissing his cheek.

Freya's throat tightens, and her face feels hot. Raven sits

across Ivan's lap and kisses his lips. A lump fills Freya's throat, and her stomach churns with acid. *Raven and my brother!* She wants to leave but Lilith urges her to stay.

'Don't you want to see them?' she asks.

The burning in her cheeks moves to her groin. She does want to see them. She wants to learn, to feel. *Most of all, I want it to be me.*

The kiss lasts forever. Freya's lower back aches and she risks changing position while Raven and Ivan are distracted by each other. Lying under the tree, curled up in a foetus position, Freya's hand plays between her legs.

At last, Raven stands up and moves into the shadows of the boathouse. Ivan turns toward her but does not follow. In the gloom, her pale skin seems to glow and her black clothes merge with the dark as though she is part of that velvety blackness.

Raven's arms make a diamond around her waist then her skirt falls to the floor and she steps out from its circle. Her legs are long and white. Neither Ivan nor Freya move; they both watch Raven entranced as she removes her top and bra with only slightly less fluid movements and stands naked, shining in the half-light— the moon.

Raven beckons to Ivan and slowly he stands up.

Is he reluctant? I hope so. What if he is saving himself for me?

He takes a step forward. Freya wants to shout to him to stop, but he would never forgive her for spying on him. Every step he takes toward Raven prickles Freya's cheeks and heats her desire at the same time. If it were anyone but Ivan, she would enjoy the show, but her lust hurts.

I love him.

'Maybe we should wait,' Ivan says. At least Freya hopes that's what he says. His voice is so low she struggles to hear it over her own panting. He is eighteen, and Raven is beautiful.

Why would he say that?

'Wait for what?' Raven asks him. Her face is soft and open, not a trace of frustration.

Does Raven love him, too?

He shrugs. Whatever reason he had for waiting a moment ago has slipped away. He shakes his head. Freya cannot see his face, but she feels his beautiful smile and watches the reflection of it break across Raven's face.

Raven drops to her knees. Ivan grasps at her hair as she sinks. He holds huge bunches of it in each fist.

So much hair.

Raven's head moves back and forth, a swaying cobra. Freya strains to imagine what that feels like, what it tastes like. She pushes her fingers into her mouth. They reek of her sex and feel too big. She stops, afraid she might tear the corners of her lips. Sucking her thumb, she imagines it swelling. Back and forth, back and forth like Raven and her brother. Hearing a soft groan, she looks at them. Ivan shivers then Raven uncurls her long legs and stands in front of him once more, smiling; she looks peaceful— content.

No! That can't be all there is. There should be more.

Raven dresses then she and Ivan walk away from the boathouse arm in arm. She leans on his shoulder as if needing support, and he wraps his arm around her protectively.

I know she needs neither his support nor his protection. She wants to feel his strength and smell his body, just like me.

CHAPTER THIRTEEN

WHEN SATORI wakes, the room is dark. Alone in Paul's bed, he stares at the clock, willing his eyes to focus on the faint glow of the numbers. Nine o'clock. *How long have I been alone? Did Paul sleep or leave me the moment I closed my eyes?*

The other side of the bed is cold. He reaches for the bedside lamp. The room is freezing, and his manhood, large and proud a few hours before, has shrivelled and is hiding in a mass of curls. He looks for his clothes and finds them among the discarded condoms scattered around the divan.

The room is silent. Satori knows this is a quiet house, no phone, no television, and a stereo that has remained mute for the duration of his stay so far. Even so, the depth of the silence unnerves him. He hurries to dress and opens the bedroom door.

The gallery is unlit, as is the staircase and hallway below. A triangle of light from the kitchen sweeps across the floor. It provides enough illumination to safely creep down the stairs. *Someone else is in the house. Should I look for a weapon? What if it is Lilith? What use would a weapon be against her?*

He was supposed to have found a weapon in words and ceremony, but distractions and ineptitude stalled him. *What now? What if it is her? What can I do? Am I going to die?*

Breathing hard, he descends and walks to the half-open door. At first, the room looks empty then, near the island unit, he sees fingertips and thinking that Paul has collapsed or fallen, he rushes to help him. As soon as he sees the half-naked body, he knows he is too late— Paul is dead. The man's genitals have been severed, and a pool of dark blood has gathered between his open legs. His cock and balls have been stuffed into his open mouth.

Satori turns away and vomits. Doubled over, he crouches, powerless, emptying his stomach of all its contents. He coughs and splutters until his stomach stops contracting. Skirting around the body, careful not to look, he reaches the sink and splashes water over his face. When he turns off the tap, the dense silence descends. His teeth chatter and his body shakes. Without turning, he can still see Paul's mutilated form, dark and sticky in a lake of gore.

He rotates slowly, keeping his ears alert to any noise and stares at the corpse. A thousand questions plague his mind, but the most insistent of them makes his neck tingle: *is the killer still in the house?*

He pulls a butcher's knife from the metal block and begins his search. Every time he opens a door to a darkened room, he fears attack. Holding his breath, he reaches for each light switch; eyes primed to look for shadows he does not recognise. Finally, he is convinced he is alone and drops the knife at his feet.

He falls to the floor beside it. Hands gripping his hair, he leans forward and presses his chest against his thighs. *Why?*

Tears blind him as he rocks back and forth. Images flit through his mind of Paul begging for his life. *Why didn't I hear him scream?* He pulls hard at the roots of his hair. *I should phone the police.* He tries to stand up, but his legs have lost all strength.

Paul's mutilated body flashes in his head like a strobe. *No!* He tries to shake the image away, but it insists on being seen. 'You will be blamed for this,' it tells him.

I will be blamed. DNA evidence will show they fucked, and Paul was killed in such a sexual way that the connection would be obvious. *Fuck! What do I do? Run? No.* Running from the scene, even though every instinct screams at him to do so, would be an admission of guilt in the eyes of the police. *Who did this?* Answers whisper in his ear— *an old lover, homophobes, Lilith!*

Bury the body, run away, and hope no one ever finds me? That would be the smart thing to do. *But can I? Paul deserves better.*

'What choice do you have?' the voice asks.

I don't know. I don't know. Leave me alone.

'Bury him. Buy some time to figure it all out. When Lilith is gone, you can phone the police. Do it!'

Satori looks up from his knees. The dark hallway is empty. The voice is in his head. He sighs and rubs his eyes. Whatever the voice is— instinct, deep self, guardian, demon, it is right. He will be blamed, and Lilith will escape. *I must bury Paul, but where?* Without a car, his choices of burying spots are house or garden. Satori returns to the kitchen to work out a plan.

He forces himself to look once more at the obscene corpse. In his mind, he replays all the police dramas he has ever seen. If he buries it outside, a dog might dig up Paul's body. If he hides it in the house, the smell will eventually alert suspicion. *Acid? Yes, that would work. Where can I buy large quantities of hydrochloric acid? No, too great a risk if anyone does get suspicious.*

This is insane. Satori kneels beside Paul's hand. He holds the cold, rubbery fingers. *This is my friend.* 'I am so sorry. I don't know what else to do. Tell me what to do, Paul.'

There is no answer from the corpse, but a light flicks on in his mind. *I can do this. It's a magical puzzle. I need to strip the bones, what can do that? Of course— scarab beetles.*

He rushes around the empty house again, gathering the supplies he needs from the library, practice room, and stores. The ancient Egyptian statue he grabs from Paul's living room will make a fine tribute. He opens a book of Egyptian ceremonies and gods on the kitchen counter. Silently, he reads through a passage which describes the ritual. Strange excitement temporarily replaces his fear and grief. A thin smile whispers around the corners of his mouth.

Standing in front of his dead friend, he closes his eyes and breathes. He feels the air and energy cleanse his mind and muscles of stress and fear. He is ready. Holding the fetish in his right hand, he recites the words. He calls on Osiris, powerful god of the underworld, to send him scarab beetles to dispose of the blood and gore. When the passage is complete, he opens his eyes and waits.

Tick, tick, tick, tick. Black creatures the size of his hand drop onto the kitchen floor. Shuddering, he smiles. The scene fills him with both awe and terror. Thousands of flesh-eating bugs writhe over each other, across the kitchen floor, and all around him.

As one dark mass, they converge on the dead body, coming from all corners of the room, some taking shortcuts across Satori's bare feet. He is repulsed but stands perfectly still. He needs to concentrate. Their wriggling bodies reanimate Paul in their frenzy. Dead arms lift as the robe sleeves fill with life and movement. The hands change from pink to black then red and finally white as skin and muscle are stripped from bone. The same process happens everywhere. When the skeletal body is ready, the scarab beetles move away, eager to explore the rest of the room. Satori sees them sense him and dismisses them before they can reach his feet.

He finishes the ritual and offers Osiris his tribute, thanking and paying his respects to the god.

The work finished, Satori's calm deserts him, and he retches again. His stomach is empty, but painful spasms fold his body. When the nausea subsides, he strips the bones of its dressing gown and takes the garment to the dining room. A huge fireplace dominates one wall and, hoping the chimney is clear, Satori arranges logs and paper in the grate. His shaking hands snap the first match and the second. It's the same with the next and the one after that. Furious and terrified, he works through ten matches before one catches and flares into a dancing flame. When the fire is lit, he throws the silk into the flames and watches it burn.

The next task is to clean away his vomit, so he returns to the kitchen. The stench fills his nostrils, and he swallows back new waves of sickness. Except for the lily-white bones lying on the floor, all traces of the crime have been erased, and Satori no longer sees his friend in the remains. The pile is devoid of humanity, and he feels his strength return.

Fear, guilt, and grief wait on the outskirts of Satori's mind; they will have their fun with him later. For now, he is calm, and he knows what he must do. He will need some tools to finish the job. He unlocks the kitchen door and sprints to the shed.

CHAPTER FOURTEEN

FREYA LISTENS for noises around the house. It is silent. Her mother and father will be fast asleep, and Ivan will be listening to music. She checks the clock again— ten past twelve. A motorbike coughs outside, and she runs to the window. He is there. *This is it.* Grabbing her satchel, she heads for the door. Each footstep is pre-planned. She knows which stairs will creak and groan under her weight and how far she can open the door before it scratches at the carpet. She will leave silently as long as she can reach the door before he knocks. *Please don't let him knock. Make him remember what I said.*

Pulling the front door closed with a soft click, Freya waves at Dave. His helmet is under his arm, and his long, blond hair shines under the streetlamp. He passes a helmet to Freya, and she pushes it down over her ribbons and hair. He smiles as she tries to tighten the strap beneath her chin with shaking hands. He puts an arm around her waist and pulls her closer. Looking at her eyes all the time, he fastens it for her.

She straddles the bike behind him and pushes her face into his leather jacket. Breathing deeply, the smells of leather and motor oil mixed with cigarettes and patchouli fill her. Putting her hands around his waist, she clings to him as he opens the throttle and drives away from her house.

When they reach the woods, Freya sees five other bikes, black leather and gleaming chrome, parked proudly side by side. *So, it really is a party.* She had hoped it was an excuse for Dave to get her alone. Disappointed, she wonders whether she can entice him away from his friends.

Dave pulls up at the far end of the row and kicks the bike stand into place. Freya lets him get off first and holds out her hand so he can help her dismount. He pulls his leather glove from his hand and grasps her fingers. His strength and warmth send shocks through her body.

'Can we go somewhere quieter?' she asks him.

His eyes widen, and he looks delighted for a moment before confusion darkens his features. 'It's Jack's birthday. Can we just stay for a few minutes?'

'Yes, of course,' Freya answers. A lump in her throat makes the words sound weak and false.

'I didn't realise. I should have asked you out sooner,' Dave tells her. He is smiling again. Leaning toward her, he carefully unbuckles her helmet and presses his lips against hers.

She feels weak, unable to believe that it could happen to-night. She has waited so long for this moment that it feels surreal, pressing her body against his, pushing her tongue into his mouth. He grabs her hair with his free hand, and she sinks to her knees, just as she watched Raven do.

'Nohohooo,' he says, shaking his head. 'There's no rush, Freya. Everything in its own time.'

Her face prickles, and she wants to run. He must sense this because he grabs her arm and holds her steady. They lean toward the bike as he hooks his helmet over the handlebars then strokes her hair and kisses her eyes. His breath smells of cigarettes. Freya imagines curls of smoke rising from their bodies as they kiss again. She nods once and looks at the floor, at his big boots and the leather trousers wrapped around his calves. His rejection, temporary or not, tears at her stomach. She feels angry. Clutching her satchel, she realises she wants to hurt him. *I know I can, I will. I just have to wait a little longer.*

There are seven people, five men and two women, dressed in leather. Some sit and others lie around the small bonfire. Bottles and cans make links between them, completing their circle. Two of the men are smoking pungent-smelling joints. They all nod and smile at Freya and Dave as they approach. Dave leans over and grasps the forearm of a bearded man.

'Happy fucking birthday, mate,' he says, handing the man a white carrier bag.

'Cheers, Dave. Come and join the party. Introduce us to your beautiful friend.'

'I'm Freya.' Maybe her voice is too soft because she hears Dave repeat it and watches them all nod in acknowledgement.

Dave joins the circle while Freya hovers behind him. He keeps looking over his shoulder at her, frowning.

She shifts her bag from hand to hand, watching it swing like a pendulum. She imagines herself hypnotising Dave, forcing him to obey her. The bastard just sits there with his friends talking about bikes and bike parts, music, and other things she has no interest in. *Why won't he hurry?*

Pouting, she wanders from the group and sits down in front of a large tree. She can still feel the warmth of the fire and hear the edges of their conversation. Taking a torch and the book from her bag, she reads. The words are beautiful. They transport her to other worlds, other times. She wants to commune with her goddess, but Lilith has been silent for a while now. Freya has her instructions. She knows what she must do to win Lilith back.

His silhouette blocks the fire's warmth, and she feels her body shiver before she sees him standing above her.

'You okay?' he asks.

Freya nods. She stares at him, willing him to sense her anger, her defiance. He is blind to both. He sees only what he wants to see.

'Wanna go?' He crouches down beside her. His fingers linger for a moment on her thigh, and he exhales.

She drowns in the stench of beer and smoke. *Is it worth it? Maybe I should just go home.* Standing up, she brushes twigs and dirt from the back of her skirt. He goes to help her. His hand brushes the swell of her buttocks, and she realises she will not ask to go home. Her breathing is ragged, and her stomach aches. She feels cold and hot. Her skin tingles. She sees only his face, his brown eyes and his blond hair, his pale but long eyelashes, his wide, crooked nose and his self-assured smile. Freya is sixteen, and she is about to lose her virginity.

She takes his hand and pulls him into the darkness between the trees. She uses the torch to guide them. Their world shrinks until all that exists is his hand within hers, the fire inside her, and the patch of blanched ground before them. She keeps walking. All hope that she will know where to stop, where to pull him to the ground, fades. She wonders whether it matters if she never finds the willow tree. *Will the spell fail?*

Instinct tells her to head left. She walks in this new direction, but Dave pulls her back.

'Why not here?' he asks.

'I waited,' she answers. 'Now it's your turn.'

He stops resisting and follows. The beam of torchlight catches the trailing branches of the willow tree, Freya's goal. She pulls Dave beneath its cage, kissing him. He presses her between his eager body and the willow's narrow trunk. She clings to him as his mouth brushes against her ear, her cheek, her throat. Her nostrils grasp at his powerful scent as she licks his warm skin and tastes the salt of his sweat. Letting her bag drop to the floor, all her thoughts and her plan are wiped from her mind. She is lost. Her brain refuses to direct her. The only will she knows is his will. She senses only his urgency and allows her own to match it.

Her skirt is lifted, her underwear tugged down, her thighs pushed apart, and she feels the pressure of him, a burning and tearing pain then the movement of him within her as though in a dream, too far away to mean anything. When it stops, he holds her, kissing her again, and she realises her face is wet with tears. She turns away from him. Her goddess has not come. She is alone.

CHAPTER FIFTEEN

Satori gathers a spade, crowbar, and sledgehammer from the tool shed outside. His eyes dart around the garden as he carries the tools back to the house. It feels as though he is being watched, but he sees no one.

First the tools and then Paul's bones are carried to the cellar. Wandering from wall to wall, he examines every flagstone and decides on the best ones to lift. There are a few to the edge of the room, which look looser than the rest. He bends and tries to lift them with his fingers. They are too close together, and he cannot get the right purchase.

He tries the crowbar next. The hook slips under the granite square, and he pulls it up, bending his knees, holding the slab close to his chest before swinging it around so he can pile it on top of a neighbour. He does this four times until he feels the gap is big enough. Below is a mixture of dirt and sand. Perfect. Plunging the spade into the earth, he pushes down on it with his foot, careful to pile the soil in one place as he digs.

About a foot below the surface, he lifts a pale stick with the scoop of his shovel. He stops digging and picks the object up for a closer look. It is a bone. From its size and shape, he believes it is a child's femur.

He finds more bones as he digs, more than one skeleton worth. There are so many. Satori tries to catch his breath. His throat tightens, and a terrible thought grips him. *Paul killed them and scattered their bones here in the exact spot I am now hiding his remains.*

Dizziness claims him, and he sits down among the stones

and dirt.

Were the children used as sacrifices by a power-hungry sorcerer travelling on the left-hand path?

Satori wonders whether Paul found pleasure in the killings. He shudders. Skin so recently caressed by his now-dead friend crawls as he imagines the same fingers squeezing the life from a young boy's throat. *Could Paul have murdered these children? Am I any better?*

As he replaces the children's bones in the soil and adds those of Paul, he prays that he will not be responsible for any more death. This done, he scoops the dirt back into place and lays the flagstones on top. Even though he is careful, the stones look recently disturbed. He whispers a spell, a simple glamour to hide the truth from prying eyes until the dust has a chance to settle over the grave.

The wooden staircase groans as he climbs. With filthy fingers, he pours himself a whisky. He wants to sleep, but he has work to do. The demon must be stopped, and he has already wasted too much time. Instead of sleep, he chooses coffee.

He returns to the library. Driven by fear and guilt, he searches the pages of book after book looking for an answer. Accompanied by the angry cacophony of his growling stomach, he works through the night and deep into the following day, only falling into bed when his eyes refuse to focus on the words before him.

Satori wakes to the sound of Paul's doorbell. Checking the time, he realises he has slept late, yet he still feels exhausted. He peers out of the window and quickly pulls away again.

It is Star. She would never understand what he had done last night. Neither will she go away without seeing him. *She could ruin everything.*

He bites down on his bottom lip, trying desperately to think of some solution. The doorbell rings again, a longer buzz this time, angry and insistent. He must act quickly. He can do this.

Satori runs down the staircase and into the hallway. With a few whispered words and a sweep of his hand, his face is temporarily transformed: the perfect glamour.

CHAPTER SIXTEEN

ON THURSDAY and Friday, Sarah tries Satori's number again. Despite his assurances, his phone is still switched off. *Typical.*

She cannot concentrate at work. Her mind flits back to the grand house hiding Satori from her. An all-consuming fear for his safety cannot be quashed. The murder Paul spoke of with authority five days ago has just been reported.

How did Paul know about it? Is he a killer? The killing was sexual, perverted, horrible. What if...

After lunch, Sarah tells her boss she isn't feeling well. Wendy keeps her distance; perhaps the memories of Tuesday are still too fresh, the stuff of nightmares. She's wearing different shoes; did Sarah ruin Tuesday's pumps? All the same, Wendy does not seem satisfied by Sarah's explanation.

'Are you pregnant?' Wendy asks.

Sarah shakes her head. *No, I couldn't be, could I?* 'Absolutely not, no. My house mates have been sick too. It must be a bug.'

'Go then,' Wendy says, frowning. 'I'll speak to HR and see if we can dock your pay, and Sarah... I don't want this happening again. Do you understand?'

Sarah's face reddens. Biting down hard on her bottom lip, she tells herself to keep quiet. Leaving work, her conscience is heavier than her bag. She catches a bus to Snuff Mills and Paul's mansion.

Outside Paul's front door, she waits impatiently. *Answer, damn it.*

She looks up and thinks she sees movement in one of the windows. She rings the doorbell again, holding the button down and letting it ring long and loud.

At last, she hears footsteps behind the door, and it swings open.

There is a strange look in Paul's eyes; he looks haunted.

'Where is he?' she asks, trying to push past Paul.

He smells different than before, familiar. He smells of Satori.

'What have you done with him?' she screams, hoping her voice will carry across the street and into one of the other houses.

'Nothing, he's fine. Calm down.' Paul's eyes glisten with tears, but his lips curve in a smile.

'I want to see him. I won't leave here until I do.'

'I'm sorry, Star. He left this morning. He said he had to go to Gloucester then he would head home. He told me he'd call you. I guess he hasn't yet.'

Paul's tone sounds so reasonable, soft, and patient like a therapist. Sarah does not trust it. The tone is meant to subdue her.

Memories of years spent in psychoanalysis reawaken inside her.

'Would you like to come inside and take a look?' Paul asks.

'Pardon?'

'I said, would you like to come inside and look around? Reassure yourself that Satori isn't hidden away somewhere?'

Paul shifts to his right. The doorway is no longer blocked. Sarah could step inside.

Go inside with you? When I've just accused you of hurting Satori? Sarah backs away and shakes her head.

'No, thank you. I'll phone his mum and find out when he's due back. Sorry to have wasted your time.' She turns and runs down the curved driveway and out on to the street.

When she has turned the corner, she grabs her mobile phone from her bag. She dials Marian's number, but there is no reply. She leaves a message on the machine asking her whether she has seen or heard from Steve, begging her to call back when she gets home.

She considers calling the police. *What would I tell them?*

That my ex-boyfriend is staying at a man's house who I suspect is a murderer? She can imagine their reply.

Staring at the useless gadget in one hand, she bites the nails of the other. She stands that way for minutes, feeling like Rodin's statue. The blue screen mocks her. Her riddle has no answer. Shaking her head, she drops the phone back into her bag.

Wandering aimlessly with nowhere to go, she spots a café and stops for a while to drink a cup of black coffee. The room is quiet, and she feels everyone's eyes on her as she sits down. The caffeine does nothing to settle her nerves.

She can think of nothing but Satori. Two weeks ago, she wanted to never think about him again, and now this… this all-consuming obsession. It is not merely fear for his safety that makes her feel sick. The constant ache between her thighs whenever she thinks of him forces her to acknowledge a truth she would prefer to bury.

Thinking back to what led to her decision to leave him, she concentrates on his negative points. The way he frightened her when he got angry, which was often near the end. He never hit her, but sometimes a shadow would come over him, and she would see a vicious darkness in his eyes, a powerful hatred that would make her run from him.

There were other things, too. Not frightening things like his anger, but annoying things that, when added together, made his company intolerable. Like the way he sometimes wouldn't care about his appearance at all, meeting her at the club with un-brushed and filthy hair, wearing an unwashed t-shirt and broken trainers. Or the way he could spend hours getting ready on other nights, painting liquid eyeliner around his eyes with painful delicacy while she waited in his room. How he might leave her side suddenly to talk to a friend and not return for the entire evening, and the way he would drink too much then sob into her hair, declaring his undying love or complaining that his life wasn't worth living.

Raven loves him, of course, but her other friends congratulated her on leaving him, they agree— he is crazy, impossible, not worth the trouble. The ache between her legs subsides.

Even so, this litany of mistakes and oversights does not explain how she feels. *Why am I so afraid of you?* Staring at the coffee, she feels her mind fall into its dark depths— a priest, a bible, her mother weeping. Her mind recoils. 'What the fuck?'

People whisper their agitation.

'Terrible.'

'No respect.'

'What language!'

Trying to ignore the other customers, Sarah traces the lip of her coffee cup with her index finger. Should she try it again? *No,* she closes her eyes. *No!* Ignoring the urge to stare at the black liquid, she sips her coffee. Yes, she did the right thing leaving him.

Her thoughts betray her. *Despite everything, he could be amazing. The most intelligent man I have ever met. Satori can talk about almost anything and sound like an expert. He is beautiful, and the way he makes me feel when he's close, it's like the hum of electricity awakening every nerve ending in my body. His taste in clothing is sublime, Satori and his sartorial elegance,* she smiles at the thought.

She misses him, but she does not want him back. When she is with him, she fades into the background. *It is never us, it's always Him.* She cannot put herself through all that again. If he is in trouble, she wants to help him then say goodbye.

People are staring at her again. She realises she is crying. Brushing away her tears, she stands up, leaving her coffee and heads for the door.

'Excuse me, Miss,' an insistent voice behind her calls.

She looks around at the waitress. Realising she hasn't paid for the coffee, she sighs and digs into her bag.

'Sorry,' she mutters as she hands over the coins.

The waitress looks at her tight-lipped. Sarah blushes and hurries away.

Outside, she looks at her watch. It is only four o'clock. With no idea what time Marian leaves work but no other place to go, she decides to wait in Satori's front garden. The house looks empty when she arrives, but she rings the doorbell. There is no answer, so she sinks onto the step. It is too cold to sit so she squats instead. Her long, black skirt opens into a circle around her legs, and she looks as though she is stuck in a puddle of tar. Startled by the shrill ringing of her mobile phone, she fishes through her bag for it and puts it to her ear without checking the caller ID.

'Hi, Star,' Satori's voice calls through the speaker.

Her sense of relief is so intense that she loses her balance and has to put her arm out to stop herself falling over. The phone hits the step with a clunk and for a terrible moment she worries it might be broken. Cursing, she fumbles to retrieve it.

'… that?'

What did he say?

'I'm sorry, I dropped the phone. How are you?'

'I'm fine. Sorry I didn't phone before. My battery died. Did you worry?'

'A little maybe. Where are you?' She breathes into the phone. The signal sounds so clear he could be next to her.

'On my way back from Gloucester. Just needed a few things. Paul lent me the most useful books so I'm going back home. I won't be back until late, though. Why don't you come round tomorrow… unless you're busy?'

His question at the end of his soliloquy takes her by surprise, and she thinks for a moment before answering. 'Okay, what time?'

'Um, ten? Does that sound good?' he asks.

Does it? The relief of hearing him alive and well is replaced by a fear of getting close to him again, but she did promise to help him, and it would seem weird to say no now.

'Ten, yeah, cool. I'll see you soon,' she says as much to herself as to him.

CHAPTER SEVENTEEN

SATORI HIDES. He watches Star as he speaks to her. He almost blew everything a few minutes ago, jaunting around that corner, unthinking. Luckily, her face was turned away from him and he had time to see her and retreat. If she sees him now, in the same clothes Paul wore when he answered the door to her, she will ask questions.

The mobile signal is so clear and crisp, she must have heard his question, but her answer seems to take forever.

Does she have plans already?

At last, her reply: it's yes. She will come back tomorrow. He disconnects and smiles. She is getting up now, so he hurries back to the next street for a better hiding place. *If she's going home, she won't come this way.*

Huddled behind a garden wall in the next street, he waits for over ten minutes. He is too close to success to risk ruining things now. She might have stopped to phone someone else and still be standing there in his garden, or a neighbour might have caught her to discover the latest gossip.

Eventually, he creeps back to his own street and finds she has gone.

Inside the house, Satori pours himself a large whisky. He doesn't want to think about anything, but memories and emotions from the last twenty-four hours battle inside his mind: grief, fear, repulsion, guilt, lust, amazement, and joy. The moment he feels ready to tackle one the others push past it, jostling for his attention.

The alcohol slows his mind. He pours another and lets the memories resurface. The first to come is Paul's corpse. Automatically, his mind fights against the image. *Let it come*, Satori tells his consciousness. *I have to face it.*

The image jars. So much red, darker than claret, the colour of an aged ruby port but thick and sticky; it congeals in smears across Paul's stomach and thighs. The open wounds remain wet and glossy. Satori's face is reflected in the vicious hole between his friend's legs. *It should have been me.* On the edge of Satori's perception, he hears Lilith's laugh, harsh and sharp like a bark.

Satori's mind gives him a needle and thread. He removes the slippery organs from Paul's throat, places them where they belong, and, using small and precise stitches, sews flesh back onto flesh and makes the man whole again. A bucket and sponge appear beside him. Satori wets the sponge and washes away the blood. He moves it across Paul's body gently as if afraid to wake him.

When his work is finished, he stands next to the body. Paul's white skin and hair gleam in the half-light. Red wings of blood spread out from beneath him. He looks like a fallen angel, and only the broken mouth remains as evidence of his violent death.

Crouching again at Paul's side, Satori places his fingers on the body's cold, motionless chest. He closes his eyes and whispers old, magical words over and over again. Opening his eyes, he looks at Paul. The skin beneath Satori's fingers glows.

'Can you hear me?' Satori asks.

'Yes,' replies a voice, Paul's voice, although his huge mouth does not move.

'Did Lilith do this?' Satori asks.

'Do you need to ask me that?' Paul answers. 'Are you afraid it was you?'

Satori shakes his head. His throat feels tight. 'I… I know it wasn't me.' His forehead creases and his eyes darken. 'No, it wasn't…'

'Lilith did this,' Paul answers, breaking Satori's chant.

'Why?'

'To get your attention,' is Paul's reply.

Satori's throat constricts further. He fights to breathe. *It's my fault.* Memories of burying Paul in the cellar push past the guilt. He grasps onto them.

'But the bones! Paul, why are there bones buried in your cellar?' Silence. For a moment, Satori wonders whether the spell is broken, but Paul's chest still glows. 'Tell me,' he demands.

'You don't want to know.'

'Yes, I do. What did you do, Paul? Did you kill those children?'

'Yes.'

'Why? Why did you do it?' Satori's voice is high, choked by the lump that's rising slowly toward his windpipe.

'For power, for pleasure, maybe both. Don't hate me, Satori. I couldn't stand it. Whatever I've done, whatever mistakes I've made, I do love you. Let me rest in peace, without your fury.'

'Be gone!' Satori shouts.

First, the light in Paul's chest dulls and dies then the body dissolves into vapour. Satori kneels on the floor. His hands shake. He reaches for his drink and finishes it in one gulp.

'I'm sorry you died like that, you old bastard,' Satori tells his empty glass. 'But now I know what you've done, I cannot mourn for you.'

The scratch and click of keys unlocking the front door makes Satori look up.

'Hi, Mum,' he calls, rubbing his face with his sleeve.

'Steve, you're home.' Marian walks into the room and sets her laptop and briefcase down on an empty chair. 'You'd better phone Sarah and let her know you're okay. She seems to have got a bit needy. I thought you'd split up.'

'It's complicated. Can I pour you a drink?' Satori lifts his glass and makes his way to the liquor cabinet.

'No thanks, love. I've got friends coming over. You're not using this room, are you?'

Satori grabs the whisky bottle by its neck. 'It's fine. I'll be upstairs.'

No doubt, her guests will be those strange women who often spend evenings cackling with Marian. The old one always makes him nervous; it's as though she can peer into his soul when she narrows her blind eyes. He is happy to stay out of their way.

'Thanks, love. We'll talk later,' she assures him.

Settling on his bed, Satori pours himself another drink, and the memories of his and Paul's lovemaking resurface. The blind passion he felt last night makes him nauseous. *Why didn't I sense something?* He quells the thoughts with another fiery gulp. *Lust makes us fools. I wish I didn't have a dick.* His eyes dart around the room, and he covers his groin with his pillow. 'I didn't mean it,' he whispers to the walls.

A fourth whisky dulls his thoughts, and he lies back on his bed, closing his heavy eyelids, pillow still resting on his pelvis.

'What a day.'

He remembers Star's furious face as she stood in Paul's doorway, demanding to see him and purses his lips to kiss the chimera. When she left, he rifled through Paul's library, searching for books to take home, elated and devastated all at once and with the uneasy feeling that he was still being watched.

The doorbell rang again. He remembers how tempted he was to ignore it, instead he renewed the glamour and crossed the hallway.

A policeman and woman filled the doorway. Satori started to sweat, and his mouth would not work.

'It's okay, sir. Nothing to worry about,' the policeman said. 'May we come in?'

Satori nodded and led them into the living room. They sat on separate chairs, facing each other. Both constables had their open notebooks on their laps. His head swam as the woman eyed him curiously. Realising he was holding his breath, Satori exhaled. The sound was much louder than he expected.

'Oh?' he managed to squeak.

'There's been a report of a large dog, running around the neighbourhood,' the policeman continued.

'Do you own a dog, sir?' the policewoman asked.

Satori shook his head. 'No.' His mouth was painfully dry. 'Drink?' he offered.

'I'll get them,' said the policewoman, leaving the room before he could protest.

'Did you see a large, black dog in the area on Wednesday night, sir?' the policeman asked.

Satori tore his eyes away from the empty doorway. He could hear the policewoman moving about in the kitchen. *Is everything as it should be in there?* he wondered.

Turning toward the policeman, he studied the shiny face; he was about Satori's age and had closely cropped strawberry-blond hair.

'What?' Satori asked.

'A large dog. Did you see any large dogs the night before last, Mr…'

Two amber eyes burned at him through the kitchen doors as he watched the scarab beetles devour his murdered friend. He hadn't paid attention at the time, but they had been there in the garden, he was certain.

He shivered and forced himself to focus on the policeman. 'No, I didn't,' he said at last.

The policewoman returned to the room empty-handed and nodded. Her colleague stood up and thanked Satori for his time.

'If you remember anything, sir, or if you see a large dog, please call us straight away.'

Satori tried to give the officers a casual smile and followed them to the front door, locking it behind them. His strength deserted him, and he fell to the floor, weeping silently.

'To Star.' Satori lifts another glass of whisky and salutes the empty room.

Drink dulls the horror and terror of the day, but the spark of possibility burns as brightly as before— Star.

'I love you,' he murmurs into his glass. 'I love you, and you came back.'

Remembering her defiance at Paul's doorstep, he smiles even as tears gather in his eyes. She still loves him, yet he constantly betrays her trust, lies to her, manipulates her, and he doesn't know whether he can stop. It's like a disease.

'Star, you have such power inside you. Why can't you see it?'

I want to show you what you're capable of. These visions of yours, they're the tip of an iceberg, my love. You have such beautiful, terrible depths.

'Let me help you accept yourself. Come back to me.'

He sees her face on his pillow and kisses her insubstantial lips.

'I want you,' he tells the phantom. 'Cleanse me, purify me. I've lost my way. Take me back.'

His fingers trace the outline of her curls, and she smiles. Without undressing, he rubs his body back and forth along the mattress, repeating her name, smiling and crying.

That night, he can hardly sleep. Lilith and fear of death eclipsed by feelings of excitement. Star. Beautiful, intelligent, independent. He loves the way she always refused to be cowed by him, and how she purred when they made love.

When she arrives tomorrow, he will seduce her, and he will never let her go.

CHAPTER EIGHTEEN

Satori wakes from fitful sleep at six am. Only four hours until she is due to arrive. After eating a bowl of cereal, his first jobs are to shave and shower. He is meticulous about this— spending ten minutes soaping and washing under his genitals. He rubs his dermis until it prickles, his pink skin hot beneath the sponge. One by one, he cleans his ears, nose and between his toes. His hair is washed three times. He must be perfect.

Drying himself, although quicker, is equally systematic. He counts as he towels each toe and finger. He uses a light powder, expensive deodorant, and her favourite cologne, the one she bought him for his last birthday. He ties his hair back and brushes each tooth and his tongue then gargles with mouthwash.

While his hair dries, he paints his face. Normally, he would save makeup for club-nights, but today he wants to look his very best for Star. He remembers how she would watch him get ready and realises he has never watched her apply makeup. He wonders how long she takes.

After stroking fragrant oil into his now dry hair, he flattens it between red hot straighteners. His hair shines like a dark halo around his face. Gazing at his mirror image, he smiles.

It is only nine o'clock. He paces the bedroom, willing it to be ten. He checks the clock and is disappointed when he realises his will has not accelerated the passing of time. Snorting, he sits on the bed. His mind clears, and he sits motionless for ten minutes before he remembers *why* Star is coming: Lilith.

From his bag he pulls out the half-dozen books he took from Paul's library, arranging them around the room. Some he opens while others remain closed and stacked in pairs. The effect is one of a person lost in endless study.

He selects a *Dead Can Dance* album. Deep, tribal music washes over him like the ocean of an exotic country. The baseline is the perfect rhythm for sex.

Something small hits his window. He opens it and looks outside.

'Didn't you hear the doorbell?' Star shouts up at him.

'Sorry,' he calls back. 'The music, I'll be right down.'

He follows her up the stairs. Now as always, he loves watching the way her hips move as she mounts each one. His fingers itch to touch her buttocks as they sway right then left and right again, but he knows it is too soon.

Entering the room, she pauses as if unsure of herself. Then, perhaps spotting an open book on his bed, she crosses the floor. She sits on his black duvet and picks up the tome.

'Have you found anything?' she asks, skimming its pages.

He smiles. 'First, would you like anything to drink?'

'Um, yes please. Water would be great.'

He leaves her reading, doubting she will understand a word.

He puts ice and a slice of lemon in the mineral water he pours for her. He blows it a kiss, a small charm for luck, then pours his own glass from the tap and heads back.

Hovering in the open doorway, he watches her. Her finger strokes each line as she tries to make sense of the ancient words. If it were anyone else, he would chastise them for spreading acid over a book worth more than the house around them, but not her and not today.

He studies the small movements of her body. The slide of her hand across the page, the movement of her throat as she swallows, the rise and fall of her eyelids and the way her nostrils expand and contract as she breathes in and out, they all enchant him. Maybe she feels his gaze because she glances up and smiles.

'Thank you,' she says.

He sits next to her on the bed. Not too close, but close enough so that he can feel the energy around her body bump into his own.

'Do you understand any of it?' he asks.

'No,' she says, sighing.

'Would you like me to teach you?'

She closes the book and turns her entire body to face him. 'I think we have more pressing problems, don't you?'

'Of course,' he answers, nodding. 'I don't have the answer yet.'

Her face falls, and he sees accusation in her eyes. She thinks he's been wasting time. Feelings of guilt burn his throat.

'But I'm close to finding it,' he says. 'These books must contain the solution, but they're riddles. Nothing in old magic is ever simple. I'm trying to work it out. I know I'm getting close.'

'Okay,' she says, lowering her eyes.

Her disappointment cuts him. This isn't how he planned it. He needs to get her back.

'Can I help?' she asks.

Yes, he screams inside his mind, *yes, yes, yes*.

'Of course, you can help,' he says aloud. 'I could use your help…' *with what, with what*? 'with looking through this book for any references to Lilith. If you see her name anywhere mark the page number on… this notebook.'

He leans across to his bedside table drawer and removes a leather-bound pocketbook.

He flicks to an empty page and writes in a careful, elegant script. 'This is what it will look like.'

'What language is this, Satori?' she asks.

Pleasure tickles him, hearing her speak his chosen name without prompting. 'It's Ancient Hebrew,' he answers.

'You can read Hebrew?' She looks up at him through wide eyes.

He feels her respect licking his ego. 'Only a little,' he says. 'The rest I have to use a dictionary for.'

'I didn't know.' She sounds astonished.

He wants to tell her more. Explain how the language is numerical and how meanings are layered upon meanings in each passage. Feeling like a child eager for his parents' approval, he wants to tell her the other ancient languages he taught himself to understand and replay that look of wonder and admiration again and again.

She is reading again. Swallowing his words, he gazes at her delicate fingers. They hover over the page. Her movements are faster now she can dismiss all information except the one word for which she searches.

He breathes deeply; her scent, mingled with that of the musty knowledge she holds, intoxicates him. He feels dizzy and screws his eyes up tight to break his trance. *Start working*, he tells himself and reaches for a book.

Absorbed in the mysteries he is researching, time rushes past. A gurgling noise brings him back to the material world.

'What was that?' he asks.

Star blushes. 'I'm sorry, it was my stomach. I skipped breakfast this morning.'

He grins at her. 'I like it,' he says. 'It's like your body is talking to me.'

He puts his book to one side, using a faded ribbon to mark his place for later. Boldly, he stretches his hand out toward her.

'Come, I'll make you some lunch. Mum went shopping last night so there'll be loads to eat.'

She looks at his hand as if wondering whether to take it.

Satori senses her confusion and steps back, lowering his hand to his side. He bows his head in a way he hopes will say, *as you wish. I am as always, your humble and grateful servant.*

She stands up and smiles. He is sure she wants to say something but is too frightened or shy. He hopes the unspoken words are a message of love. They could be. The possibility of it is in the air. The chemistry between them is obvious.

Just take things slowly, he warns himself, *all things come...*

Satori prepares an enormous lunch by grabbing armfuls of food, packets of cheeses, hummus, dips, and salad from the American-style double door refrigerator, bringing them to the kitchen table and laying them before Star like offerings to a goddess. He takes a packet of pita breads from the cupboard, two plates and a new glass of water for each of them, fills and switches on the kettle.

'Marian working today?' Star asks, looking around the silent room.

'Yep. The life of a lonely, only child, eh?' he jokes.

She nods, smiling again. She has smiled a lot today. More than Satori can remember her doing for a long time.

'I feel your pain,' she says.

He opens the bag of pitas for her and watches as she fills one with hummus and salad leaves. He unwraps a block of cheese and heads for the knife drawer.

She watches him slice it. He forces himself to look at the knife rather than her. He does not want to end this shared moment in a pool of blood.

'Would you like some?' he offers, passing a slice of cheese across the table.

She shakes her head, still chewing, her mouth stuffed with food, then licks the hummus from her fingers. As he watches each digit enter her mouth, his pulse quickens. He licks his lips, and she blushes.

'Are you going to Club Midian tonight?' she asks.

He shrugs. 'I thought I'd keep looking through these books. Are you?'

She frowns, 'I haven't decided yet. Donna mentioned some play she got tickets for. I think it's tonight.'

'Are you sure Raven'll let you miss club night?' he says, grinning.

Star snorts a half-laugh then sighs. 'Steve… Satori… whatever. I'm not sure what *this* is. But it isn't a date, okay? I'm not coming back to you. I can't… I won't… I'm sorry.'

She pushes her plate away and gulps her drink.

'Back to the books,' she says and walks out of the kitchen without offering to help him clear up.

Puzzled, he puts the open packets of food away and stuffs the plates in the dishwasher. Before following her upstairs, he takes a few moments to meditate. Sucking deep, cleansing breaths through his nose and blowing hot air through pursed lips. He faces east and visualises sunlight entering him through his skull. With his forefinger and thumb, he touches his forehead, chest, and groin, his left then right shoulder and finally he places both hands across his chest. He feels the light fill his body. Energy crackles at his fingers, then he discharges all the darkness through his feet and into the earth.

Smiling, he jogs up the stairs and joins Star in his room. She is already deep within the book, scouring its pages for the demon's name.

CHAPTER NINETEEN

'I'M MAKING myself some lunch, Raven. Want anything?'

Raven looks up from her book. Her eyes look tired even through the perfect makeup. 'Uhh, yes, I've got some Miso soup in there somewhere.'

'I know where it is. Are you okay?' Donna frowns at her flat mate.

Raven's fingers tremble as she turns the page of her book.

'Sure, yeah, I'll be fine. You know…'

Sighing, Donna stands up from the velvet sofa and stretches.

It is three o'clock already. Time passes too quickly at the weekend. A mountain of washing, a scribbled shopping list, and a dirty bathroom demand somebody's attention. They will all have to wait. Today is the day Donna, Raven, and Star find peace from the soul-destroying working week— a day for reading, music, movies sometimes, not a day for housework. That will be tackled tomorrow with hushed voices and dark shades and the shopping, well it can always be purchased online.

The galley kitchen is tiny. Clusters of plates and dishes, full of cold, foamy water, crouch on the worktop and in the sink, waiting.

'What a dump,' Donna whispers, flicking on the kettle.

'Where's Star?' Raven's voice pierces through the thickening haze of steam.

Donna shrugs and pours the boiling water onto a small pile of powder in the bottom of Raven's black mug. 'I don't know, but she's been acting strangely all week.'

'It'll be a man,' Raven answers. 'It's always a man. They

fuck you up.'

'Amen to that,' Donna whispers as she stirs the powder into a thin and insubstantial looking soup. 'How do you have any energy at all, living on this crap?'

'Hmmm?' Raven's voice sounds automatic. She isn't listening. A world of New Orleans' vampires, futuristic pagans, or Victorian drug addicts must have dragged her back into the pages.

Donna wishes she could consume books as quickly. She wishes she could concentrate on anything other than the growing dread that Sarah is in trouble. *I am not her keeper. I have to let her make her own mistakes.* She knows though that what is easily said is not so easily done.

Where are you? The temptation to phone Sarah's mobile rises for the eighth time since Donna woke two hours ago. Once more, she pushes it aside and pokes her nose inside the fridge to search for something edible: old pizza, perfect.

'Is this gonna be enough?' Donna asks, passing over the steaming mug.

'What?' Raven shakes her head. Her forehead crinkles into her trademark scowl, and she peers up at Donna. 'Yes. It'll be fine… thank you.'

Donna takes a bite of the cold pizza. It always tastes much better on the second day, when the cheese is hard and rubberised. Raven is vegan and Star eats so little that a large pizza can last for days. Strings of cheese hang from the serrated edge. Donna licks a film of grease from her lips and shrugs back into the soft couch.

A contented sigh escapes her before she remembers that she cannot be happy until she knows Sarah's okay.

'You're all tense again, Belladonna,' Raven says, her eyes peering above the sepia pages. 'Why do you worry so much?'

So, it is Storm Constantine's post-apocalyptic techno-pagans again. Hermetech, one of Raven's comfort blankets and a book she returns to at least twice a year. Donna shrugs and takes another bite.

'I blame the dairy. It makes you twitchy. Give it up and see how much better you feel.'

'It's not the dairy, Raven. I'm just worried about Sarah.' Donna stares at Raven, willing her to understand the source of her tension. The message falls on closed ears.

'Star's an adult. If she's with Satori, I say good for her. She's been without it for too long. It just isn't natural. Speaking of which… when do you plan to reach sexual maturity?'

'Miaow, that hurts. Fuck, you can be a bitch sometimes, Raven.' Playfully kicking her friend's hip, Donna chews her pizza with a theatrical volume. It has the effect she desires, and Raven recoils behind her book.

'Cough, lesbian,' Raven says, giggling.

'Cough, slut,' Donna replies.

'Seriously girl, you need to get some. If you're not careful, you'll be a dried-up old hag by the time you're thirty.'

Raven has closed the book and put it on her lap. Her eyes are fixed on Donna's face waiting for a reaction.

'I've seen too many women lose themselves in bad relationships, Raven. Look at you and he who shall remain nameless, you're one of the strongest women I know, but you've hardly stopped crying. Is it worth it? What can you gain that is so valuable it's worth losing yourself?'

Donna returns Raven's stare, watching her friend's nose wrinkle and her eyes narrow. They stare at each other in pregnant silence for what seems like hours but is only a few minutes. Neither woman has an answer.

Eventually, the lines across Raven's nose unfold, and she shrugs. 'I don't know. I can't help myself, Donna. When I fall for a man, I fall hard. It's the most wonderful feeling. It's the real magic. I wouldn't change it if I could. I wish you could feel it, too.'

'Maybe I do. I think I'm in love with Sarah.' Donna bites her lip. She shouldn't have said it. *Can Raven be trusted with the truth?*

'Oh, sweet Belladonna, I know, but you don't have a chance, my love. Star's a poster child for the straight life. She's never gotten over Satori. I doubt she ever will. Those two will end up married with half a dozen kids and just as many cats. Goddess knows I'm as jealous as you are, for different reasons, of course. We have to accept it. She's our friend. She should be happy.'

'He doesn't make her happy.' Donna's eyes feel hot.

This isn't fair. You don't get to be the sensitive caring one. You're an emotional cripple. How can you tell what will make Sarah happy?

'He could if she let him,' Raven answers. Breaking eye contact, she picks her book up again and opens it.

You're wrong, Raven, but I could make her happy. I could make her forget her parents, all those lonely years when no one cared enough. She could paint, and I would work, and we'd be happy, holed up in our cottage, complete with rose garden. We could have cats.

Donna picks up her plate and Raven's empty mug and carries them in one hand, allowing the glazes to scrape against each other. The sound is a howl of anguish. She pretends not to hear Raven's complaints. With as much noise as possible, Donna empties the kitchen sink and fills it with water and detergent. Glass knocks against glass, metal against metal as she churns foamy liquid around the dirty plates and dishes. The act of washing the dirt away, bowl after bowl, glass after glass settles her.

She feels calmer when the work is done, ready to read. Silently, she flops onto the sofa beside Raven and picks up her book.

CHAPTER TWENTY

SARAH MAKES her apologies at five o'clock and gathers her bag and coat. She sees Satori hovering. He is so close. *Does he plan to kiss me?* She edges away from him and lifts her hand to wave.

'Can you come back tomorrow?' he asks.

Her hand hovers in front of her eyes. She looks away from Satori's eager smile and at her forefinger. The print from the Kaballic volume has gathered at the tip. It is not, however, smudged black or grey. Instead, tiny letters and symbols cling to her skin.

'What are you looking at?' he asks.

She holds out her palm, but he shrugs, either not seeing or not understanding. She looks again at the traces of language on her skin.

'Nothing,' she says, shaking her head.

'So, can you?' he asks again.

'Um… maybe. I'll call you,' she says and walks to the front door.

She can feel his eyes follow her as she walks away.

'Goodbye,' he calls.

Donna and Raven are sitting, with drinks and cigarettes, in the living room when Sarah returns. There are bowls of chips, onion rings, and bean burgers on the coffee table.

'May I?' Sarah asks Raven.

Raven nods. She looks tired. Another hard week at work,

Sarah suspects, but she knows better than to ask.

'Where have you been all day?' Donna asks her.

Sarah hesitates before answering. She knows the reactions her news will inspire before she opens her mouth.

'Steve's,' she says.

Raven lifts her head and smiles. Donna frowns.

'Oh, Sarah,' Donna says. Disappointment drips from every syllable.

Sarah fills her mouth with food and looks at her feet. The bean burger sticks to her tongue. Chewing it makes her jaw ache. Her stomach rebels, and gasses gather in her oesophagus. She decides to forget food and use the bathroom before it is claimed by the others.

'I'll have my bath now so we're not all queuing for it later,' she tells them.

Donna's frown deepens, and Sarah wants to scream, *no I didn't fuck him*, but she decides not to justify her actions and leaves her friend to her thoughts.

At the door to the bathroom, she lingers for a moment. Her friends speak in hushed tones. She knows she's the subject. When she was going out with Satori things got a little crazy. One evening, Donna came home from work to find her passed out. Another time, Raven caught a glimpse of the little cuts along her arms, the ones she always tried to conceal. They blamed it on Satori, maybe they were right.

Or maybe it isn't only Steve who is wrong for me.

She runs a bath and sinks into the scalding water. Her skin feels alive in the heat. She submerges her head, watching the bubbles escape her lips one by one until she has to rise and gasp for dry air. The cuts on her arms are healing into tiny white lines. The fresh cuts on her thighs sting in the hot water.

Cleansed, she leaves the bathroom, a towel wrapped around her wet body. Her hair needs to be dried quickly or her natural curls become unruly. Shivering with cold, she blasts her head with hot air and teases the curls into wild ringlets, then aggressively rubs herself dry. Naked, she stands in front of the mirror.

Stretching her limbs out in turn, she rotates like an ice-skater to view every inch of her skin.

Her body is slim without being waif-like; she doesn't hate it although she wishes her breasts could be bigger like Raven's, which rise proudly above her corsets and bustiers.

Cross-legged on the floor in front of the mirror, she glances at her pubis. Its unruly auburn hair contrasts with the ebony on her crown.

She pulls her makeup bag closer and leans forward. First, she applies white foundation mixed with a touch of pale trans-lucent, not quite white skin but so pale as to look dangerously anaemic— her signature shade.

She draws over her pale eyebrows with a *nearly black* pencil and paints heavy lines of black liquid eyeliner over her eyelids, she finishes these in a small flourish, ivy-like spirals tonight. Above this line, she carefully brushes potent red, shading as she applies the colour. She adds a touch of the same shade to the skin below each eye, just where they meet the bridge of her nose.

Finally, she adds mascara to create dark and dangerous lashes. Not as dramatic as Raven's false eyelashes, but she tried those once, and her eyes ran all evening. She hasn't touched them since.

Realising she hasn't chosen what to wear, she opens a ward-robe crowded with velvet, lace, net, and shiny PVC. Every item is black: shadows to hide behind.

She owns nothing like Donna's long white dress, which glows under the black light of the nightclub. It takes too much courage to be seen. Donna looks amazing wearing it, of course. Her friend's individual sense of style shines from under the cloud of rules and regulations. Yet, Sarah has never heard Raven crit-icise any of *Donna's* outfits.

Sarah returns her attention to her wardrobe and pulls a knee length net tutu from the crush of clothes. It springs into life. She spots a micromesh sleeved bustier on the higher rail and lifts it off the hanger. It catches on a buckle as she pulls, so she lets go, fearing it might tear. She pushes the swivel chair from her computer desk across and balances precariously on the seat. The top freed, she examines it closely. There is a slight wrinkle on the back. She tries to smooth it out, pulling the fibres back to their proper positions. Satisfied that it looks okay, she spreads it out on her bed with the skirt.

She searches her drawers for the black strapless bra and shorts plus black and red striped over knee socks. Jewellery next— she selects a large, silver ankh pendant and eight silver rings including her favourite Whitby jet. Opening another cupboard, she looks at her choice of boots and shoes.

All her spare money is spent on clothing and footwear. She has eight pairs of boots and four pairs of shoes. Arranged in two rows, they face forward for inspection. She picks up a pair of black *New Rocks*.

Saturday evenings, the only time her existence is more than a series of mundane chores. The life she grinds away each day at work is restored to her in full during these few hours before the nightclub.

It is almost half-past eight. She checks her nail polish. The shiny black lacquer is chipped on one nail. She fixes it and blows on the paint until it dries hard. Time to get dressed.

At five minutes past nine, she relaxes in the living room with a long glass of absinthe and 7up, listening to *Baby Turns Blue*. Raven and Donna are still getting ready.

Donna arrives next, sinks onto the velvet couch beside Sarah, and grabs her hand.

'Are you okay?' Donna asks.

Sarah nods.

'You know, I didn't mean to upset you earlier— push you away,' Donna says.

'I know. I just didn't…'

'Expect the Spanish Inquisition?' Donna finishes.

They both laugh, and Donna's finger automatically brushes over her scar— a constant reminder of what it means to be Goth.

They had been in a bar celebrating Donna's promotion. A drunken boy, young and yet full of rage, pushed into them. It had happened so quickly, the glass smashing, the bottle slicing the air. They'd been told Donna was lucky not to have lost her eye. *Lucky!*

'Does my makeup look okay?' Sarah asks.

'Beautiful,' Donna answers.

Donna's stare burns as she reaches out and brushes something from the top of Sarah's cheek. A perfect sphere of water rests on the tip of Donna's finger.

'You're always so sad,' Donna says. 'Why?'

Sarah shakes her head. 'I don't know. I guess, maybe… oh, I… I didn't expect the…'

'Spanish Inquisition,' they say together.

'I'm here. Whatever it is, Sarah, I'll listen. You can't carry on like this. Where's the vivacious, young perky Goth I know and love?'

'Don't make me cry. I'll have to do my makeup again.'

Donna nods and lifts her glass to her lips. Before taking a large gulp, she whispers. 'I love you.'

They huddle together, drinking and waiting. At half-past-nine the doorbell announces Freya's arrival.

Donna arranges bottles and glasses on the coffin-shaped table: vodka, absinthe, orange, Jagermeister, and four bottles of Bud. Freya sits alone in a high-backed chair, shuffling her pixie boots across the wooden floor. She has tied purple ribbons in her hair, which look great against the blonde.

Sarah tells her this.

'Thanks,' Freya mutters, staring at her footwear.

'So, what have you been up to today?' Donna asks Freya.

'Ivan was competing in this kayaking race in the Gower. We went to cheer him on,' Freya says. 'He came second. We only got home at seven. Didn't think I'd even make it tonight.'

'Second, that's great,' Sarah says.

'Yep, we're all proud of him. You know Ivan. Things come easily for him.' Freya looks at the door.

'She won't be much longer,' says Donna.

'Huh?' Freya grunts, absentmindedly.

'Raven'll be ready soon. Do you wanna drink?' Donna asks, nodding at the alcohol-laden coffee table.

Freya reaches for a beer and the bottle opener. She drinks the cold beer straight from the bottle.

Sarah watches her. She cannot understand Freya. A newcomer to the scene, she quickly adopted Raven as a mentor, yet remains unchanged by Raven's cajoling— unmarked— still blonde and still Freya.

Silence settles over the room. Sarah realises she is shaking. Her throat feels as though she has swallowed something big and sharp, and it's caught half-way down. Taking another sip of absinthe, she watches Freya through narrowed eyes.

'Here,' says Raven, shimmying into the room in her PVC corset and buckled hobble skirt. A powdered arm, heavy with silver bracelets, reaches out and lifts the bottle of vodka. Raven uses a straw to preserve the perfection of her painted lips.

The woman looks incredible. Her figure and height scream power and beauty. Realising she is staring, Sarah looks away.

'So, Star, spill the beans, how did it go with Satori?' Raven's tongue licks the front of her teeth.

'Okay I guess,' Sarah answers.

'Okay? I don't believe you, Star. Satori is heavenly. Don't spare any of the details. You know, since he who shall remain nameless, I've been living my love-life by proxy. You have to tell me everything.'

Sarah shudders. Images of the unnameable man flash through her mind. The bruises Raven inflicted, the broken nose and torn earlobe, stand testament to an act of violence Sarah struggles to comprehend.

How could a person tear another apart like that?

Tilting her face, she looks again at her friend—five-foot-ten in bare feet with a generous hour-glass figure. It is true that jealousy turns love to madness, and Raven's height and Amazonian build lend strength to her fury.

Never cross her, she thinks, shaking her head.

Sarah cannot control her shaking hands. 'It wasn't like that,

Raven.'

She doesn't want to say what it was like. Even if the details were less confused, she would not want to share them.

Raven looks disappointed for a moment. She sucks her straw then checks her watch.

'I have something Ivy needs for her set tonight. So, I'm afraid we'll have to get to the club early. Drink up, girls.'

Sarah always wants to get to the club early despite Raven's assurances that only losers arrive before eleven; the "beautiful people" swan in after the pubs close.

Club Midian has two resident DJs, one of them plays Trad Goth, the likes of *The Sisters of Mercy* and *The Cure*, the other plays Industrial and EBM, *Combichrist, Covenant,* and *VNV Nation*.

Sarah loves the melodic, dark, and slow Trad Goth. Johnny O who spins these disks for her listening pleasure is on from ten until eleven and again from twelve until one. He always starts the night with the dark eighties music she adores.

Poison Ivy, the other DJ, plays the floor fillers from eleven until twelve and from one until the club closes at two.

Most nights, Raven insists that they arrive later.

Without complaint, Freya, Donna, and Sarah stand up. They tidy away their bottles and glasses in the kitchen and shrug into their coats. Sarah gasps as she sees Raven's new jacket. It is black satin with a luxurious fur trim around the collar and hem. Raven smiles and picks up her coffin-shaped handbag. Together, the four of them head to the club.

CHAPTER TWENTY-ONE

A QUEUE has formed outside the club. Raven stares at the end of it, a look of horror on her face. Sarah scans along it, searching for familiar faces. The *kids* are here, their faces hidden behind long fringes. There are more t-shirts and jeans than she would like to see, although there is the glint of PVC under some of the jackets and coats. Raven is right. In the club hierarchy, these patrons occupy the lower tiers. The idea that Raven might know what she is talking about amuses Sarah, and she stifles a giggle.

'I can't queue,' Raven declares. She shakes her head as if trying to dispel the memory of a nightmare.

Raven strides to the door, Sarah and the others follow her. Two doormen stand by the closed entrance; both have shaved heads, and their bare arms are crossed over their sculpted chests. She approaches the nearest man. His arms are covered in tattoos, and his ear lobes have been stretched by thick, black plugs. He is tall, but in her heeled boots, Raven's height is equal to his. She leans forward to whisper in his ear. Sarah watches her friend's forefinger stroke the man's bicep as she speaks to him. She turns back to her friends smiling as the bouncer opens the door.

Great job, Raven. They pay for their entry as the first group of misfits swell in behind them. Their coats are checked, and their first drinks purchased before anyone else reaches the top of the stairs.

Sarah sits on a sticky vinyl seat, swaying her torso in time to the gentle music. Raven leaves her drink on the table and marches to the DJ's pulpit. Johnny spins a Dead Can Dance track, a beautiful song, but it reminds Sarah of Satori. She takes a large sip of her drink and prays to the goddess he does not come tonight.

The intro to *Lullaby* chimes through the foggy club air, and Sarah leaps up.

'Come on,' she mouths at her friends. Freya shakes her head.

Donna stands up and follows Sarah to the dance floor. 'So, what about Steve?'

'I'm not seeing him again,' Sarah says, still shaking her head.

'But you were with him today?'

'Last Saturday and today,' Sarah admits, nodding slowly in case her words are lost in the music.

'Why? You know the guy's bad news.' Donna moves closer. 'It's okay, Sarah. We'll work it out.'

'What?' Sarah asks, twisting her neck to face her friend.

'You're pregnant,' Donna says.

In spite of herself, Sarah laughs. She laughs so hard her body bends double. When she comes back up for air, Donna is staring at her; a look of confusion has a stranglehold over her face.

'I'm not,' Sarah manages to say. 'The truth is so strange you'd never believe it.'

'Try me,' Donna insists.

'Bathroom break,' Sarah says, leaving the dance floor.

Club Midian's toilets are infamous. At best a den of vice even Vermelho Road struggles to match, at worst flooded with urine, vomit, and faeces. However, the night is young, and the only patron is reapplying makeup.

Donna and Sarah huddle into the corner. It is easier to talk in whispers here. Although the music can still be heard, it is an insubstantial echo— a siren, enticing patrons back to the dance floor.

'So,' Donna says when Sarah struggles to find the words. 'You saw Steve, your ex-boyfriend; the man you fell totally in love with and who drove you half-crazed, psychotic and potentially suicidal, last weekend.'

'And today.'

'But that's okay because you're not going out with him anymore?'

Sarah smiles. 'Yeah, that's right. I guess when you put it like that, there's no reason to fear for my sanity at all.'

Donna hugs her tight. 'You're not insane. You're hormonal.'

'I promise you, Donna,' Sarah says, serious now. 'There was no sex, no kissing even. I'm helping him.'

Donna steps back, and Sarah feels the physical separation like a bottomless chasm opening between them.

The woman by the mirror shuffles a little then leaves the bathroom. They are alone.

'Did I tell you about my vision?'

Donna nods.

'Well, it really happened. Steve summoned a demon, and she's out there somewhere, killing people— at least one man, maybe more. That gruesome murder by the tobacco factory, did you hear about that?' Sarah looks around the room, realising how crazed she sounds. *What was Donna's word? Psychotic. I sound psychotic.*

She looks at her friend's sympathetic face and feels more alone than she has ever felt in her life.

Donna will not believe me, how could she? Demons don't exist.

'Did Steve tell you this?' Donna asks, pronouncing each word with care.

Sarah snorts with laughter, her eyes dart from side to side searching for truth.

'I'm crazy, aren't I?'

'No no, my love, you aren't crazy. Maybe a little… gullible.'

Sarah tries to remember whether she mentioned her vision first.

Is it all an elaborate lie to get me back into his bed? What about the room, the markings all over Steve's body?

'Aargh!' she screams, pounding the heels of her hands hard against each temple, trying to squeeze out the confusion.

'Shh, it's okay,' Donna says, moving Sarah's hands and

stroking her face. 'Men, they fuck you up. Come and dance it all out.'

Sarah nods and follows her friend back to the dance floor. When they return, Raven has finished with Ivy and is scanning the room for them. She nods when she spots them and goes back to her drink. Looking across at the table, Sarah calculates it's her third drink of the evening, excluding the half bottle at home.

Alice is playing. Sarah loves this song. She mouths the words as she dances. Goth music— the soundtrack to her insane life. The music resonates in the deepest parts of her. It tells her she is not the only person who feels this way.

CHAPTER TWENTY-TWO

TONIGHT, LILITH feels free. She's surprised the magician hasn't found her. *What's keeping him? Is he hiding somewhere, terrified to see me again? He can't have given up already— time perhaps for a change of tactics.*

She concentrates on the image of her outfit. It must be perfect. As the picture forms in her mind, so her body changes to reflect her will, and clothes wrap themselves around her thighs and stomach. Her skirt is made of a dense silk that caresses her thighs, tight-fitting until it reaches her knees then flaring like a fish's tail; the heavy, liquid-looking material is long enough to cover her feet; above that, she creates a highly polished latex corset with curved horn shapes that frame her exaggerated breasts— black and reflective, an obsidian mirror; opera gloves, made from the same silk as the skirt, encompass her slender arms.

Her hair darkens until it reaches the blue-black shade of raven feathers. It thickens, too, achieving an impressive volume. Her makeup alters. Deep red lipstick on porn-star full lips, her skin a flawless alabaster, and her eyes drawn like Cleopatra's with heavy lashes casting shadows across her cheeks. Finally, she stretches her neck and binds it in a latex collar which moves like her own skin.

She admires the effect— pure villainess, *the* femme fatale.

When she arrives at *Club Midian,* a group of smokers outside halt their conversation and stare. They too stand tall and pale, black hair framing their own painted faces yet somehow the effect she achieves manages to eclipse their efforts. She hears them hold their breath as she glides across the threshold, up the stairs, and out of their sight.

The club is dark and full of a sweet-smelling mist. Lilith cannot see the magician in the swarm of black wrapped bodies. Standing at the edge of the dance floor, she scans the room. Dancers' teeth glow, as do the white and neon flyers on every table. Drinks shine like lanterns under the black light. It feels like home.

A man bounces across the dance floor. He wears a black trench coat and shiny jeans; the skin just below his mouth is pierced with a small metal spike. Admiring the look, she adopts it as her own. Her spike is ebony and wags like a tail as she licks her lips.

The music is fast, it pounds so furiously that her natural rhythm has to adjust to keep up with the beat.

Bodies and hair bounce in unison. In the centre, four girls dance together.

One towers above the others. Her hairstyle is similar to Lilith's, and she moves in an uncoordinated way— Raven.

Another, the blonde girl from the rum bar with purple ribbons in her hair, sways slowly to the music, carefully moving out of Raven's way whenever she staggers too close.

The other two jump up and down with the rest of their tribe. Like a live volcano, swelling and shrinking as one bubbling mass before finally exploding. One of the girls has short black hair, the other an abundance of dark ringlets, she is the one Lilith is interested in. The magician's female— Star.

Star bounces in perfect time. Her enormous boots look weightless. Lilith can only see the back of her. The thick black curls of her hair rise and fall as she leaps. Her shoulders and throat revealed with each descent. Her skirt lifts too, each time she falls back down to earth, like the petals of an exotic night flower, tempting insects to its core.

The music changes, Star and her group leave the dance floor and cross to a table of drinks not far from where Lilith stands. The blonde and Raven fall onto the couch together, giggling. The other two stand behind stools and move their bodies in time to the music. They cradle drinks, but their movements are too controlled to spill the liquid.

Violent lyrics repeat over a metallic drumbeat. Lilith smiles, thinking back to the man by the factories: her first kill in this brave new world and sweetest so far. The others feel less exquisite in her memory, but the next one— she nods and smiles, watching Star enjoy the evening. She will take her time, become the corrupter of spirit rather than flesh.

Three of the girls return to the dance floor as soft keyboards wash across the nightclub. The square of wooden boards fills, and bodies crush together. Some stand still, others sway as the soft vocals sing of regret and the passage of time. As the pace builds behind the voice, the movements of the dancers become more exaggerated, then the bouncing starts again. Faces filled with joy blur with their rapid rises and falls.

Star's face is as rapt as any other. *Is this worship? To which god do these souls lay themselves bare, offering their tributes of sweat?*

Lilith does not join them. The music confuses her. She enjoys the role of voyeur for the moment.

At midnight, the music slows. The strains of a great organ replace the keyboard. The music sways as do the bodies still clinging to the wooden boards after others have deserted them for drinks or rest. Star remains. The woman's body curves and arches, her thinly veiled arms rising above her head then twisting like ivy down to frame her face before descending further to cross her chest. The ritual is repeated again and again.

Lilith looks at Star's face; her eyes are closed, and she looks as if in sexual ecstasy, writhing in pleasure at an unseen touch.

Entranced, Lilith joins the dancers. She sways across the floor like a snake. Like *the* snake.

Well, it worked with Eve.

When Star opens her eyes, Lilith is dancing beside her. Her body matching Star's deep curls and twists, the pheromones in her scent mingling with the dry ice.

CHAPTER TWENTY-THREE

SARAH STOPS bouncing and sways her hips like a belly dancer on slow play. Johnny O has taken his place in the DJ booth, and the harsh whisper of *Moonchild* fills her head.

She closes her eyes and lets the melody fill her body while her hands flutter around her face like falling leaves. She hears Freya move away to join Raven.

Her heart quickens and her nostrils strain to grasp the meaning behind a heady new scent. She licks her lips, feeling hot, panting. She opens her eyes, attempting to break the spell.

It takes a moment to focus. Faces and bodies swim past her through the swirling mist. Donna is there, hands stroking her own breasts and circling pert nipples. Such lewd behaviour would not be permissible in any other public place but is appreciated in this safe haven.

A movement on her right catches Sarah's eye. The most beautiful woman she has ever seen moves so gracefully she might be liquid or a zephyr, swirling and changing shape. The woman is as tall as Raven, but slender. Her clothes reflect the purple glow of lights and something else, a mystery upon which Sarah cannot quite focus. Her dark lips smile.

Blinking, Sarah smiles back, and the mysterious woman moves closer. The scent gets stronger. It is incredible.

Sarah has never felt attracted to a member of her own sex before. She appreciates beauty whatever its source and can comfortably admire a woman's figure or face, but never has she felt such an overwhelming desire to suck on a woman's tongue or undress her and stroke every part of her body with eager hands.

The woman leans in and whispers in her ear. Sarah stops breathing and becomes a giant aural organ that exists only to listen. The woman's hot, sweet breath tickles her ear and cheek as she speaks.

'Would you like to get a drink?'

The woman inches away, and the sense of loss is profound. It takes a moment for Sarah to understand the question. When she does, she stretches up to whisper back. Her fingertips touch the latex collar wrapped around the woman's throat. It feels like quicksand, pulling her hands into the woman's body.

'I'd love to,' she answers.

The woman walks away.

Sarah remembers her friend and pulls on Donna's elbow to shout in her ear. 'I'll be back in a minute.'

Registering Donna's nod of understanding, she rushes after her quarry.

'What's your name?' Sarah asks.

After a moment's pause, the woman answers. 'Lilith.'

'Lilith,' Sarah repeats the name. The word feels familiar in her mouth.

'What's yours?'

Sarah seems such an ordinary name, and she feels extraordinary this evening. Anything could be possible on a night like this.

'Star,' she says.

Lilith smiles and nods in approval. 'What do you drink?'

Star has drunk enough already, and she doesn't want to spend the rest of the evening heaving in swampy toilets.

Will Lilith think less of me if I don't ask for alcohol? She checks herself. *Is this the new friend I want to make— another Raven, who I constantly need to impress?*

'Red Bull, please.'

If Lilith is disappointed, she gives no sign as she turns and heads for the bar. A minute later, she returns, and they are together again. Lilith passes the drink to Star who cradles it in her hands.

'Can we find some seats?' Star asks.

Lilith motions for her to follow. She walks to a couch filled with people and bends over the mousy girl at the end of the row, whispering in her ear. The girl nods and passes the message to the next person who does the same in turn. When the whispers are complete, the group stand up as one and wander to the dance floor.

Lilith sits, leaving plenty of room for Star to join her. The couch is soft and far more comfortable than her usual vinyl stool. She sits so close to Lilith that she feels the woman's arm brush hers as she reaches for her drink. The sensation leaves her breathless.

Does Lilith want me, too, or is she looking for a friend?

She stares at the table, shivering and sipping her drink.

What should I say? Please, not something lame.

'I haven't seen you here before,' Star eventually says. 'Are you new to town?'

They are words, and they might get Lilith talking; she desperately wants to hear the woman's rich voice again; but they seem so cliché, and she wishes she thought of something better.

'I am, but I'm very glad I came here tonight.' Lilith's face shines with pleasure. Her smile is wide and welcoming; not a trace of judgment clouds her eyes.

'So am I,' Star answers.

'It's too noisy to talk, don't you think?' Lilith asks. 'Would you like to dance or go somewhere quieter?'

Star's throat swells, and she finds it hard to swallow. The music is amazing and being here with Lilith feels like a dream.

Would the dream be broken outside this room?

If I ask to dance, and our bodies move as one on the dance floor for the next two hours, will Lilith make the same offer a second time?

'Where do you wanna go?' Star asks.

Lilith smiles again, a beautiful smile which washes over Star, telling her everything will be wonderful.

'I have a room near here. It's nothing much but it's warm and quiet.'

Star shivers as she exhales.

This is it. This beautiful woman is offering me her body, and I don't know what I want to do.

This is crazy. Why is everything so muddled?

'I have to let my friends know I'm leaving.'

'Give me your cloakroom ticket. I'll get your coat,' Lilith offers.

Star rushes across the dance floor, bumping into dancers and mouthing apologies at their fierce faces. She cannot feel the floor under her feet. It's as though she is gliding, skimming the ceiling with her hair. The bodies below seem distant and insubstantial.

She reaches Raven's table, and three frowns turn to meet her.

'Where have you been?' Raven's voice sounds cold, and her words are clipped.

'You said you'd only be a minute,' Donna says, shaking her head.

'I… I've met someone. We're leaving,' Star replies.

Raven's eyes narrow to penetrate the fog as they scan the club.

'Who?' she asks.

'The woman in the latex bodice. I was dancing with her earlier. She's gone to get our coats.'

'Really? Why are you leaving?' Raven stares into Star's eyes. 'But… but you've never been with a woman. Let me see her.'

As Star walks unsteadily toward the cloakroom, her three friends follow. Lilith waits by the stairs, Star's coat draped over her arm.

Raven nudges Star and whispers. 'She's gorgeous. You must tell me all about it tomorrow.'

The three walk away from her back to the music.

CHAPTER TWENTY-FOUR

SATORI LOOKS up from his books and feels a shiver of dread. Gasping, he holds his chest. Something is wrong.

He clears a space to meditate. Even though he tries to empty his mind, Star's face lingers there, unwilling to give him peace. *Is Star in trouble?*

He dials her mobile number. It rings, but she doesn't answer. It is eleven thirty, plenty of time to get changed and check out the club. She's probably there.

He decides to take care over his appearance. Star never seemed happy when he arrived at the club in his old clothes. He straightens his hair and chooses a pair of skin-tight jeans and the red silk shirt she always loved.

It is almost midnight by the time he leaves, and when he reaches the bus stop, the last one has just left. He hurries along the main street toward the club, hoping to catch a taxi on the way. His walk is brisk, and he reaches the club at half-past-twelve. The bouncers nod as he passes them.

Without stopping to check his coat, he bounds up the staircase and into the mist. It seems foggier than usual this evening, and he can hardly see a thing. He walks toward the dance floor.

She isn't dancing, but he can see two of her friends. Donna and Freya are swaying to *Suspiria*. They look tired and listless.

Searching for Raven and Star, he spots Raven slumped in her usual spot. He crosses to her and pats her hand.

Her eyes flicker open, and she smiles at him. 'Satori.'

'Where's Star?' he asks.

Raven's eyes swim in their sockets as though she is finding

it impossible to think and focus on his face at the same time.

'Star?' he asks again.

'Oh, Satori. My darling Satori. I'll never know what you see in that girl,' she answers eventually.

He feels his temper rise and struggles to control it. 'Is Star here tonight?'

'She was,' Raven answers, her words thick and slurred.

'Was? Where did she go?' Panic breaks his voice into squeaks and whispers.

Raven slumps back down with a contented smile on her face. 'Satori, why her?'

He leaves her question unanswered and rushes to the dancers.

'Donna, Freya,' he asks, summoning a look of humility he hopes will charm them. 'I think Star's in trouble. Where did she go?'

Donna frowns and shakes her head. Freya looks to her friend then back at Satori and shrugs.

'For fuck's sake, Donna. I know you hate me. Although fuck knows why, but this is Star we're talking about. You love Star for Chrissake, why won't you tell me where she is?'

Freya touches his shoulder. 'She left with a woman.'

'Who?' He looks from one girl to the next. They do not answer.

He runs back to Raven. 'Who did she leave with?' he growls into her face.

Raven's eyelids flutter.

He looks around him. He wants to scream, but he needs to stop panicking. He cannot think if he isn't calm. Shaking, he tries to force the fear down from his chest and through his stomach, out of his body. It sticks and digs into his gut with tearing claws, twisting and writhing.

The bouncers, maybe they know.

He jumps down the stairs, three at a time, and greets them at the bottom with a strained smile.

'Did you see where Star went?' he asks.

'Your girl? De one wid de curls?' the taller man asks.

'Yes, yes.' He nods frantically.

'Ah, yes, she go dat way,' the doorman replies, pointing to the archway that leads to Vermelho Road.

'Thank you,' Satori shouts over his shoulder as he runs.

The bridge casts deep shadows over the road as Satori tears under it. It is an age-old landmark that separates the city of commerce from the city of vice.

He's been along this road before. It's where everyone goes to purchase mind-altering substances when the travellers aren't in town, but he has never been here alone.

The first houses are barricaded— no signs of life— a portal transporting and delivering.

The lights of Vermelho Road shine a few metres away. He runs harder.

He sprints into a street full of life. Noises and smells surround him; exhaust fumes mix with the greasy stench of fried chicken while music crashes through car and house windows. People shout to be heard above the heavy basslines. Lining the street on either side are women, young and old, dressed in short skirts, furs, and high heels. Their makeup heavy and their faces tired. Groups of men stand in doorways, chatting and watching the cars crawl past.

He approaches the first woman. Her short hair is blonde and her lips vivid red. She stubs out her cigarette as he walks toward her.

'Hello, darling,' she says. 'Looking for something?'

'I'm looking for my girlfriend. She came this way with another woman. Have you seen her?'

'We makes it our policy not to notice people, lover.'

'Thanks, anyway,' he says, jogging toward the next woman.

One of the men in the doorway calls to Satori. 'Yow girl, you lookin' fine!'

'Fuck, it's a batty bwoy,' another of the group says.

Shit! Just keep walking.

Three men intercept Satori before he reaches the next woman.

'Bwoy, you look like a girl.'

'You gave my parri a fucking boner.'

'What'cha doing here, pretty boy?'

'I'm looking for someone I know,' Satori tries to explain.

'Who dat be?' the first man asks.

'A girl, this high,' he puts his hand to his shoulder to indicate her height. 'With black curly hair.'

'White chick?' the man asks.

'Yes, have you seen her?'

The man smiles and shakes his head, turning away.

'You betta get outta here bwoy,' he says. 'You no business roun' here.'

'I have to find her,' Satori says.

Other men join them. The first man whispers to the second, and they all move forward.

'No, I don't have time for this. I need to find her,' Satori yells.

A fist connects with his nose, and he hits the floor.

When satori wakes, the street is quiet. The air is freezing, and the sky has a pre-dawn paleness. He stands up, wiping his nose on his sleeve and looks around— empty. Looking at his wrist, he realises his watch has gone. He checks his pockets and discovers his wallet and mobile are missing too. Wiping his itchy nose again, he stumbles across the street. Every step makes him wince with pain. He looks at the boarded and paper-covered windows. *No hope of finding her now*.

He walks home. Every step away from Vermelho Road and knowledge of Star's safety is agony. Angry words echo through his head. He has lost her. *Who is she with?* A deep part of him already knows. *Star is with Lilith.*

He chastises himself for his arrogance, *if only…*

As he moves through the city, he forces himself to think of solutions. Maybe he can summon Lilith again. Bring her back to his room. Find some way of binding her. It will be dangerous, madness perhaps, but… His steps are quicker now he is moving toward rather than away.

He doesn't need much to summon her this time. The glyphs were useless, so he does not replicate them. The tribute— the only thing he knows *she* will respond to— semen.

He stands within his circle and calls to Lilith, succubus, serpent, temptress of Eve, first wife of Adam, dark mother.

He jerks his hand back and forth as he calls to her, his voice becoming more urgent with every stroke of his fingers. As his seed shoots across the room, she appears.

Naked and long-limbed, black hair wild, eyes angry, she materialises before him.

'Magician,' she screams. 'What are you doing? I was busy.'

'A trade,' he says. 'Will you make a trade?'

'You for her?' she asks, snarling.

He nods.

Lilith turns and crosses to the wet trail across the wall. She wipes the spunk with her forefinger and brings it to her lips. Satori watches, transfixed, as her curved tongue flicks out to taste the wetness. She draws her finger inside her mouth and sucks at the tip. He gulps as he watches her: more aroused than horrified.

'What a waste,' she says. 'What use is a tribute that's been splattered over your wall?'

'I have more,' he says.

She steps closer.

'What will you give me if I give it all to you?' he asks her.

'Hmm, a night with her? You want that don't you? She won't come back to you, you know.'

'I don't care. I love her, and I won't let you hurt her.'

Lilith laughs. 'Who says I'm hurting her? She's having the time of her life.'

She reaches him in three strides. She clasps his balls in the palm of her hand. Her nails bite into his tender skin.

'Would you sacrifice what all men value most?' she asks.

He is silent.

'I thought not,' she says. She waves her hand as if flicking away an annoying fly.

'Wait,' he pleads. 'You said I could have a night with her.'

'Yes, I did.' She nods and disappears.

No, she hasn't disappeared, he's moved. He faces the way she had been facing.

He tries to turn his head to look behind him, but he cannot will his muscles into action. He feels her presence. Lilith is close. She is all around him.

Oh fuck. I'm inside her. Lilith's body is his prison, and he has no control over its movements.

He feels his right leg move as she steps forward. As his foot touches the floor, a different room appears around them, a dark room with a grimy looking bed. Star sleeps there, wrapped in filthy blankets. Her shoulders and chest are exposed and covered in small bruises.

'What have you done?' he asks in his mind.

Only what she wanted, comes the mocking reply.

Lilith pulls back the blankets, exposing Star's body. The sleeping woman stirs, shifts position, and falls back into a deeper slumber. Satori imagines licking his lips. His tongue will not move, and his mouth still feels dry.

He looks through Lilith's eyes at the woman he loves. That she is lying naked and unaware of him is a powerful aphrodisiac. Her legs are bent at the knee, and she lies half on her back and half on her right side. Her pale thighs and calves are splayed. Above and between them, her triangle of ginger beckons him. He wants to nuzzle there, smell her tangy musk, and lose himself within her. Her stomach is small and soft. He imagines his seed inside her, sowing new life that will bind them together for perpetuity. Her breasts and their alert pink nipples, he could feed on them forever and never need to eat again, but the most painfully beautiful part to look at is her face. A face that worshipped him once and saw wonders in him. Her mouth formed words of undying love. He wants to bend over that face, whisper into her ear to run and never look back, but it seems he is only a voyeur.

Lilith reaches across the bed for Star's ankles. Satori feels them too, delicate and smooth. She pulls her toward them, legs spread across the dark sheets. Star seems to wake. She smiles at them, and Satori wonders whose face she is seeing. She is so tired, though, that her eyes flutter down again within seconds of opening.

Satori feels himself respond to the closeness of her sex. He hardens, and Lilith's body stretches to accommodate him.

Her eyes look down at their eagerly bobbing cock. Satori sees it too and feels the smile, which spreads across Lilith's face.

This is why she brought him here— her dildo and her witness. He feels frightened for himself and Star, but that fear does nothing to dampen his ardour.

As Lilith sucks Star's breasts, Satori feels his own tongue caress the hardening nipples. He loses himself in the motion of licking and pulling, gorging himself on her.

Am I doing this or is it Lilith?

The boundaries are blurred; they both want the same thing.

Gentle moans of pleasure escape Star's lips, but her eyes remain closed.

They move up her body and press their lips against her eyelids.

Her eyes move quickly beneath. She is dreaming.

Is she dreaming of this?

They fasten their mouth to hers. Her lips taste like honey. Their tongue flicks inside her mouth, hungry, eager for a response. She moves her tongue with theirs, a soporific dance.

Their fingers stroke her hair then tug it. Gentle movements grow stronger until she opens her eyes again. Star grasps their head and pulls it closer, attempting to swallow their tongue in her passion.

The hand moves from Star's hair to her breast, kneading the flesh. She gasps at the strength of their grip and digs her fingernails into their shoulders. The pain makes them shudder.

Breaking the kiss, they stand at the end of the bed. Star raises her hips off the mattress in expectation, and they kiss her wet lips, letting her sweet juices run down their chin and throat. Her body twists on the bed, and they push deeper. Lilith's tongue takes Satori's own farther into the pulsing orifice. Their tongue is a serpent, exploring the warm, ridged cave, finding a new home. Star reaches an arm toward them, but they push it back onto the bed. She surrenders willingly.

Their tongue flicks from this hole to its tighter neighbour. Star gasps in surprise and pleasure, pushing her body toward them, opening herself up to their exploration.

The Lilith/Satori satyr straightens again and looks upon Star's beautiful, flushed face. With a flick of hands, the woman is flipped on to her front, and they pull her hips up, staring with mounting delight and excitement at the welcoming tunnels.

As they push their conjoined flesh inside her, she looks over her shoulder. An expression of shock and wonder crosses her face.

'How?' she whispers but does not resist. Her eyes narrow, and her groans grow louder and thicker as she abandons the mystery to embrace her pleasure.

Yesssss, yesssss, yesssss. Words echo around his brain. *Are they mine or Lilith's, silent or cried aloud?*

They push harder and deeper. Flesh expands with Lilith's magic until they fill Star and the void within.

Satori closes his eyes and enjoys the singular sensation. His balls tighten as the pressure mounts, then, with a flood, it is released. He growls as he hovers there, giving everything he has to give. When he opens his eyes again, Star is staring at him.

'Who are you?' Star's voice is full of accusation.

Then he is alone in his room, and the smell of his come fills the air.

'Star,' he cries.

CHAPTER TWENTY-FIVE

'It's getting dark, love. Won't you come in?' The silhouette of Freya's mother lingers in the kitchen doorway, shifting her weight from one foot to the other and back again.

'In a minute,' Freya answers.

The garden is full of sound. Grasshoppers chirrup, and a soft breeze hisses through the tree. Ribbons dance in the branches. She holds the image of their waltz in her mind. Ivan told her why he attaches them; they are gifts of thanks. Their mother hates them, but she stopped complaining years ago. Ivan told Freya he has a tree in his head: a great oak tree that he can touch, smell, and taste if he wants. Its colours are more vibrant than nature, and the depth is compressed, like this moment in time.

Freya asks him about magic more and more. She shares his excitement. Her desire to understand a world controlled entirely by will grows stronger by the day. She dreams about other worlds, hidden powers, and unseen realities, and she wants to travel inside her head, like Ivan. Her *Book of Lilith* does not show her the way. She needs his help.

Her brother is reticent, sensing perhaps that her interests are darker, more like Satori's. Ivan says Satori does not travel. He brings everything to him. Freya tried that with her experiment in the woods, but it failed, and now she feels empty, reluctant to try again. That night and the way she felt— still feels a year later— haunts her dreams. Dave called a few times but stopped when her father threatened him.

Every time Freya tries to speak to Satori, he brushes her aside. *He treats me like a child. I'm not that young.* Freedom calls to Freya from beyond the prison bars that her parents constructed and maintain. *I'm eighteen. I shouldn't be sneaking around.*

A glimpse of movement in his window, and her train of thought is abandoned. An arm and shoulder come into view; he's topless again. Freya squeezes her thighs together. Her mouth feels dry, and she licks her lips. He is so strong.

Oh, to be held by those arms. It would be real, and my goddess would hear my cries of ecstasy.

Freya senses her mother's frown.

Does she know I'm spying on Ivan?

The cold grass splinters under approaching feet.

I should move. It's best if she doesn't know who I'm watching.

Freya tries to turn, tear her gaze away from his window.

Her mother is at her shoulder. The older woman looks up and makes a strange choking sound as if she cannot catch her breath.

Ivan glances toward them, but the garden is dark, their shapes obscured by shadow.

Freya looks at her mother's pale, almost grey face. *Should I call Dad?*

She's pointing at me.

Colour rises in the woman's cheeks— a hot flush that is pierced with eyes as dark as coals.

'He's your brother,' her mother says, shaking. She steps forward and slaps Freya's face.

Freya's eyes widen and fill with tears. It stings like crazy, a throbbing heat.

She stares at her mother, defiantly. 'You never let me see anyone else. What do you expect?'

She rolls a ball of spit inside her mouth and launches it, watching it connect with her mother's face. Freya charges into the house, grabs her jacket, and leaves.

Freya passes groups of women dressed in sparkling outfits and giggling together. A lone runner sprints past her, and the air rushes with him, rustling her clothes and moving her hair. A giant dog takes its mistress for a walk. The woman's arm is stretched so far it looks as though it might pop out from her shoulder socket at any moment.

Freya turns a corner and sees curls of smoke snaking from a privet hedge. A voice in the back of her head warns her to cross the road. A man might be waiting there for someone like her. Breathing in, she stretches her spine, lifts her chin, and walks slower. Each step is thrilling. Every time her thighs stroke against each other her groin is on fire.

I want him to grab me. No, I want him to follow. Let this feeling of anticipation last a little longer.

She smiles and stops, letting images fill her head.

I want to do what Raven did to my brother in the park. I want to drop to my knees in front of this man. I want to hear his gasp of surprise as I open the zip to his jeans. I want to feel his penis expand as I touch it; pull it through the open fly.

I will gaze up at his beautiful face and see a look of adoration in his eyes. I will wrap my lips around him, taste him, and let him fill my mouth. I want to hear him pant. I want to know what semen tastes like, then I'll stand up and walk away, leave him hanging from his trousers.

She feels paralysed by desire. *Not again!* She chastises herself. *Don't be passive. Do this, make this yours, your act, your desire— not his.*

Feet heavy as tombstones, she takes the next step forward. Leaves rustle and brittle branches break. A head extends from the corner of the hedge. It reminds Freya of a turtle poking out from his shell. Long hair.

The face turns toward her. It's a woman. *A fucking woman!* Freya's feet lose their weight, and she rushes away. *I need a drink. Please, let Raven be home.*

CHAPTER TWENTY-SIX

STAR SITS upright on the bed and studies the room. It is almost empty, like Satori's but prettier. The cream silk sheets, lying creased beneath her, are as soft as Lilith's skin, and red walls lend it the feeling of passionate security. Lilith stands naked at the end of the bed. Star feels the sticky fluids of their coupling.

'Are you all right, Lilith?' she asks. Lilith smiles. 'Just perfect.'

'I thought…' Star hesitates.

'Tell me.' Lilith's face is open and loving.

Instead of answering, Star kneels before her. She touches Lilith's cheek, marvelling at her exquisite beauty. She licks her lips and leans forward, kissing her lover's mouth, gently at first then more passionately.

Lilith responds, putting her hand against the small of Star's back and drawing her body closer. Their breasts rub against each other, and the movement hardens their nipples. Skin tingles and warms under each other's tender touches. Their lovemaking is gentle. They explore, sharing rather than possessing each other's bodies.

'Will I see you again?' Star asks when the kiss breaks for a moment.

'My darling, you never have to leave here.'

Star settles back onto the bed. Lilith lies next to her, stroking her hair. She licks the tears from Star's face.

'What is it?' Lilith asks.

'If I ask you something and you think I'm crazy, will you still want me?'

Lilith laughs. 'There are many crazy things in this world

and the next, but you, my beautiful child, are not one of them.'

'I could change your mind.'

Lilith shakes her head. 'Never.'

'Did you feel strange earlier?' Star asks tentatively.

'I don't understand,' Lilith replies. Her eyes are wide as if trying to read the truth behind the question.

'I used to date a guy, Steve. He was... different. He could do things, make things happen which defied logic. Earlier, when you woke me, and we made love like... that. Had he... how on earth do I ask this? Was he inside you? I thought for a minute...'

'I thought I was imagining it,' Lilith answers, her body relaxing. 'I felt... strange. Like I could see what I was doing but wasn't controlling it. At first, I thought it was just the passion, then I was inside you. Really... inside. It was amazing. I thought it was a dream.'

'Bastard,' Star growls. 'I'm so sorry, Lilith.'

'Well, it's just us here now,' Lilith assures her. 'Will you speak to him?'

'I'm not sure. It might make things worse. Oh fuck, what should I do?'

'Ignore him. Act like he isn't even there.'

'Yes, yes, I think you're right,' Star says. She embraces Lilith, nuzzling her face in the woman's scented hair. 'When can I see you again?'

'Whenever you want to,' Lilith answers.

'I have so much to do, but I want to fall asleep in your arms.'

Lilith kisses her shoulder. 'Stay, work tomorrow.'

Star falls asleep quickly. In her dream, she sees Satori shouting at her from beyond a gossamer veil. She cannot hear his words, but his eyes are wide with fear. A stream of light rushes from his body into hers. It burns, and she tries to cover herself to stop it penetrating her skin. It keeps coming. Her body swells and aches. When she screams at him to stop, he shakes his head. He looks confused, not defiant, as though the light is not of his making. The light stops, and Satori falls to the floor. Star's fingers are covered with blood. A scream rattles in her lungs, bursting to be free. Opening her mouth wide, she tries to release it, but a serpent wraps itself around her chest, crushing the sound in its coils.

She wakes up. Lilith is still beside her with one arm draped over Star's stomach, her face nestled against her back. The room is dark.

'I have to go,' Star says. 'Will you be here at four tomorrow?'

'Yes,' Lilith says. 'Let me walk with you. I don't think this is the safest place.'

'Okay,' Star replies, glad of the company.

They hold hands as they walk along Vermelho Road. If anyone notices the affection, it is not mocked. No one bothers them even as they walk through the shadows beneath the bridge. It is only as they join the street beyond that Star feels people stare at them, judging them.

'Fucking lesbos,' a man shouts from the window of a passing car.

Star feels Lilith's grip stiffen at the words.

'They're not worth it,' Star whispers.

'Maybe we should give them something to shout about,' Lilith suggests, cupping Star's chin and kissing her.

Star pulls away. She does not feel safe. 'Not here.' Her cheeks redden, and she feels ashamed that she cares about the opinions of strangers.

Lilith smiles. 'Okay.'

They walk together in silence to the bus stop. Their hands no longer grasp each other. They rely instead on the accidental brushing of fingers against fingers as they walk.

Waving goodbye to her lover at the bus stop, Star's body feels tender from their lovemaking; the desire within her is a flame that burns away all other thoughts. She is not hungry even though she has not eaten for more than a day, nor is she thirsty. Her head feels light, and she finds it hard to focus. She is a ball of lust rolling away from its only source of satisfaction, travelling toward a hollow life.

Allowing the shops and restaurants to drift by before they

transform into multi-coloured, urban blocks of flats and blackened town houses, Star switches on her mobile phone. A dozen beeps follow each other— text messages. There are missed calls too— from Satori and Donna. She checks the messages.

One from Donna: 'Steve lookin 4 u told him to F off xxx.' Lots were sent by Raven, all asking how things went with Lilith. Star calls Donna.

'Hi, Star,' Donna says brightly. 'How are you? I thought you'd disappeared.'

'Sorry to leave you alone last night,' Star says. 'I just needed…'

'Haha, I know exactly what you needed.' There's an edge to Donna's voice that Star cannot identify. *Is it jealousy?* 'So, spill the beans, lover. How did it go?'

'Not now, Donna, I'm on the bus.' She laughs.

'When you get back… I want a stroke-by-stroke account.'

'All right, soon.'

'Love you.'

'Love you, too,' Star whispers back.

Star does not want to face those questions yet. She can feel her friends' curiosity gouging into her as she unlocks the front door. The stairs loom above her. Gripping the handrail, she mounts them one by one. The wooden treads transform into her lover's spine, and she bends to kiss Lilith's back.

'What the fuck? Are you okay?' Raven calls from the landing.

Star glances up, and the stairs swim back into view.

'You look terrible, Star,' Raven says as she descends.

Donna pokes her head around the corner and frowns at her friend's prostrate body.

'Did you fall?' Donna asks.

Star shakes her head and takes Raven's offered hand. 'I'm just exhausted,' she says.

'A drink then bed,' Raven tells her. 'You can tell us in the morning.'

Donna pouts and withdraws from view.

When Star wakes at five the next morning, the others are

still asleep. She makes her breakfast in silence, glad to avoid their questions.

How can I describe my time with Lilith?

To try to form the words to make them understand would be to stick pins through a live butterfly and set it on display. Its delicate wings would be torn as she fumbled with inadequate phrases, and the vibrancy of those hours would be destroyed by her clumsy hands.

She eats with the hunger of someone who might not see food again then showers and packs a few things.

Unwilling to wake her friend, she sends Donna a text. 'I'm moving out for a while. I'll see you soon. Love you.'

CHAPTER TWENTY-SEVEN

After Star leaves, Lilith prowls the city streets, daring anyone to speak to her. The humiliation of the taunts and stares weighs heavily on her.

Would they still laugh with my fist and forearm tearing down their throats?

It confuses her why Star worries about what small-minded strangers think. There is no shame in love, only completion.

Why has that burden of shame, first felt in The Garden, not yet been lifted? Humans are meant to fuck. Their bodies are covered in nerve endings all screaming to be touched. Why do they hide from their desires?

Lilith walks full circle and returns to the bus stop. She needs to feel, to fuck or kill. Sex and death, just two points on the same continuum.

She hears the wails of sirens and, with nothing better to do, starts walking toward their source. A car slows beside her.

A group of four teenage boys sit within its steel frame.

'Got room for one more,' one of them says as she passes.

'Where are you heading?' she asks.

'Anywhere you want,' they promise, giggling.

One boy opens a rear door and climbs out. She sits between two teens. The driver grins at her over his shoulder before he puts the car in gear and drives. Lilith is crowded in the back. The boys keep breathing on her face, their breath rank from alcohol and cigarettes.

A boy's arm encircles her as she stares at the blur of office blocks then houses and finally trees through the window. The car slows and turns a sharp right then heads up a steep hill. The driver brakes and switches the engine off. He turns to her, leering through eyes glazed with lust.

'You might think this is your lucky day guys, but it's not,' she warns.

The car doors open. The boy to her left drags her out. Fabric tightens around her arms as he yanks at her. She stands tall among them and, when she smiles, they stop grinning. They shuffle about, staring at their trainers— like actors who have forgotten their lines.

The driver speaks first. 'Goth girls are always hot to trot.'

His words break the spell, and they descend on her like wolves. Lips and teeth bounce off her skin. It is as though her body no longer belongs to her. Someone else has claimed her flesh shell as their puppet and is moving its limbs without her consent. *Is this how the magician felt inside my skin?* He seemed to enjoy the experience, for her it has already grown tiresome.

'Come now, guys. Are we not gentlemen? Let's not crowd the lady,' says the tallest. His smug grin will be the first she grinds under her heel. 'Let her choose who she wants first.'

The wall of boys parts around her. Spotting the arrogant bastard, she walks across to him and challenges him with her stare. He smiles, confident in his masculine power.

'You,' she says and pushes him.

He falls heavily and grabs his arm, yelping in pain. She lifts her boot and smashes it down through his teeth. Bones crunch under her heel, and she spins around to stare at the other pale and fearful faces.

'Who's next?' she asks the three.

They run from her. The driver is already at the car, pulling open the door. He starts the engine and, in his blind panic, reverses into a tree, crushing the breath from another of his friends. Dazed, he looks into the rear-view mirror and sees his pal spitting blood. Changing into first, he wheel-spins away. Lilith turns her attention to the last one. The air reeks of his fear. She finds him cowering behind an oak tree. Crouching down, she stares at his ashen face, watching beads of sweat trickle from his brow into his eyes.

'I'm sorry,' he says, blinking.

'Yes, you are,' she replies.

She zips open his jacket and tears his t-shirt. His heart hammers rapidly beneath his ribcage. He struggles to breathe, adrenaline poisoning him, preparing him for fight or flight when he is powerless to do either. She rests a nail against his chest then digs into his skin. He yelps as she draws back a slender strip of flesh, pulling it further and further down like a second zip, leaving his chest, from collar bone to navel, wet with scarlet. He stares beyond her as if his fear has blinded him.

'I'm here sweetheart,' she whispers in his ear. He struggles to push himself away, but his back is pinned against the tree.

'Please…' he says.

'You aren't going to live,' she tells him.

'Make it quick,' he pleads.

She places the palms of her hands on either side of his jaw and twists. His neck snaps, and his body slumps into the fallen leaves.

CHAPTER TWENTY-EIGHT

A FEW minutes after nine in the morning, Star arrives at Lilith's flat.

Vermelho Road has transformed yet again, and a community buzzes through the street. Children play in the generous front gardens of Victorian town houses. Mothers and grandmothers gather, chatting together in a rich patois, the sense of which is lost on Star. Shops are open, and the variety of vegetables and fruit arrayed outside eclipses any she has seen before. Familiar fruits: melons, oranges, and pineapples, nestle beside a mass of vivid green bananas and large, yellow, alien-looking spheres.

The door from the street is unlocked, and Star disappears inside, mounting the steps with the eagerness of a long absent lover. She knocks on Lilith's door, gently at first then more insistently and hears a movement within the room.

'Lilith, it's Star,' she calls through the keyhole.

As she stands up again, the door opens.

'I'm sorry to come back so early.' Star stares at the woman's face, frightened that she will be sent away. Her suitcase is heavy in her hand, and she feels foolish.

Lilith's smile is reassuring as she reaches for Star. 'Stay with me. It's what I want. It's what we both want.'

'It is. It is what I want.' Star grabs the extended fingers, smiling.

'If that's true, why the sadness?' Lilith strokes a tear from Star's cheek.

'This isn't sadness. It's relief and joy.'

Lilith drags her through the doorway and into the dark room.

They kiss and fall onto the bed in a tangle of limbs. Each eager body searching for its twin, they merge until they forget where one starts and the other ends, stroking their own bodies as often as each other— a melting pot of lust and need. Their coupling lasts hours, each moment of which seems to stretch for an eternity. Tongues and fingers explore, tasting and feeling.

When they fall asleep in each other's arms, it is two o'clock. The cool rays of the autumn sun do not penetrate the room, however, and it could be any time. As Star shuts her eyes, she wonders for the first time why the room is so dark, but the question does not trouble her enough to keep her eyes from closing.

Two hours later, she wakes again. Lilith's face rests on the pillow beside her, eyes open. Star smiles, and her lover smiles back, a mirror of emotion.

'Did you sleep well?' Lilith asks.

Star laughs and nods, moving closer. Her nipples touch Lilith's, and as they breathe, the soft tips move against each other. The sensation is as calming as it is arousing. She feels languid, content to look, wanting to commit each feature of her lover's face to memory: green eyes, oval with heavy lashes and perfectly shaped eyebrows above; the tone of Lilith's skin, like creamy milk even without makeup, and the way it stretches over her cheekbones as she smiles; full lips are soft purple, supple yet dry, wrinkling when she pouts and smoothing out over perfect teeth with each smile. Below her mouth, she has a single piercing, a black labret. It bobs as she moves, swaying like a cobra's head or a phallus. The way it felt, knocking against her when they drank from each other, was electrifying. Star licks her lips and sucks the spike. She tastes herself on its cool surface.

'Again?' Lilith asks, eyes bright and full of humour.

'No,' says Star. 'I want to know you. Not just your beautiful body, all of you. Have you ever played truth or dare?'

'No, but don't you think you should eat? When did you last have any food?'

Star shrugs. 'Sure, let's eat first.'

Getting dressed takes Star an age. Clothes, discarded around the room, are hunted down. To Star's surprise, Lilith dresses alone, strange that the woman feels shy *now*.

They cross to the grocers. The street is full of children in all manner of scary and beautiful costumes.

'Is it Halloween already?' Star asks.

Lilith's face wrinkles, and she shrugs her shoulders.

They grab sandwiches and fruit from the shop and head back to the flat to consume their feast. Crumbs fall from their mouths onto the covers. They lick plum juice from each other's chins. A date in the finest restaurant could not be more pleasurable than the meal they share.

'So, how do you play?' Lilith asks.

It takes a moment for Star to understand.

'We ask each other questions. Some can be silly, others intimate. We answer truthfully or ask for a dare.' Her first question is forming in her mind already.

'Okay, and what if I say dare?'

'I'll dare you to do something, and you have to do it.' Lilith nods.

'You start, what do you want to ask me?' Star's heart quickens.

Lilith creases her brow trying to think of a question. 'Do you like dogs?' she asks at last.

Star falls back in a fit of giggles. 'You can ask me anything, and you ask if I like dogs? Yeah, I guess they're okay… My turn, what's your real name?'

'What do you mean?' Lilith appears genuinely confused.

'Well mine's Sarah, I just call myself Star. I don't know what Raven's real name is. I want to know yours.'

'It's Lilith,' she answers. 'I've always had that name. Why do you call yourself Star?'

'Hmm, a better question. When I met Raven, she was— well still is— this big uber-Goth. She made Donna and me change our names.'

'Made? How could she make you change your name?' Lilith asks.

'Not so fast, Lilith,' Star says. 'It's my turn. Am I the first woman you've ever been with?'

'Yes,' Lilith answers. 'Okay, how did Raven make you change your name?'

'I guess I saw her as this perfect image of who I wanted to be. I did it because she wanted me to, and I wanted to please her.' Star laughs dryly. 'Unfortunately, I can't stand being near her now. How old are you?'

'Dare,' Lilith answers, quickly.

Star smiles. 'Kiss me,' she says.

'I should have said dare sooner,' Lilith says as she lifts Star's face to her own and kisses her.

'I won't make them all as easy,' Star says. 'I want you to tell me about yourself.'

'You know, I've killed softer-hearted people.'

Star laughs. 'It's fun. What's your next question?'

'Who was your lover before me?' Lilith asks.

Star goes white. 'I don't want to talk about him.'

'Then say dare.'

'Okay, dare.' Star holds her breath. The thrill of not knowing what Lilith will demand makes her body tingle.

'Carve my name in your leg,' Lilith tells her.

'What? Uh, I mean, with what?'

Lilith shrugs. 'Don't I have a knife around here somewhere? Okay, how about your nail scissors?'

Shaking, Star fetches them from her makeup bag. She looks at Lilith's face as she pulls up her skirt and holds the scissors next to her skin. They are not clean. They could poison her blood. Wishing for a moment that she had brought her razorblades to this new life, she hesitates.

'Do you have any alcohol?' Star asks.

'It's not your turn,' Lilith answers, licking her lips.

Staring at her criss-crossed thighs, Star realises she might die. The thought fills her with a romantic longing to perish fulfilling her lover's wish. Star pushes the point of the scissors into her thigh. She winces as she drags it along her skin. A vermillion L rises to the surface.

Star glares at Lilith, who stares at the wounded thigh. Breathing deeply, Star returns the scissors to her skin. She presses harder, and the burning becomes a sting. A ribbon of blood weaves down her leg.

'Should I carry on?' Star asks.

Lilith nods.

Star shakes.

Cutting the letters of my lover's name into my skin, it's a mark of ownership, a wedding ring that can never be removed. Am I ready for this? Is this what I want? It isn't like an anonymous notch in the bedstead. Her name will mark me as hers. When the wounds, heal her name will be my scar.

'I'm sorry. I don't think I can,' Star whispers.

'Okay, stop the game,' Lilith says.

Star swallows her doubts. A tear forms in the corner of her eye, and she brushes it away.

Cutting will release me. If I change my mind, I can obscure the word with fresh cuts and set myself free.

'No. I'll do it.'

Lilith watches as Star carves the five remaining letters into her thigh.

The pain is intense. Sweat trickles down Star's face and breasts. With the pain comes familiar pleasure; all she knows is the penetration of metal into her flesh while doubts and worries flee. The mutilation is sensual. Endorphins surge, making her light-headed. Both women watch in silence as the letters rise on Star's skin.

'Now you'll never forget me.' Lilith's voice is a soft purr.

'I never will,' Star answers.

Blood flows freely, obscuring the word— Lilith. Red letters swim in Star's vision, shifting and changing. The writing is strange, foreign, Hebrew, but the meaning is the same. Star's finger prickles, and she holds it to her face— different letters but the same name. Struggling to understand, Star looks to her lover for reassurance.

Lilith takes the finger and wraps her lips around it, licking its tip and sucking. Desire spreads from Star's finger to her groin. Her train of thought is lost, and she floats above the pain and confusion.

'Maybe you ought to clean that,' Lilith says, bringing Star back to earth.

'You do it,' Star replies. Her breathing is ragged as she stares defiantly into Lilith's eyes. She feels her own strength and power building. *Could I become someone to be proud of in this woman's arms?*

Lilith licks the wounds clean.

The desire to be cleansed all over by that tongue tightens Star's throat. Her next question is asked in a ragged whisper. 'How many men have you had sex with?'

Lilith lifts her face from Star's leg. 'I'm bored of this game,' she protests and returns her mouth to Star's thigh.

'I want to know you,' Star says.

Sitting up, Lilith asks, 'Wouldn't it be more fun to find out the important things about me rather than be told?'

'Ah, I think you're just trying to avoid more questions. Do you have something better in mind?'

'Yes, I do,' she answers, pushing Star back onto the bed covers.

'Itchy crumbs,' Star protests.

'Forget them,' Lilith demands.

CHAPTER TWENTY-NINE

LOST IN his studies, Satori feels further than ever from the answer. His reading has taken him through the books of the Kabbalah, to Crowley and even Paul's old favourite— Gilles de Rais, but they aren't enough, not alone. Eventually, he discards Paul's books and returns to his own. He reads the Necronomicon again, certain the answer lies here, in the words of the mad Arab.

'Steve, there's someone at the door asking for you,' his mother shouts.

'Okay,' he says. He closes the books, pushes them under his bed, and runs down the stairs.

'Raven,' he says. 'How are you? Come in, come in.' He leads her upstairs and into his room.

'I suppose you've heard about Star,' Raven says, sitting on Satori's bed and bouncing.

'About her quitting work and disappearing?' he asks. 'Donna came round a few days ago. Made a scene. She thinks I'm hiding her.'

'But you're not, are you,' Raven says. Her tone makes it clear this is a statement rather than a question. 'Freya reckons she's gone to live with that woman she met.'

'The one from the club?' The same thought had crossed his mind.

'Yes, her,' says Raven, smiling. 'Can you imagine? Meeting someone and moving in with them the next day?'

She watches him closely, looking for chinks in his armour perhaps. He tries to hide his pain.

'I'm sorry,' she says. 'I forgot. I guess you don't want to hear about her.'

'It's all right,' he mutters.

'Maybe you've moved on. You were always too good for her. Are you seeing anyone?'

She has made a real effort to look good for him. As always, her makeup is immaculate. Her hair and lips are dark and full—an extraordinarily attractive woman, in her own way.

'I just thought.' She bites her lip and looks up at him through wide eyes. It's disarming. 'I miss her, and you miss her. Maybe we could help each other. You know…'

'Feel less lonely,' he finishes the sentence for her.

'Yes,' she says, smiling.

He sits next to her. Her heavy lashes cast shadows over her blue eyes. He sighs.

'We'll help each other,' he repeats, staring at her face, his pulse racing.

'Yes,' she whispers.

'Just for tonight,' he says.

She does not answer. Instead, she reaches across and touches his cheek. Moving her face toward his and opening her mouth, she flicks her tongue over his lips. He opens his mouth to let it slip inside. As they kiss, her hands are busy with her buttons, unfastening her jacket, then her top and bra.

He reaches forward and cups her heavy breasts.

'You're beautiful,' he tells her.

He makes spirals with his fingers toward the centre of each one. He feels metal and stops kissing her to look. 'Nipple rings. Do you have any more piercings?'

'That's for me to know…'

'And me to find out.' His lips curl into a wolfish grin.

She licks his cheek, and he returns to the kiss. He pulls up her skirt and pushes it over her hips. He feels between her legs. She is shaven. His fingers find metal. He tugs the piercing gently, and she moans with pleasure. He smiles and does it again.

'I could do this all day,' he says. He knows Raven has always wanted him, since before he met Star, long before. He wants this bedding to become the stuff of legend, knowing she will be too proud to keep it a secret.

'Please, Satori,' she says, almost breathless with desire. 'Whatever you want to do to me, I'm yours— body and soul. Just tell me you'll fuck me.'

'I'll fuck you,' he promises.

With one hand, he squeezes her breast hard enough to bruise it, with the other he tugs on her clit piercing. Her body is arched, and her head hangs behind her, long hair whipping her back. Pain and pleasure flash across her face like the zeros and ones of binary code. He watches her, marvelling at the magic of her transformation, from icy goddess to rabid animal, ready to tear him to pieces with her excesses if he let her.

'Bite me,' he says.

She sinks her teeth into his neck; the pain makes him shudder, and he grinds his teeth, growling softly. Desire threatens to take over, but he pulls away and stands beside the bed. She looks up at him, her narrowed eyes willing him to return.

'Undress,' he tells her.

She takes her time, bending her arms behind her to let the open shirt and bra fall to the floor. Her exaggerated posture pushes her breasts upward. He watches them, transfixed. He loves the way they ripple and the tiny hypnotic movements of the rings bouncing against them. She unzips her skirt and lets it drop to the floor. Only her stockings and boots remain.

'Keep them on,' he says. 'Now undress me.'

Smiling, she takes a step toward him. She unbuttons his shirt, kissing the skin beneath. She licks his ear then bites it gently. The silver rings chime as they knock against her teeth.

With her forefinger, she traces a red scar across his shoulder. 'What's this?' she asks.

'A magical war wound. I'll tell you later,' he says.

She nods and moves her fingers downward. She unfastens his jeans and pushes them over his slender hips. She kneels before him, rolling the tight denim down his legs to his ankles. The seams leave marks along his thighs; she licks them, and he shivers with pleasure.

She pauses a moment to unbuckle his boots then removes the rest of his clothing and looks up. As she moves back up his body, she leans forward so her breasts rub against his legs. His hairs become newly awakened fingers, reaching out to tickle her skin. Remaining on her knees, she brushes her lips against his engorged manhood.

He stands silently.

Without his instruction, she hesitates. Then she wraps her lips around him and pulls him into her mouth and throat.

He wraps a lock of her hair around his fingers and pulls, slowly but firmly. She does not stop her exploration of him with her tongue, so he stands above her, pulling her hair and enjoying the intense pleasure.

'Stop,' he says.

She looks up at him.

He lies on the bed, his eager cock heavy on his belly, and motions for her to join him. After stopping to get a packet from her bag, she does. She bites through the metallic casing and withdraws a black circle of latex. Slowly, she unrolls it over him then straddles his hips. Grasping it in her steady hand, she pushes his member inside her. Her breasts blur in continual movement as she bounces. With each descent she gasps.

He reaches up to her throat and squeezes. She stares at him, shocked for one moment then groaning softly with pleasure the next.

When he eventually comes, she lies on his chest, holding him inside her while he shrinks. He turns away from her, and she nestles into his back, her breath hot on his neck.

'So,' Raven whispers into his shoulder.

'So, what?' he replies.

Was that insensitive? I don't want to sound dismissive. I should clarify, quick, before I hurt her feelings.

'What do you mean?'

'You promised to tell me about your magical war wound.'

'Ah, yes,' he says.

He turns to face the ceiling and tries to form the right words. *How do I tell her what she wants to know without it sounding like one of those riddles Star would always complain about?* He nods a few times, closes his eyes, and taps his lips with his index finger.

When the words start to form, he points up. 'Yeah. Okay… well, there are some things in magic which are like play time. They're fun, and they make you feel good. But… there are other things… like the Great Rites… which aren't like play time at all.' He scratches his cheek and faces her.

She nods.

'If you start the Great Rites, you build up this power source. Imagine a rechargeable battery… okay… each day, twice a day, you charge the battery. It gets more and more powerful. It's something separate to you— this other entity, made entirely of power. If you complete the Rites, you get the power. It's supposed to be incredible, but if you fail to complete them perfectly… well, I guess I'm lucky to be alive.'

'How did you fail?' she asks.

A grin spreads across his face. 'I overslept.'

Raven laughs. The sound delights Satori. He kisses her on the nose. Her full lips are soft purple, her white powder less obvious than before, and a hint of colour brightens her cheeks. A soft sigh escapes his lips.

'Are you thinking about her?' she asks.

He strokes her cheek; his momentary sadness has passed.

'Who?'

She kisses him.

When he wakes up, she is still next to him. He touches her cool skin. It feels good to have something real to hold in his arms rather than an abstraction.

CHAPTER THIRTY

LILITH STROKED the polished scales of the snake as it dangled from a willow branch. It blinked at her, its forked tongue licking the air between them. The heat was unbearable. Her cave much cooler and darker than the shade provided by the feathery branches.

'A new bride, you say.' Lilith's words hissed around them. She didn't need to speak out loud, but she enjoyed the sound of her voice. Far richer than it ever sounded in The Garden. Far stronger, even in a whisper, than any cry of frustration or anger she had uttered within those high walls. 'What is she like?'

The serpent cocked its head. Maybe it didn't understand her question or perhaps it knew that any answer risked a violent response.

Lilith dug her toes into the sandy earth. 'I don't care, of course. I wouldn't go back there if God himself begged me. I was just asking… because… well, it doesn't matter, does it? I have more than I need right here. I have my freedom.'

The snake bobbed its head and coiled itself around the branch once more, resting its head on its tail. Its eyes closed.

Lilith stared at her dirty toes. Images of crushing Adam's skull beneath her tiny foot made her grin.

Thinking back to her time in The Garden, Adam's beauty seemed more vibrant, more breathtaking. Weeks of solitude fed her desire and gave a golden glow to remembered fragments. His assertion of his desires and ignorance of hers felt, at a distance, like a form of worship, a devotion to that part of her body which pleased him more than any other. If only he had let her teach him, submitted even a fragment of his control, what wonders she could have shared.

Of course, God took his side. When the choice was made and The Garden's peace had to be restored, who was told to leave? Lilith had shed her humanity at the gate. That choice, at least, was hers. With a deafening screech, she spread her wings and returned to her cave. What was life without choice? Who could exist under someone else's control?

The freedom she cherished surrounded her. Choices filled her mind, so many possibilities.

Now, what does a demon desired by two males, controlled by neither, do?

Lilith's smile became a sneer.

Apparently, she sits in the shade of a willow tree speaking to snakes, wondering whether the new bride of a man as beautiful as the sun will fare any better. I'll bet she is silent, docile, yielding. She has no knowledge of any other way. Made new for the pleasure of her master. This could be fun.

Lilith strokes Star's cheek as the girl drifts off to sleep. She does not know how much longer she can play happy families. She imagines scratching Star's cheek, tearing at the soft, innocent skin with her fingernails, stripping away the girl's shell of lies and exposing her. When they kiss or make love, Lilith is filled with such pure desire that she wonders if this might be what love feels like, but when she looks at Star, studies her without the glaze of passion, she sees two people— the one exposed, the lie, is cracked and crumbling like baked earth, unable to sustain or nourish— a mask Star holds up to the world, even to Lilith. Beneath the mask, a little girl cries for a father who will never love her.

When Star complains about her life, Lilith feels oceans away from the girl. She wants to smash open the barren cracks and see how deeply they penetrate, destroy Star's innocence, tear it from her and laugh as she tries to cling to it, watch her run naked, weeping with shame. Lilith is sick of love and needs to be cured of it, but her plan involves Star, so she waits.

Star's time will come. Eventually, Lilith will make sure there is nothing left for her to hide behind. Either Star will accept the truth, or it will destroy her. Lilith hardly cares which if it means an end to this weakness, whining, and insecurity.

The violence wells up inside her again. She presses her thumb against the girl's throat. Star moans, and Lilith releases the pressure. *I want to kill you. I want to squeeze your throat and watch your eyes glaze over.*

Standing up, she moves away from the bed, staring at Star's naked body through narrowed eyes. *I need some air. I can't stay here and watch you breathe.*

Lilith steps out of the room. Her magical step takes her to the edge of a large park. Skeletal trees scratch at the violet sky as if trying to climb to heaven. A crescent of large houses skirts the edge of the green. They are tall and elegant Georgian town-houses, their golden Bath stone lit from below. Almost all of them have been split into apartments now, but there is still wealth and power within these walls.

She scans the front of each, moving slowly from right to left along the row. Lives are being played out within them, people fucking, people crying, babies stirring in their cots. Some couples are finishing a meal, others starting one. A few apartments are empty. *There. That's the one.*

As quick as thought, she steps into a bedroom on the second floor of the third house from the left. Inside, a teenage girl gets dressed for bed. Her day clothes lie discarded at her feet, and she pulls a nightdress over her head. Her lifted arms reveal small breasts, still forming, her body almost hair-free. The room in which she stands is huge with high ceilings and rich furnishings. Her bed is draped with a velvet cover and on it a few soft toys are arranged. A mass of auburn curls spring up as she pulls the nightdress down.

The girl's face registers shock at seeing a strange woman in her room. Before she can scream, Lilith pulls her through space into the centre of the park below.

The girl shivers in the chill November air. 'Who are you?' she asks.

'Lilith.'

'What do you want?'

'I want to hurt you and silence the torment inside my mind, for a moment at least.'

The girl shudders and steps back. They walk together, Lilith striding forward while the other stumbles back, shaking in her nightgown, until she falls onto the wet grass.

The girl lifts her arms trying to hold the woman at bay. Lilith watches her, amused. She crouches down next to the girl, avoiding blows and scratches, parrying as fists and nails are raised. Staring at the girl's face, she doesn't see the kick coming and is knocked over.

The girl scrambles to stand up. Continually looking back, she runs blindly across the grass then stumbles and falls to her knees. Muscles strain as she tries to push herself back up. She lurches on, her ankle twisting awkwardly with each step, but she keeps going, desperate to reach civilisation.

Lilith lets her run. The girl fought back, and that is enough to buy her freedom.

CHAPTER THIRTY-ONE

'MUM,' FREYA shouts into the silent house.

If her mother hears, she does not answer. Freya hangs up her jacket and sits on the bottom step, staring at her boots, chest tight with unshed tears. *So, this is freedom. This is what I have been craving.*

The day after her mother found her in the garden, leering through her brother's window, Freya tried to tell her that it wasn't what she thought. Childish tales of spying and war games spewed from her mouth. They came too late.

Lilith calls to Freya through the pages of the book and in dreams of lust and blood. She tells Freya she can make things better, but Freya knows it is a lie. Lilith cannot help her repair this wound, only make her forget, and she does not want to forget, not yet.

Wandering into the kitchen, she sees her mother smoking by the window.

'Mum, I'm sorry. What do you want me to do?' Freya's eyes plead.

Her mother tries to focus on her face. Her stare is ugly, hungry for a sacrifice. She has been waiting for this moment.

Freya feels herself falling into a trap and struggles like a fish on a hook.

'I think you should see someone,' is all her mother says before she walks away.

Freya reaches for a chair and lowers herself onto the seat.

My mother thinks I'm insane. Can she force me into therapy?

Without the overwhelming desire to tear her brother's clothes with her hands and his skin with her teeth, she might no longer be Freya, but some hollow shell. Fulfilling this powerful need to be one with him and her goddess, may be the only way she can feel whole.

Would she be happier if every nerve ending wasn't screaming to be touched and every breath wasn't a lust filled pant?

Visions of nothing but darkness and a slumped figure drooling in her lap fill Freya's frightened mind.

She shakes her head. *No. Lilith, I accept your help. I welcome you into my heart and mind. Make me strong.*

Freya leaves the house. She considers heading to Satori's, but he would probably call her brother, and the thought of visiting Dave makes her shudder. She must do this alone.

Skirt waving like a flag in her wake, she runs to the place she feels closest to Lilith: the lake in the park and the weeping willow where she sat and watched Raven and Ivan. It seems so long ago when she drew the symbol on the boathouse. She wonders if it's still there. Staring at the spot, since repainted, she feels it glow hot beneath the surface.

The mark is easy to reproduce. She holds its shape in her head and moves her hand slowly. Curves and waves, dots and points, all are reproduced perfectly. When the work is done, she squats in front of it and empties her mind of all but the drawing. The scrolls unfurl inside her body. The lines are like fingers. Sharpened points penetrate her skin. Her fear vanishes, and she feels warm. It brushes her shame away with gentle strokes. Her body and mind are pure. Love can never be shameful. Self-love, love for others, and the need to make connections are the most natural, most holy feelings of all.

When Freya opens her eyes, the world seems brighter and smells sweeter than she remembers. She sucks great gulps of air into her lungs while her eyes absorb the beauty of the trees and grass.

How many shades of green are there? She has never seen such colours.

The lake shimmers silver, and the sun dances across its

gentle waves. A breeze, fragranced by late roses, caresses her hair and face. Its touch is gentle, reverent, as if nature worships *her*. She wants to taste everything: lick the trees, drink the water.

She runs excitedly around the park, experiencing anew things she has ignored since childhood. She hears laughter then realises it is her own.

Grey and brown figures are blisters on the park's beauty. They walk their dogs or run along labyrinthine pathways. She sees them, but they lack lustre compared to the surreal hues of the plants and earth. She passes them, neither noticing nor caring if they stare at her in confusion or fear.

She lets her knees fold beneath her and rubs her face in the grass, smelling its sweetness. Dew cleanses her face. Kissing the crumbly dirt, she laughs.

'Are you okay, love?' someone asks.

She has forgotten how to speak. *My laughter must show him I feel fine.*

His shadow blocks the sunlight from her skin. *Why doesn't he move away?* She looks up and sees a man with a caring smile painted across his face.

'Let me help you up,' he says, holding a hand toward her.

She shakes her head and crawls a few feet away. The sunlight warms her skin again and contentment fills her. The man retreats.

'They're on their way,' another voice says.

Two men stare at her. *Who is on their way?*

Something tells her she does not want to be here when *they* arrive. A voice urges her to run. She pushes herself to her feet and sprints across the grass. Without thinking, she runs home. She leaps up the stairs, taking two at a time, and throws herself onto her bed. She thinks about the park, remembering everything. Imagining that her mattress is a bed of moss in the centre of a forest, she falls asleep.

CHAPTER THIRTY-TWO

'Let's not go to Club Midian tonight. I feel tired, and I have nothing to wear.' Star rushes her makeup, using the only mirror in Lilith's bedsit: a tiny, cracked, tile-sized mirror attached to the bathroom wall. She stands in the bathtub and leans across, trying not to slip and fall.

In the bedroom, Lilith is pouting. 'I want to go. I want to show you off.' She has already changed her clothes and applied her makeup perfectly. 'For one night, I want to be with you, outside this box, in a place where you are comfortable touching me.'

'Lilith, my love, can't we go next time? I just want to sleep.'

'What if I solve both your problems?' Lilith asks. 'Just give me a moment.'

Alone in Lilith's room, Star peers at the fine muslin drapes at the window, unable to understand how such sheer material is opaque. When she tries to brush them aside, they feel like liquid and coat her fingers with a damp and sticky residue; she shrinks back and rushes to the bathroom to wash.

Star returns to the curtains to ponder the mystery but cannot find an answer, so she sits on the bed amidst her creased clothing to await Lilith's return.

Lilith grins as she opens the door, holding a small packet and a black lace dress. She hands over the packet first. 'Swallow it.'

'Speed?'

Lilith nods, and Star does as she is told. She creases her face as she swallows the bitter white powder. 'What else have you got?'

Lilith offers the dress for inspection. Star admires the way the soft fabric falls. It fits perfectly. She smiles, spinning on the balls of her feet.

'It's amazing,' she says. 'Are you sure I can borrow it? It looks expensive.'

'It's fine,' Lilith answers. 'Woman owes me a favour. It's yours now.'

'I'm ready.' Star spins, and the skirt opens like petals around her ankles.

This is why I'm a Goth! The eternal glamour, where adults can play dress-up, be a princess or goddess every day.

'Coat?' Lilith asks, handing Star her jacket.

They walk together. When Lilith tries to hold Star's hand, Star shakes her head.

The amphetamine takes effect as they walk, and tiny crystals of energy spread across her body. Her hair follicles prickle, and she grinds her teeth. She tells Lilith about everything her life was before and everything it will be in the future, her voice so fast it blurs into white noise.

Above their heads, the sky flashes green, silver, and red. Explosions echo through the street. Beyond the haze of street-lamps, the night is alive with colour, an echo of a turbulent past and a celebration of the enduring status quo.

'Bonfire night,' Star whispers.

The moment they enter the nightclub, Star transforms. She grabs Lilith's hand and pulls her onto the dance floor. They dance face to face, bodies swaying in time with each other, sometimes inches apart and other times with no distance between them.

Dancers move around them, appearing between clouds of dry ice and smoke then vanishing again as Star's attention is drawn back to the beautiful woman who is hers and hers alone. She feels she's dancing within a dream, and her body seems to rise until she is floating above the floor, twisting around and around her lover. Bodies coiled together like pythons.

A faster track follows, and her body sinks. The deep rhythm pulses through her feet and brings with it memories of their lovemaking; that strange first night when she'd thought Satori had somehow possessed Lilith. The beats, like those thrusts, make her body shiver. It seems so long ago, and she doubts her memory.

Satori's world had been too strange for me to exist within, but Lilith's is far stranger— body parts grow out of nothing, muslin blocks sunlight, and clothing appears without a wardrobe?

Madness beckons, but she ignores its call. She loves Lilith and is determined to accept everything.

When Johnny O finishes his set and Ivy takes over, Lilith buys two glasses of absinthe, and they sit together, huddling close, arms wrapped around each other. They giggle at private jokes and sip their potent drinks.

She feels connected to this woman and curses herself for tarnishing it with feelings of confusion, wanting desperately to embrace everything Lilith is, however strange.

Being a Goth, more than the clothing, the music, and the sense of freedom, is about accepting the strange and unusual, drawing it into myself as part and parcel of life. She clings to this idea as they drink and talk about the other dancers, the music, and themselves and how they have both changed over the last week.

'I never thought I'd be sharing that room with anyone,' Lilith says.

'How does it feel?' Star asks.

'Not being alone? Wonderful.'

Their arms wrap around each other's shoulders, and they kiss.

Star's body rebels. She needs to use the bathroom. 'I'll just be a moment,' she says.

As Star squats above the toilet, unwilling to touch the seat with any part of her body, she feels again the effects of the speed. Her legs tremble, her pulse quickens, and her teeth rub together. When she is finished, she looks for toilet paper but finds none so shakes herself then flushes. It takes an age to straighten her skirt, but she doesn't rush.

She opens the stall door and sees Raven. Star wants to embrace her old friend and share with her the wonders of her new relationship; describe in detail the passions she is experiencing.

She reaches over to touch her flatmate's arm, but Raven moves away— a single step but the rejection cuts Star like a knife.

Narrowing her eyes, she looks at Raven's face. Her makeup, perfectly drawn, depicts a trio of bats around one eye. Her lips are almost black with only a hint of deep purple berry, ripe and full, ready to be eaten. She desires this image of Gothic perfection but fights it. She loves Lilith, and a life with Raven would be no life.

'I fucked Satori,' Raven says proudly, her words full of poison.

Star stares at her. The words echo around her mind, each syllable floating like an autumn leaf caught in a zephyr. They dance in the air until the weight of them crashes through her skull. Raven fucked Satori. Raven waited until Star was out of the way and took him. Star shakes her head to deny the image of Raven and Satori's bodies moving together. It fills her brain.

Something wakens in Star's belly and writhes with a fury that energises her arms. She grabs Raven by the shoulders and pulls her into the stall. Raven's ankles buckle as her boots slip on the wet surface. Star is upon her. Lifting the woman's head by her hair, Star smashes Raven's cheek against the porcelain toilet. She lifts the once-immaculate face and forces it down again and again, pummelling her against the grubby white seat, now streaked with ribbons of red.

When Star releases her grip, Raven slouches onto the floor. Star hurries out of the stall and stares in the mirror. Blood is splattered across her arm and shoulders.

'Fuck,' she curses and grabs green paper towels to wet them in the sink.

She rubs at her skin, trying to erase the stain. The paper's roughness scratches her; she feels its burn but the red just deepens in tone. Growling, she throws the towel to the floor.

People are chatting outside the bathroom door. Head bowed; she rushes past them.

The stairs seem to move as she reaches them. She clings to the rail. The rise and fall of each tread make her feel sick; her head spins and blood pounds in her ears. She cannot hear the music. All she can hear is the crack of Raven's skull as it breaks.

Reaching the bottom, she stands swaying.

Which direction?

She sees a swirl of bodies on the dance floor. Donna and Freya are there. They face each other, enjoying the music. She starts toward them then remembers she came with Lilith. Her eyes search the darkened room for her lover. *There, sat at a table near the bar.*

'We have to go,' she whispers urgently into Lilith's ear.

'Why? What's happened?'

'I think I killed Raven,' Star whispers.

Lilith laughs.

'I'm not joking. We need to leave now.'

Leaving the jacket unclaimed in the cloakroom, they hurry out of the club.

Lilith is still smiling as they walk under the bridge to Vermelho Road. Star burns with frustration and anger. *Doesn't she believe me?*

'Why are you grinning?' Star yells.

'You don't have an aggressive bone in your body, love,' Lilith answers. 'Why would you kill your friend?'

Star stops walking and stands in the shadows. She needs to be in the darkness, not wanting to see the expression on her lover's face when she makes this confession. *Will Lilith leave me, or will she take pity and help me through this?*

'She told me she fucked Satori.'

'Satori?'

'Steve, my ex,' Star clarifies.

'The magician?'

Star nods. Not a title she would have used, but she supposes it does describe him. Now she regrets the darkness. She wants to know what thoughts Lilith is hiding from her.

'You know him?' Star asks, starting to walk again.

Lilith keeps pace. 'Only from your numerous and vivid descriptions.'

Is that jealousy?

'I'm sorry,' she whispers.

'It's okay,' Lilith soothes. 'In France, it would be a crime of passion.'

'Here it's murder. I have to get away.' Star pauses. 'Will you come with me? If I promise never to mention Steve or Raven again, will you come? I don't think I can do this alone. I'm frightened.'

They are under the streetlights, and Star sees Lilith's nod.

'Gather what you need from my room. I'll get some transport.'

Walking along Vermelho Road without Lilith beside her, Star sees far more of the underbelly of the city than she would have liked. She passes women, pinned against brick and stone walls, being pumped by strangers. Each face resting on their aggressor's shoulder has eyes either closed or glazed in some drug-induced fugue. She spots bodies sprawled in bliss with needles still attached to their arms, and men in doorways bristling with the threat of violence.

She hurries past them all and up the stairs to Lilith's bedsit. For the second time in a week, she packs. Her velvet bag is stuffed with clothing. Looking at the items she brought into this new life, she realises that none of them are practical; they are all pure vanity. *Is that what my life is now?*

She rushes back down the stairs and is met by Lilith in a black estate car. Without question, she settles in the passenger's side and hauls the bag onto her lap.

'Throw it in the back,' Lilith says.

'I'm okay,' Star says. 'Let's just get out of here.'

They move away and join the motorway at the next roundabout. Star cuddles her bag, staring through the window at the passing lights of houses and, when they leave the city behind, the lights of stars.

'Wales or Scotland?' Lilith asks her as they approach the merging of two motorways, two routes to different lives.

'Scotland,' Star answers.

Lilith increases her speed and joins the M5.

CHAPTER THIRTY-THREE

IN A valley, nestled between mountains of black clothes, lies a woman. Her eyes are closed but she is not asleep.

The wardrobe and drawers hang open, gaping at Donna in disbelief. Textiles, books, and CDs are strewn across the unmade bed. Donna tries to remember the room tidy, but it feels like years since she last sat here with her friend. Her memories are hazy, but she is certain this is not how Sarah's bedroom usually looks.

Sarah's parents will arrive tomorrow, and the maelstrom might be one too many blows for them. Donna is not certain whether Sarah or the police made the mess. The door remained locked until yesterday. Donna had not wanted to betray her friend's trust.

What does that matter now? What does anything matter? Sarah and Raven are gone, and Donna is alone.

She does not bother to sit up when she hears the doorbell.

It is him— bastard! Well, he can just fuck off and crawl under his stone like the slimy, evil fucker he is.

Fuck off! Fuck off! Fuck off! I'm not getting up. I'm not letting you in.

When the glass smashes, Donna jolts upright, heart pounding, her mouth dry as desert sand. She cannot swallow. Shaking her head to deny him entry, she stares defiantly at Sarah's bedroom door.

For five minutes, she sits frozen, heart racing ahead of the music, hands balled into fists, until she realises Satori is not inside the house and falls back between the clothes, breathing deeply. Sarah's smell, still clinging to the unwashed clothes, fills

Donna's nostrils.

'Why?' she asks.

Opposing desires juxtapose themselves in Donna's head. Part of her wants to get drunk and fall asleep here, among Sarah's belongings. Feel close to her friend before she is evicted from the flat— from this life. Another part wants to hunt for Sarah, shake her and slap her until she tells Donna the truth about what happened. A third part wants to help, tidy the room, meet with Sarah's parents, be strong for her friend— now, when she is needed most. Pushing them all aside for the moment, Donna reaches for the boxes beneath Sarah's bed: her paintings.

Fingers close around empty air, and she jams her head under the divan, waiting for her eyes to adjust to the gloom.

Sarah's boxes are gone, her paintings, her paints, and her other box, the one Sarah thought she kept secret: the razor blades. Where others might coast through life, Sarah struggles; her art is broken somehow— incomplete, as though some piece of it and her is missing.

What did she lose, and why did she never tell me, her best friend?

Donna imagines the police poring over Sarah's paintings, analysing them, making judgments. *What will they make of the black and red portraits?*

Donna shudders. *What will they think when they see Sarah's face and the demons jabbing, tearing her scalp with spears and claws?* It's one of Donna's favourite pieces. One she wishes she could have kept.

The painting is beautiful and disturbing, like all Sarah's fine art. Damning though to anyone who doesn't know the context, and part of that context will arrive tomorrow.

Donna's experience of parental love is unconditional. Her mother accepts everything and still loves her but, from the few stories she shared when they drank or got stoned together, it seems as though Sarah's parents are different. Perhaps because Sarah is an only child or because her parents were almost forty when she was born, already set in their ways. Maybe, in part at least, it could be these things. But Donna blames it on religion, Sarah's bohemian lifestyle and her obsession with the unusual, anathema to their Christian faith.

Donna cannot imagine such a family. At the time, she had brushed it aside as fantasy and hyperbole, the product of a young woman's despair at not being heard, not being understood. Now Donna isn't certain and, if she stays here, she will meet the ogres tomorrow.

One plan of action is scored through in her mind. She will not tidy for them. Let them see the disarray, it represents their baby well.

Two choices remain: to follow or lie here and remember. Donna tries to remember Sarah happy. Memories of them skipping along the streets, arms linked, singing 'we're off to see the wizard', flood into her head. Pressing Sarah's mesh bodice top to her face, she cries. As the fabric dampens, Sarah's scent fades and saltiness, like the sea in winter, replaces it.

Donna grabs another garment from the pile: a stocking.

'I love you,' she whispers.

Donna felt Star's fingers in her hair and heard the hiss of straighteners.

'I love you, too. I don't know what I'd do without you,' Sarah replied. 'There… beautiful.'

Donna turned to face her friend. 'Thank you.'

'So, what do you think of him?' Sarah grinned, her eyes wide, hopeful, expectant.

'Who, Steve?'

Sarah nodded. 'Satori.'

'I've heard he's really weird.'

'Oh?' Sarah replied, looking hurt. 'He seems nice to me, intelligent, gentle. He's interested in what I think.'

'Aren't they all at first? Look, it's just I've heard he's into magic.'

'What kind? Tricks or magick?' Sarah emphasized the final k with a click of her tongue.

'Magick. Alistair Crowley, the word is the law; heavy fucking shit, Sarah.'

Sarah scratched the base of her skull, staring intently at the floor. 'He doesn't seem…'

'I'm just saying what I heard. I hardly know the guy.'

Why didn't I tell her not to date him? Would Sarah have listened? Would she still be here? I should have stopped her.

'He goes to Club Midian every week. He doesn't have a job. I think Freya's brother knows him pretty well. You could ask her.'

Sarah nodded. 'Magick.'

'That's what I heard.' Donna's heart softened. 'Of course, it could be lies and exaggeration. You know how people are.'

Sarah glowed; for a single moment, no longer than a blink, her skin flashed with golden light, then it was gone, and Donna never saw it again.

Why didn't I talk to her about it? Why did I pretend nothing happened?

Donna considers asking Sarah's parents when they arrive, but she is certain it would do no good.

'Where are you?' Donna asks.

The room offers no reply.

How do you follow someone if you don't know where they're going?

The urge to see her friend makes her scalp prickle.

If Sarah was here, what would I do? What would I say?

Donna imagines Sarah sitting at the end of the bed. Questions form but dissolve on her tongue. Accusations stick in her throat.

She reaches across and takes Sarah's hand. It feels cold and insubstantial. There is no solidity in the illusion.

Donna concentrates harder, trying to feel cool, slender fingers grip her hand. One by one, the fingers form. Donna feels their gentle pressure against her skin. Trying to focus only on the sensation, she breathes deeply. She wants to move closer, feel her friend's arms around her, but she doubts her imagination could create an illusion big enough.

Her extended arm aches. Gravity tugs at its weight. The fingers fade.

Unable to hold onto them, she yells. 'Fuck!'

There is no holding back the tears, she does not even try; she hopes they might wash away a little of the sorrow. Rocking herself, back and forth, tears choking her until the words sound like hiccups, she sings a slow, haunting melody from Sarah's favourite band. The lyrics and screams of frustration echo around her swaying torso.

Sarah is gone. Sarah is gone, and she is not coming back.

The telephone rings six times before the spell is broken, and Donna races to answer. 'Hello?' *Let it be her.*

'Donna, it's Freya. I was starting to worry. Satori's been here. He might come to you.'

'He's already been here. He smashed the front door.'

'Shit! Are you okay?'

'He didn't get in… You wanna come over?' Donna asks.

Silence. 'I… I can't. I can't… it's too… oh, I don't know what I'm trying to say.'

'I understand,' Donna says.

'Raven was my best friend. She was like a…' The words trail off into harsh and rasping sobs from a throat scorched by hours of crying.

'I'm sorry,' Donna replies.

'Do you want to come here?' Freya asks.

'I'm not sure I could leave the flat.'

'Ivan'll pick you up if you want,' Freya offers. 'You should come. Get out of there for a while. Please.'

Donna looks at Sarah's bedroom door. It hangs ajar but the clothes and bed cannot be seen, only darkness.

'Please come,' Freya says. 'We're worried about you.'

Donna nods. 'Okay.'

Is it the right thing to do? What if I'm out when Sarah comes back or phones? She grabs her bag from underneath the coffee table and drops her phone into it then checks her keys are there. *Do I need anything else?*

The doorbell rings.

He was quick!

Taking her bag and coat, Donna walks down the stairs. Broken glass covers the floor. As a shard crunches beneath her boot, she feels frightened by the silhouette beyond the door.

'Who is it?' Donna asks.

'Ivan.'

Grabbing the keys from her bag, she tries to unlock the door, but her hand shakes. Putting the palm of her left hand against the wooden door frame, she tries to guide metal into metal with her right. On the third attempt, she stops and rests the tip of the key against the metal surround. Keeping the pressure steady, she drags it toward the hole. The sound the key makes as it scratches the metal is the sound her soul has made since she was told that Sarah had killed Raven: a dull, insistent scream.

Closing her eyes, she tries to block out the world. Images of Sarah and Raven fill her head.

'You okay?' Ivan asks.

'I'm just trying to get the key in the lock. Give me a minute.'

'You wanna pass me the keys, and I'll unlock the door?' A tanned forearm appears through the broken panel.

She takes a step back so that his fingers do not accidentally touch her shin.

Shards of glass glint evilly beneath his arm, and Donna imagines the hand of God reaching toward her across a starlit sky.

Will he save or punish me?

The fingers wriggle, Donna remembers the keys and hands them to him.

The door opens, and she steps aside. In the doorway stands Freya's brother. His kind face is puffy from his own tears. The urge to hold him, cling to him as if he could somehow cure her of this pain, makes her shake even harder. Maybe he knows how she feels because he squeezes her shoulder.

'Come on, let's go,' he says softly. 'Freya's worried sick about you.'

Donna nods and concentrates on reaching Ivan's Citroen. She hears him lock the door, then he is at her shoulder. Ivan opens the car door for her. His skin, as it moves past her face, smells like sage. She closes her eyes and licks her lips. They sit side by side in silence as Ivan guides the car back to his parents' house.

CHAPTER THIRTY-FOUR

THE SHARP crack of glass breaking underfoot— someone is in the house. Donna's eyes adjust to the bright sunlight streaming through her open curtains. *How did I get home?* The question will have to wait, the more urgent one being— *who is downstairs?*

Pulling back her duvet cover, Donna realises she is fully dressed. Her shoes have been removed but her skirt and blouse cling to her body in a combination of sweat and static.

Clumsily, she creeps to her door, wielding a stiletto boot and grasps the handle. Her body shakes as she opens the door a few inches and glimpses an old woman dressed in various shades of brown, white hair scraped back from her narrow forehead. Donna opens her fingers, and the boot falls with a thud.

The woman looks up and sees Donna's face in the gap between the door and jamb.

'You must be Donna,' she says.

The woman's voice carries none of the emotion Donna thinks she should feel.

Is this what Sarah's parents expected? Was the murder a natural culmination of Sarah's life choices in their eyes? No one can be that prejudiced, could they?

Perhaps the woman already emptied her store of tears.

Donna can empathise; her own chest feels hollow; although she knows she has plenty more tears to cry.

'I'm so sorry,' Donna says.

The woman sighs and turns toward the top of the stairs.

An old man with granite hair rounds the corner and touches his wife's shoulder. 'Thank you, Donna. Which was her room?'

'Oh, um… here,' Donna says, pointing at the room at the end of the hall. 'I'm afraid the police left it in a mess.'

'You've been in there?' Sarah's father asks.

Donna blushes. 'Just for a moment.'

He nods and follows his wife along the corridor toward Sarah's door.

'Would you like a tea or coffee?' Donna asks.

The man's eyes are hazel, a startling combination of gold and green, and Donna feels herself shrivel under the weight of their stare.

She pulls her clothes around her, trying to create a barrier between herself and the man's disdain.

He hates me. I have never spoken to him before, and yet he hates me.

'Two teas, milk no sugar.' He walks away without another word.

Donna sinks to the floor. She crouches there, her fingers gripping the carpet, trying to calm her racing heart. A momentary sense of relief that she never had the opportunity to join his family fills her head.

She struggles to her feet and heads for her wardrobe. Grabbing a baggy jumper and ankle length skirt, she gets changed. Her mouth tastes bitter. She will brush her teeth while she waits for the kettle to boil. She fills and flicks on the kettle then tiptoes to the bathroom.

She hears them move around Sarah's room. Low whispers scratch at the periphery of her hearing. She dares not eavesdrop. Bolting the bathroom door behind her, she feels a little safer, a little less the intruder in her own home.

Her purple toothbrush rests beside Raven's black one. The neat little hole, which used to house Sarah's is empty. She douses the brush with water, squeezes too much paste onto its bristles, then scrubs her teeth until her gums bleed. Pink foam fills the basin. She knows she should stop, open the bathroom door, and make the cups of tea, but she keeps brushing while her eyes drip tears.

The urge to phone her mother overtakes her. The landing is empty. Hushed voices still seep from Sarah's room. *What are they doing in there?*

Donna searches for her phone. Checking her bedroom, she finds it at the foot of her divan. The phone feels light in her hand. She feels frightened of the weight of her words. Her mum doesn't know yet.

She carries the phone to the kitchen; its unlit screen reflects her shadow. Her own movements mesmerise her. Pouring water onto teabags, she forgets to phone her mum and remembers instead the time Sarah told her she was leaving Satori. Donna's sense of relief had been overwhelming.

She couldn't repress a smile, hoping that things would be better. She could help Sarah through this, and Sarah would see how happy Donna could make her.

Sarah saw the smile, and her anger ripped Donna from the space they shared, shooting like a meteor from the room. When Sarah emerged hours later, there was blood on the sleeves of her shirt. Donna had been more careful with her friend's feelings after that.

Leaving Satori had been the best and the worst thing Sarah had done until now.

Deep amber scum floats on the surfaces of the drinks.

Donna plunges a spoon into each cup and removes the bag, squeezing it over the sink. Trails of brown liquid drip onto the counter.

'Fuck,' she growls under her breath and reaches for a dishcloth.

It is dry, but she does not bother to wet it. Splodges spread as she tries to wipe them away. Unable to care, she returns the discoloured dishcloth to the corner of the sink.

The milk smells rancid. She hunts for another carton but all she can find is Raven's soya milk, so she uses that instead. The tea looks thin and dark, but it will have to do.

Donna considers knocking on the bedroom door but realises she is in no hurry to see those people again. Instead, she takes two trips to carry mugs and phone into the living room. Settling on the sofa, she feels Raven's presence beside her.

'I'm so sorry, Raven. For what it's worth, I miss you, too.'

Her mobile squats on the coffee table. *I should have phoned on Sunday. Why did I put it off?*

Donna takes a sip of her warm, throat-coating tea and picks up the phone.

'Mum, it's Donna,' she says as the familiar voice recites her old phone number.

'Donna! How are you? Mrs Rogers was just asking about you today. I meant to phone last week, dear, but it has been so busy here.'

Donna hears her mother's smile. She wants to listen to the chatter, the updates on people she only has the vaguest recollection of ever meeting. She doesn't want to share her news. Eventually, the excited voice finishes, and there is a pregnant silence.

What did my mother ask? Oh yes— how are you? How is Sarah?

'Not good, Mum,' Donna says at last. Her voice carries no volume. She hopes that maybe her mother might hear different words, happier words. 'Raven is dead.'

'Oh gosh, no!' Donna's mother's voice vibrates with the same shock and the same pain Donna has been feeling. This is real, the voice tells her. This is important. People care. 'When? How?'

'I... I... I don't know how to say it, Mum... but it hurts so much.' Donna shakes.

A door opens and closes in the hallway. Shadows move.

'I'm sorry, Mum. There are people here. I've got to go.'

'Baby don't go. Tell me what's wrong. Can I help? I'll get on the train, Donna. I'll be there in a couple of hours. I love you.'

'I love you too, Mum.' Donna bites her lip and severs the connection.

Sarah's mother hovers in the doorway like a hawk. Her features fixed in a tight scowl, unchanging even when Donna turns her tear-blotched face toward her.

'Your teas are here.' Donna grabs a cushion and squeezes it to her belly. Looking at her knees, she rocks herself. Her only thought is that her mum will soon arrive.

CHAPTER THIRTY-FIVE

STAR SLEEPS in the car. Her dreams are full of Raven's face cracking open like an eggshell in her hands. Rivers of blood pour from her fingertips. Her dead friend turns to her. Raven's eyes are milky white, and her right cheek and jaw are so badly smashed that her face hangs lower on that side, her mouth a triangle of pain.

'We will find you,' the horror promises.

'I'm sorry,' Star pleads.

Raven sways unsteadily on her feet. Her clothing stinks of urine; her face and shoulders are covered in blood and gore while more drips from her mouth onto her chest and boots. Star tries to leave but she is pinned against the closed toilet door. Like a drowning fish, Star's mouth opens and closes in silent pleas.

Raven presses her cold body against Star and whispers in her ear. 'The evil is inside you. They put it there. All is death and darkness. You cannot escape. Why run?'

'What else can I do?' she asks the phantom.

'Tear it out!' screams Raven.

'Are you all right?' a voice from beside her asks.

Star opens her eyes and tries to focus. It is dark, and Lilith's face is obscured by shadows. The movement of the car creates ripples across her features.

'I had a nightmare,' Star says.

'Go back to sleep. You'll have better dreams.'

Lilith is right. The dream Star slips into, as sleep lays its claim on her once more, is an erotic one.

When Star wakes again, the first light of dawn pierces through the mist.

'Do you want to stop?' Star asks. 'You've been driving all night.'

'Rest would be a welcome change,' Lilith answers.

'How far north are we?'

'We've just passed Perth. I thought we'd head for the mountains from here.'

'It looks like we're low on petrol,' Star says, noticing the dial.

'Do you have money?'

'Not enough for food and petrol.'

'There's a hotel coming up. Maybe we should swap cars.'

'Steal someone's car?' Star asks, shocked.

'Do you think this car belongs to us?' Lilith laughs.

Star sits in silence. A week ago, she was working for a call centre. Now she is on the run and riding in a stolen car with a woman she barely knows.

Little things about Lilith worry her: the strange room, her reaction to the murder, the way she changes clothes without possessing any. Things Star casually brushed aside while in the arms of her lover crowd against the gates of her sanity, trying to break through.

She is glad she is not alone. Lilith has taken charge and done things she could never have done. Without Lilith, she would be hitchhiking, risking her safety with each new driver, or in a police cell.

Lilith acts without complaint. If anything, she seems happy to do it, to give up everything for Star. Pushing her doubts into the back of her mind, Star balances her petty worries against how amazing Lilith is and leans across to kiss the woman's cheek.

'Thank you,' Star says.

'What for?'

'Everything.'

They continue north along minor roads. The new car is as nondescript as the old. Only the landscape changes. Forests are darker, grasses coarser, and the road twists between steep banks of both.

Sometimes they rise into the pale sky. At other times they

plunge toward rivers. Beneath them, the wheels bounce and stagger over uneven surfaces. Loose stones spit onto the underbelly of the car with loud cracks, the ticking of a bomb, as their journey weaves its way toward the final explosion.

As they round a hairpin bend, a remote cottage rises out of the mist. No car is parked outside, and the garden is overgrown. Lilith pulls up behind the building, careful to hide the car from the road.

'Why are we stopping here?' Star asks.

'It looks like a holiday home. Wait here if you want. I'll check it out.'

Sitting alone in the car, Star glances at the woods that surround her. Shadows between the trees are full of movement. Even now, in the mid-morning light, their darkness oppresses her. Half of her wants to stop, get clean, and rest. The other half wants to keep moving, fearing the unforgiving judgment of the forest.

The cottage is small, just one storey— the perfect size for a holiday home. The walls are grey brick and mortar, and the windows are tiny. She wonders whether there will be warmth inside, physical or emotional will suffice.

Soft taps on her window make her jump. She turns and sees Lilith grinning at her. She opens the car door and stretches her legs.

'It looks like no one has been inside for months,' Lilith says. 'Shall we?'

Star leaves her bag on the front seat and follows. There was a rose garden here in the summer months. Stalks and sharp thorns jut out at her as she skirts around the flowerbeds.

The door has been forced. Splinters of wood scratch the air. A cold, more biting than the one outside, presses against her, making her shiver. Damp air fills her nostrils.

A tiny sitting room adjoins an even smaller kitchen, and the two doors at the other end of the room promise a bathroom and bedroom.

Pulling her jumper tighter around herself, she wanders to the kitchen. The half-sized fridge is empty.

'There's a fire here,' Lilith says. 'I'll gather some wood if you're cold.'

Star nods and sinks into one of the two armchairs in front of the fireplace. She knows she should offer to go into the woods and collect branches for the fire; Lilith has not slept. Her lover should be resting while she organises these things, but she cannot drag her tired body back onto her feet.

She falls asleep feeling cold and alone but wakes feeling warm and in love. Fire dances in the grate, and Lilith sits on the chair opposite. Lilith's eyes are closed, her beautiful face relaxed, body moulded onto the chair, cradled by it, like a baby in its mother's arms. She is silent, her breathing so soft that Star cannot hear a whisper.

Star retrieves her bag from the car and checks the dash-board clock— it's five. She tries to ignore the darkness between the trees, hiding hundreds of unseen eyes that watch her every movement. Shivering, she hurries inside.

The forced door refuses to shut properly. She spots a metal box in the porch and rests it against the broken wood to keep the door closed then checks the rest of the house.

The left door leads to a bathroom with a tub that beckons her filthy frame. The stiff tap hisses and splutters. She cups her hand under the flow until she feels warm water hit her fingers. Leaving it to fill, she checks the second door.

The chimney backs onto the wall of the bedroom. The bed has been made with blankets, reminding Star of her childhood, tucked into bed by her mother with a story and a kiss. The memory feels distant, as if it belongs to another lifetime; she wonders how her mum and dad are feeling. Have they heard about Raven?

Her thoughts wander to Donna and Freya, and she feels sick to think of their suffering. Sitting on the edge of the bed, she weeps. The sound of gurgling water reminds her of the bath she has left running. She hurries to the bathroom, wiping her face on her sleeve. The bath is full but not overflowing. Before she steps into the hot water, she checks the cutlery drawer and grabs a small, sharp paring knife.

Water prickles her skin. Gritting her teeth, she sinks into the bath. She lifts her left leg and pivots it. Watching the water run in rivulets down her pale skin, she grabs the knife from the side of the bath and scratches the surface of her skin with its blade, enjoying the gentle sting. It takes a few seconds before blood pushes through the damaged surface. When it does, she plunges her leg into the hot water and gasps at the pain. It helps, but the dark thoughts are still there, just below the surface of her psyche, and she knows they are waiting to overwhelm her.

Closing her eyes, she lets her head sink under the water. Dull slaps of waves echo around her. She holds her breath, wanting desperately to remain beneath the surface. Her lungs rebel, her body shifts, and her face rises. Tiny, perfect spheres of water line her eyelashes, obscuring her sight. She sees a shadow in the room but cannot see its form.

'You've been cutting yourself again.' Lilith frowns at the threads of blood rising through the water. 'Why do you do that?'

'The pain helps. Life leaves a dull ache in my chest. Cutting externalises the pain. It feels… more manageable when it's on the outside.' She pauses. 'It's good to feel something.'

'I'll see if I can find you a towel,' Lilith says.

Star pulls out the plug. She loves feeling the water drain away, pulling the darkness with it, leaving her lighter, purer.

Lilith rubs the first towel over Star's shoulders and breasts. The feeling is luxurious. Star imagines her lover as her hand-maiden, bathing, drying, and dressing her, not in clothes but in skin and kisses.

'I love you,' she whispers into the hair at Lilith's crown. If her words are heard, Lilith does not respond. She continues rubbing and drying, working at the creases of Star's skin, her armpits and under her breasts; her knees, elbows, and her sex all get the same gentle yet thorough treatment. As Star steps out of the tub and onto the cold floor, Lilith kneels at her feet to dry between her toes.

'There's a bed,' Star says, and they run to it, throwing themselves onto the itchy blankets in a tangle of limbs and sexual abandon.

CHAPTER THIRTY-SIX

FREYA WANDERS through the forest. Trees are cast into darkness under a pale grey sky. The last remaining leaves cling to the branches, shivering in the cold. She doesn't feel discomfort from the fresh wind. It feels more like an awakening.

Ahead, Freya sees a deeper darkness within the shadows. Trees bar her way, but she pushes forward, teeth clenched, jaw jutting outward in a mask of determination. Branches claw her naked arms and legs. Blood trickles down her skin. *Why doesn't it hurt?*

Stumbling out of the forest, she pulls brambles from her knotted hair and coils of ivy from her ankles. In the mouth of a cave lies a single red rose petal. Freya reaches down to touch it, and her fingers close around the soft velvet of its skin. Sniffing it, she is reminded of a childhood vacation and a cottage in the valleys with a rose garden where three siblings played together while their parents watched from rusting wrought iron chairs. *We were happy then, all of us. Life was simple.*

She peers into the gloom. A tawny glow reflects off the walls; the source must be just around the corner: a fire perhaps. She steps inside. Toes sink into damp earth. Skin warms. While she didn't feel cold outside, she notices the heat immediately. The mud is sensuous, kissing her feet as she walks, its warmth spreading upward. Dripping water sounds like the chimes of distant bells. Walls and ceiling glisten with moisture. Mud envelops her ankles. She watches each step, not wanting to slip and fall. Yet part of her wonders how it would feel to sink to the ground and roll in this mud. The swinish, greedy thought brings a smile to her lips.

Another rose petal rests on the surface, and she wonders whether she should pick it up or leave it to mark a safe route back. Giggling, she stares at the perfect petal for a moment then crushes it into the mud with her blackened foot. She trudges onward, deeper and deeper into the cave.

A few feet ahead, the tunnel bends. Her heart quickens. Placing her hand on the cave wall, she leans forward to see what lies ahead. The surface is ridged and silver algae cling to its troughs. The slimy surface seems to move under the slight pressure, bending outward like elastic or living tissue rather than rock.

There is no fire, no sign of life other than the trail of petals leading to another bend. It is difficult to discern the exit when she glances back as if the cave merges into the forest like an ever-spreading ink blot. For a moment, she considers leaving, returning to the world outside.

There is nothing of value for me there. I need to see, to understand the truth at the centre of my life.

She pulls away from the pliant wall and takes another step. Her feet sink deeper, and mud coats her calves. Perhaps she will submerge completely before she reaches the next bend. Gritting her teeth, she tugs at each leg then lets it sink deliciously back into the mud.

It would be a luxurious death to be swallowed by this ooze. With each step, only half of Freya wishes to continue. The other half wills her heavy limbs to slide backward and propel her face first into the darkness. She matches the rhythm of her steps to the beat of her heart and urges herself to keep moving. Each beat brings her closer to the light. Everything feels easier when she works to the music of her own body, and she reaches the corner quickly.

A woman sits cross-legged within a crescent of fire, unbothered by the flames. On one side of her is a pile of red roses. Freya watches as the woman picks a new rose and teases the petals from the bloom. Some of these petals fall into her lap, which already looks blood red from her work, others catch in a mysterious breeze that Freya cannot feel, floating past her into the cave beyond.

'Do I know you?' Freya asks.

The woman does not respond. Another rose is taken and stripped. Dirty and tangled blonde hair covers the naked woman's bowed head. Freya moves closer. The cross-legged woman doesn't look up.

Freya sits in front of the naked woman and studies her face. Her features flicker: old then young, full of innocent beauty then cruel and terrible. Needing to focus on something else, Freya picks up a rose. A thorn pierces her thumb and draws a thread of blood. She sucks it and tastes the metallic warmth of her essence. Freya tugs at the first petal, but it is held firmly in place. Freya watches the way the other woman wiggles the petals and does the same. It comes free, complete and perfect, untorn. Holding it to her face, Freya stares at the petal. Beyond the red, she sees the woman's face lift. She smiles at Freya and closes her vivid green eyes.

'Goddess,' Freya whispers.

Petals fall all around her. Freya sits in a waterfall of red confetti. The scene blurs and vanishes.

She stands in her brother's room not knowing whether she is asleep or awake. His bed is covered in rose petals. It must be a dream. He sleeps on his left side, his arm obscuring his face. The navy duvet and ruined blossoms cover him. She grabs the duvet and pulls it away. Petals fall to the floor and the duvet lands in a crumpled heap.

Freya pauses.

Here lies the body she has worshipped for three years yet never touched.

Dare I touch it now, here in the safety of my dream?

His build is athletic, toned not skinny. His skin glows, and pale hairs decorate his shins. The urge to lick his legs, let the hairs tickle her tongue, almost overwhelms her. She glimpses the silhouette of his high white buttocks and shivers.

She crawls up the bed hovering above him.

If his body responds to mine, we will be touching in moments.

She traces his forehead with her thumb. A smudge of blood marks him as hers, her kin and her lover. Leaning back, arching her body, she looks up at the ceiling.

'Liebe Lilith,' she prays and lowers herself down upon him.

CHAPTER THIRTY-SEVEN

STAR FALLS asleep under the covers. The room cools quickly after the heat of their passion. The fire dwindles to a few embers and does little to warm her. Her troubled dreams are haunted again by the image of Raven, her broken mouth spitting words of venom.

Satori appears next to the phantom and embraces it, drawing its gaping jaw to his mouth. His hands caress its blood-soaked hair. She watches in fascination and horror as his penis becomes a serpent that weaves itself around Raven's body, squeezing Raven's stomach and ribs until they shift and distort. With a final crush, Raven vanishes, and Satori is alone. Dressed now in his favourite black frilled shirt and tight jeans, he points at her with the blade of his dagger.

'Cut out the evil,' he whispers.

Star hears a heavy shifting noise outside the dream world. She wants to stay with Dream-Satori, question him and learn the truth, but he evaporates as the real world beckons.

Someone or something moves around the living room. Lilith's side of the bed is cold. Maybe she is relighting the fire.

Weak rays of sunlight creep through the window. *How long did I sleep?* Her mind does not hold the answer. Her waking senses struggle to analyse the clues, the light in the window, the cold mattress, and her exhaustion. Sleep clings to her muscles as she half-walks, half-falls to the door. Cold air shrouds her naked body.

As she opens the bedroom door, she faces a grey-haired man. In his shaking arms, he cradles a rifle, pointing it at her startled face.

'Wha' the feck are youse doin' in me hoose?' he yells.

Stumbling back, she shakes her head, trying to deny his presence.

It's a dream. It has to be a dream.

As she moves, he follows. The barrel of his gun reflects her movements; its mouth sways, twisting and weaving through the air in a tight figure of eight, like a snake charmer's pungi flute.

'Is there anyone else wi' youse?' he asks, entering the room carefully, checking for a second trespasser.

She shakes her head again.

'I guess we better check though eh,' he says. 'Youse better come wi' me, lass.'

Leading him around the house, she is painfully aware of her nakedness. They check the kitchen then he motions to the bath-room door. She opens it and hurries inside. Seeing the knife still resting on the edge of the bath, she grabs it and hides it behind her thigh.

He follows her and checks the room. Satisfied they are alone, he retreats to the living room. She stands in the bathroom, shaking. Seeing her discarded clothes, she stoops to pick them up.

'I wan' youse where I can see youse,' he shouts.

She carries her clothes through the doorway.

'So wha's this pretty wee thing doin' in me hoose?' he asks her. 'A gift from the fairies perhaps?' He laughs at his own joke.

'I'm sorry,' she says. 'I thought the cottage was deserted, and I was so tired.'

'Dinnae lie. Youse kicked me door off its hinges. In wha' way did youse think it was deserted exactly? An' youse English, too.'

He spits.

Although the spittle falls short of where she stands, she feels its vitriolic power.

She wonders where Lilith is. *Has he killed her already or is she hiding outside?*

She wishes she hadn't told him she was alone, not daring to ask about her lover now for fear of maddening him further.

'What are you going to do?' she asks him. 'I'm so sorry. I just want to go. Please, let me leave.'

He looks undecided. She feels his gaze on her body and decides to dress. As she moves to do so, though, he stops her.

'Dinnae move.' He steps closer. His breath stinks of whisky and unbrushed teeth.

She sees a dribble of sweat on his brow. He drops the muzzle of the rifle to the floor and moves so close that the wool of his clothing scratches Star's skin. His eyes fix hers in their stare, and she cannot look away.

Her fingers tremble around the knife handle.

His nostrils flare as he inhales. She takes her chance and raises her hand. Distracted, perhaps by the scent of her, he does not see her fist move back. Only when the knife hits below his shoulder does he realise the danger. Staring at her through wide, disbelieving eyes, he stumbles. She moves with him, twisting the blade in his flesh.

Her heart races as she breathes in his fear. Rage swells inside her. With the heel of her hand, she slams the sticky blade deeper, pushing him to the floor, burying the knife deep between his ribs and shoulder blade.

He releases the gun, and she kicks it away. As he pulls the knife out of his shoulder, she grabs the firearm and faces him.

'Don't move.' Her demand echoes his words from moments before. 'I don't want to hurt you. I just want to leave.'

'Bitch,' he snarls. 'Youse just stabbed me. Wha' do youse mean you dinnae wanna hurt me? I'm bleedin'. I'm feckin' bleedin' to death.'

She blanches. There is a lot of blood coming from the wound. Part of her wants to help him stem the flow and call an ambulance, but the dominant part wants to run away and blot the image of him dying from her mind. Dropping the gun, she turns to leave.

Lilith is behind her. An icicle of dread slides from the base of Star's skull and down her spine as Lilith grins at the injured man. His movements, at the edge of her vision, become frantic.

'What did you do?' Lilith asks.

'He... he came home,' Star stammers. 'He had a gun, that

gun. I thought he was planning to kill me… or rape me. Maybe both.'

Lilith strides over to the man. His body is doubled up in pain. The hand, pressed against his wound, is covered in blood. He recoils, and his tear-filled eyes blink rapidly.

'Let's go,' Star says.

Lilith shakes her head. 'Were you going to rape her, you sick fuck?'

His mouth opens and closes. The only sound to escape his lips is a soft gurgle.

Lilith kicks him in the stomach. 'Answer me.'

She bends over his body and loosens his belt.

'What are you doing, Lilith?'

'Busted shoulder won't do it. There's only one way to stop a man thinking about rape.' She lifts his limp cock in one hand and grabs the knife.

Horrified, Star looks from the man's castrated groin to his face. He has passed out at least.

'Lilith,' she says, moving toward the door.

Lilith stands up and looks at Star, defiantly. 'Do you think he would have survived your attack?' she asks.

'It was self-defense,' Star says weakly.

'And what about Raven?'

Star shakes her head and backs away.

'You and I are the same, Star,' Lilith says. 'We're both full of rage.'

Star sprints out of the cottage. She stumbles into the woods and empties her guts. She has eaten so little that the retches are painful. Welcoming the pain, she lets it carry her mind away from the horrors inside the house. When she straightens up again, Lilith stands beside the car, watching her.

'Are you going to leave me?' Lilith does not shout, but her voice carries across the distance and whispers the question into Star's ears.

The pounding of Star's heart and the groaning of her stomach are silenced by the question, and she stares at the woman, this stranger with whom she has shared her body so many times, to whom she has whispered her darkest secrets and desires.

Tears cloud her vision, but she knows the image of her lover well enough to see every detail, the thick black hair, the pierced lip, the emerald eyes, the soft yet impossibly high breasts. She feels the memory of their embrace, the warmth inside her when they make love, the feeling of completion within Lilith's arms.

Slowly, she walks to the car and Lilith. Although she is still half-blind with tears, she imagines her lover's smile of triumph. Lilith hands her a pile of clothes, and Star dresses. Her bag is already on the back seat. Reaching behind her, she grasps her seat belt.

She weaves her fingers together, as if in prayer, then squeezes hard until the nails of each hand dig into the skin of the other.

The drive north is suffered in silence. The scenery gets wilder as they pass raging rivers and thick forests before winding their way upward into the mountains.

At dusk, Lilith stops the car. A landscape of peaks, valleys, and waterways spreads out before them. It is breathtaking. Star climbs out of the car and stares down. The depth of the valley below draws her vision.

'Look up,' Lilith whispers.

She does and sees green swirls of light dancing in the sky, wisps of colour of such supernatural hue that they make Star gasp. The black summits are dwarfed by towers of emerald, which fill the horizon.

'What is it?' Star asks.

'The Northern Lights,' Lilith answers. 'When you get further north, you can see other colours too.'

'It's beautiful.'

'Let's get back in the car and find somewhere to stay. There's going to be a frost tonight.'

'I don't want to break into another house,' Star says.

'Would you rather freeze?'

They follow the winding road to lower ground and find somewhere to park. They huddle together on the back seat.

Star longs to undress her lover, but moments after the engine is switched off, a biting cold permeates the space. She shivers in Lilith's arms.

'You're right,' Star says. 'We won't survive the night.'

They search for another place to stay and find a second house, which looks empty. They have reached the Cairngorms. They search the cottage thoroughly for signs of occupation and find tourist guides and heating instructions— a holiday house.

Lilith turns on the electric heating while Star searches for something to eat. There is nothing.

'I'll catch a rabbit,' Lilith tells her. 'Boil some water on the stove.'

Star sits alone in the house. Every noise outside the walls frightens her, from a howling dog to the cars that occasionally rumble past.

She makes herself a coffee and tries to ignore the sounds prising open her sanity. The noises inside her head frighten her more than those of the world outside. Phantoms push through the veil of her consciousness, and the gurgles of the man she helped kill replay in her mind.

When she lifts her hands to her face, she can still smell his blood on her fingers.

Trying to dismiss everything as a dream from which she'll soon wake, she imagines she never met Lilith, that she and Satori had worked together to dismiss his demon and had fallen in love instead.

Satori's demon— she has not thought about that for such a long time, so involved has she been with her affair. She wonders how he is getting on.

Has he found it yet? Sent it back?

She feels a pang of guilt for not helping him, but that guilt opens a gateway to remorse she has to fight to hold at bay.

What was the demon's name, ah yes— Lilith. Lilith. Lilith!

Fuck, no, it can't be.

It is. Oh shit!

Is the woman I love, who is currently gathering food for my empty stomach, is she a demon? Satori's demon?

Hairs bristle over Star's body.

She remembers what she can of the past weeks. *Lilith is a demon.* The knowledge which lay dormant inside her stretches itself, unfurling in her mind like a waking cat, luxuriating in the long-awaited acknowledgement.

The killings are on my conscience. I killed Raven, and the man wouldn't have survived even without Lilith's added mutilation.

Something twists inside Star's stomach; is it her conscience squirming or the evil from her dreams?

She looks for a knife and sits holding its weight in her hand. She takes off her jacket and lifts her jumper. The skin beneath is pale and soft. There is no sign of the taint.

With the tip of the knife, she pricks her belly. A thread of blood unravels down her stomach. Biting her lip, she tries to press harder but feels afraid. Even now she does not want to die.

She looks at the telephone. It is a pay phone. She wonders whether it will accept a 999 call without coins.

She drops the knife and crosses the room. With every step, the howls get closer. With every movement, she feels something shift inside her, urging her not to make the call.

As she lifts her leaden arm to pick up the receiver, a giant black dog with a rabbit in its jaws hurtles through the room and knocks her to the floor. She hits her head, and all is darkness.

CHAPTER THIRTY-EIGHT

HE REFUSES to believe. At dinnertime, his mum is crying at the table. Beneath her folded arms, she hides a newspaper. Satori puts his arm around her shoulder and asks her what's wrong. She shakes her head, and her sobs grow louder. He tugs at the corner of the newspaper trying to prise it away from her. Lifting her arms, she allows him to take it and turns from her son.

On the front page are two photos. One is of Raven, the other of Star. He tries to read the article. He manages to absorb the first line of the story before dropping the paper as if it burns him.

Goth bitch-fight blood bath. Girl (24) brutally murdered in toilets of local Goth club.

'No,' he cries out in denial. *It isn't true. It cannot be true.* He refuses to believe the words.

His mum stands up and tries to put her arms around him, but he pushes her away and runs out of the house. Leaving his mum to her distress makes him feel cruel and ungrateful. He cannot turn back and tell her he is sorry— be her dutiful son. There isn't time.

He goes to see Donna. She does not answer the door despite his loud rings, knocks and shouts. Filled with fury, he kicks the door, shattering a glass panel. For a moment, the sound of breaking glass makes him feel better before shame and sorrow overwhelm him again.

He runs around the streets. When he reaches Freya's house, Ivan is leaning against the garage door, smoking. His eyes are full of tears.

'You've heard,' Ivan says as he spots Satori at the end of the driveway.

He drops his cigarette, crushing it with his bare foot, and lights another. 'Want one?'

Satori shakes his head. 'How long have you known?'

'Since yesterday. Freya was at the club with Raven, Donna too.'

'How is she?' Satori asks.

'How do you think? I wouldn't go in there if I were you. Somehow, they seem to think it's your fault.'

'Maybe it is,' he says, looking at Ivan's feet.

'Why did she do it, man?' Ivan drags on his cigarette.

Satori shrugs his shoulders.

'Raven was so beautiful. She and I…' Ivan sinks onto his haunches, shaking his head. 'So beautiful. Such a waste.'

'One of a kind,' Satori replies as he tries to hold the nausea at bay.

'It's twisted, man. Why did she do it? They were friends… The reporters, they fuckin' love it. Our garden was heavin'. Did they come an' see you?'

Satori shakes his head and stares at the house, imagining the crowd of excited journalists. *Goth bitch-fight blood bath.*

'Can you get Freya so I can speak to her?' Satori asks.

'I dunno, man,' Ivan replies. 'They're all pretty pissed at you.'

'Please try. It's important.'

Satori watches Ivan lurch into the house. The man moves as if each step requires too great an effort to bear. Satori knows that feeling. It is unbearable.

He wonders what he will say to Freya. He told Ivan *it* was important, but he has no idea what *it* might be. He only hopes that seeing Freya will connect him with Star and Raven.

He hears a scream of anger from within the house and sees Freya's father swaying in the doorway. The man lunges toward him fists raised. Without a backward glance, Satori flees.

His feet take him back toward Raven and Star's apartment, and he passes the street corner where he first laid eyes on Star.

She'd been walking with Donna. Her hair bounced as she

walked and her face, when he first set eyes on it, was so open and so animated that he fell in love with her that very moment. She had been wearing her long velvet coat and a short skirt, and as she walked, the coat opened to reveal black-and-white striped legs and those huge boots she loved to wear.

He pauses for a moment, hoping to sense her presence here. He feels nothing more than the twist of pain in his stomach he has carried since seeing the newspaper report.

The air is hushed in the street as though all televisions have been silenced, all dogs muzzled, and all children put to bed. Listening hard, he believes he can hear the wails of a mother who has lost her child.

He turns his back on the street and walks home. When he opens the front door, his mother rushes to him. He shakes his head and retreats upstairs, gathers a few things in a canvas satchel— a change of clothes, his dagger, and the Necronomicon, then opens an atlas and sets his crystal ball beside it.

'Show me where they are,' he says.

The crystal's mist clears, and he sees his answer. He wraps the ball in a piece of purple velvet and places it and the atlas in his bag. He searches his clothes and room for money and fills his pockets. It will have to be enough. Bag slung over his shoulder, he heads after them.

He starts his journey hitchhiking. He wants to save the little money he has brought for when he really needs it. Luck is with him, and each time a driver drops him off, another picks him up. His head fills with their stories. He wishes to find peace but resigns himself to their temporary chatter, a small price to pay for such generous travelling companions.

He reaches Perth by dawn on Tuesday morning. The air is cold and misty. He checks the map and sees they are still some distance from him. Waiting at the bus station for a coach to Aviemore, he drinks bitter coffee and eats a stale bun. Trying to ignore the eyes of strangers, he pushes crumbs around the table's surface with his finger and tries to clear his mind. Everything seems too noisy or too bright to ignore. He hopes the bus journey will settle him.

Since he first read the headline, he has not stopped to think. Running from one place to another. Faces blurring into featureless balls of confusion.

This is his fault. Everything: the murder, Star's disappearance— it is on him.

No one would understand. No one can help.

A hole opens inside Satori's mind. Its warm darkness beckons him. His toes hang over the edge, and his body teeters and sways, wanting desperately to fall. He stares at oblivion and feels it swell and push toward him. It wants to claim its prodigal son. Whispering promises of emptiness, peace, and solace, it tugs at him with velvety claws, trying to pull him over the edge into depression. Angrily, he denies it and turns away. He has no time to wallow in self-pity.

The bus is quiet. Only two other passengers board at the station. He settles near the back and lets the vibration of the wheel beneath his seat lull him into unconsciousness.

As his body travels north on the threadbare seat, his mind soars ahead. Picturing Star's face, Satori tries to touch her mind. He feels her confusion. Her thoughts are shrouded by a dense grey weight: Lilith. Satori's mind yells at Star, trying to penetrate the psychic curtain. She does not respond, and he has no way of knowing whether she can hear or sense him. Withdrawing his mind, he allows a dream to claim him.

Raven waits for him there, just as she had in life. She rises and falls above him. Her arms lifted above her head, his hands around her throat. Her skin grows cold beneath his fingers. Her face cracks and changes. Horror fills him as she bends forward. Her cheek and mouth are smashed and gaping. Raven kisses him, and he is swallowed by her cavernous mouth. Her throat squeezes him, pushing him down. He gasps for air but there is none except a stale, bloody stench that turns his stomach. He tries to fight back, but she holds him there, inside her.

He wakes, covered in sweat. More people have joined the bus since he fell asleep; some are staring at him.

Did I scream in my sleep?

He glares at them, and they turn away.

When he eventually reaches the town of Aviemore, the place is busy with walkers. The sky is darkening and people swarm toward the numerous cafés and restaurants. Others return to their hotels and hostels.

He mounts the stairs to the Mountain Café. A wall of glass frames the breathtaking Cairngorm Mountains. Their colours are like the acrylics in Star's palette; perylene green rises to caput mortuum-violet and a titanium-white tip pierces the lamp-black sky. He remembers the way she would lovingly name each shade, like her own magical chant.

I never spent enough time watching her, listening to her wisdom. It was always about me— never her.

He orders a coffee and sits at one of the heavy wooden tables beside the window. Star is somewhere in these mountains; he is certain of it. He removes his atlas from his bag and dowses the page. Closing his eyes, his finger hovers just centimetres from the paper. He feels the tip of his finger brush the page and opens his eyes. There is a forested valley about ten miles south of where he sits now. They are there.

Showing the map to the waitress, he asks what the valley is called.

She shakes her head. 'Sorry, sorry, I not know name. Umm, I think, wait… yes, follow.'

She leads him to a huge map of the Cairngorms, which dominates an entire wall of the café.

'Here,' she says, nodding at the four by three metre map. 'Names here, see? The mountains.'

'Thank you, thank you. That's perfect.'

Satori stands in front of the map. He clears his mind and looks, not with his two grey eyes, but with his third eye— his spiritual vision.

Oblivious of the other patrons, he raises both arms and feels the map come to life. Stretching his palms toward the wall, he senses the icy tips of the mountains and hears splashing rivers descend them.

A spot glows in a valley. Satori steps closer.

The mountains part for him, and he places his finger on the spot. It is close to a small hamlet. He squints at the name, switching back to his two eyes. Straanruie. Straanruie— he will head there to find them. He notes the name of the hamlet on the cover of his atlas and finishes his coffee. The warm and nutty taste soothes and refreshes him. It is four o'clock.

Outside, the streetlights are already lit, and the mountains loom menacingly, shoulder to shoulder. Their dark shadows pierce the starlight: a god's bodyguards.

Looking left and right along the busy street, he sees a tourist information sign. The woman behind the desk is full of smiles as she greets him. Her Scottish accent is clipped and precise. He asks for the best way to reach Straanruie.

'Taxi,' she tells him. 'Or a hire car. The buses don't go there.'

Nodding, he checks his wallet. He has just enough money for a taxi, but he will need some way of getting Star and himself back here.

Who knows what weakened state Star might be in by now?

'I'll hitchhike,' he tells her.

'Leave it until morning,' she warns him. 'No one heads into the mountains after dark.'

'I have nowhere to stay,' he argues. 'And I need to get there now.'

She shakes her head. 'I can give you a place to sleep. You won't reach Straanruie tonight.'

'I'll try,' he says.

'I'm here 'til five. Come back if you still need somewhere to stay.'

He thanks her and heads for the mouth of the road leading up into the mountains. Traffic converges on the town. Nothing heads toward the dark peaks. Standing at the roadside, he shivers as the mist descends around him.

Eventually, he gives in and returns to the tourist office only to discover the time is six o'clock, and the office is already closed.

With a sense of fatalism, he counts his money. He has just over sixty pounds in his pockets. Wandering along the high street, he grabs some sandwiches and a drink from a supermarket. The shop is busy as walkers buy food and beer to see them through the *après marche*. Taking his carrier bag of provisions with him to the youth hostel, he asks a middle-aged man behind the desk for a bed. The man frowns, the place is full, but he will not let him spend a night outdoors.

'Aviemore in November is nae place for sleepin' under the stars,' he assures Satori. 'Stay here 'til me shift ends at ten. The name's Douglas.'

'Thank you. Where are you heading when you finish?' Satori asks.

'Youse askin' for a bed or a lift?' Douglas' eyes twinkle with humour.

'Either, but a lift to Straanruie would be preferable.'

'Ack that's up in the mountains, son. You'll nae be wantin' to head there after dark.'

'Why?' Satori asks.

'It's affa treacherous. The roads twist and turn. When the mist settles, you can lose yer way. Drive off a cliff before you know what's happening.'

'I need to get there,' Satori insists.

'Patience, lad,' I'll drive youse mi'sell in the morn.' Douglas' wide smile tells Satori there will be no negotiation.

'Thank you. Thank you so much.'

'Now settle down wi' yer cuppa and let me finish this paper-work.'

Satori reads through the ritual again. He knows every word, every nuance, but there is no room for error. It is all theory, of course. It might not work at all, but he needs to try. He needs to save Star.

Douglas' house is a single-storey cottage in Carrbridge. When they arrive at ten thirty, Satori is greeted by a wife and hound. The former makes a fuss of him and wants to hear the romantic tale of his search for Star. He edits heavily, removing any mention of demons, magic, or murder, but it still excites in her a shock he did not expect.

'Yer girlfriend left you for a woman,' she repeats again as if trying hard to make sense of an impossible riddle. 'Youse English live the strangest lives.'

The dog licks his fingers as he drifts off to sleep in a huge armchair.

CHAPTER THIRTY-NINE

STAR WAKES with a thumping head. She struggles to open her eyes, and when she does, the image is blurred.

'Is that you, Lilith?' she asks the dark shape at the end of the bed.

'Yes, my darling.' The shadow grows, and Lilith kisses Star's forehead. 'How are you feeling?'

'Strange, I can't quite focus. What happened?'

'You fell. You were on the floor when I got back.'

'A dog,' she says. 'I remember a dog.'

'There's no dog, my darling. Maybe you were dreaming.'

Star turns over, holding her head in her hands. The memory does not come to her, and it hurts when she tries to concentrate.

'Would you like some food?' Lilith asks.

'I just want to sleep,' Star answers.

Sleep comes without dreams. In odd moments between consciousness and unconsciousness, she hears movements around the room but ignores them. A hand, shaking her shoulder, wakes her.

'You should eat,' Lilith says. 'Does your head still hurt?'

Star feels a cold, wet, towel touch her forehead. It eases the pain, but she struggles to stay awake. Mumbling a few words, she falls back to sleep. This time she dreams.

She sees Steve. His naked body is covered in strange markings. He holds a knife above his head and thrusts the blade down. The air tears, and Lilith steps through the rift.

Star sits bolt upright. She focuses on Lilith's face. 'I saw you.'

'I'm here,' Lilith answers.

'You're not real,' she says, hugging her knees tight against her chest.

'Of course, I'm real,' Lilith answers patiently. 'You just hit your head, that's all.'

'No.' Star shakes her head, eyes wide with fear.

'Shush my love,' Lilith says, stroking her knee. 'Here, I made some broth. Please, eat.'

'But...' Star drifts into silence as she forgets her train of thought.

The food smells delicious, and her stomach is empty. She takes the bowl of soup from Lilith's hand and shovels spoonfuls into her mouth. It drips onto her chest, soaking her clothing. Lilith watches her from the edge of the bed.

'Why did you come with me?' Star asks when the soup is finished.

'Is it truth or dare again?' Lilith jokes.

'Are you a demon?'

Lilith takes the empty bowl from Star's hand and leaves the room. Star follows Lilith into the kitchen, holding walls and furniture for support. Her legs feel weak, and the room swims in and out of focus, but she needs to know.

Lilith leans over the sink and seems absorbed by the domestic duties.

'How can you ask me such a question?' Lilith asks without turning. 'All I've ever done is love you. Haven't I given you everything you wanted?'

'I've changed, Lilith. I think you changed me.'

'What's changing you isn't inside *me*,' Lilith answers, still facing the sink.

'You mean it's inside me?' Star asks.

Raven had said that to her in her dreams. *The evil is inside you, cut it out.*

'Haven't you felt its movements?'

'Face me, for fuck's sake, Lilith. I want to see your eyes when you tell me this.'

Lilith turns around. Her green eyes shine with a religious zeal. 'You're carrying our baby.'

Lilith's wide grin frightens Star, and she backs away.

'That's impossible,' Star says, shaking her head. 'You're a woman.'

'No, I'm not,' Lilith answers. 'You've said it already. I'm a demon, a god, and you're carrying our child.'

Star laughs. She clutches her stomach and bends double. Her laugh shakes every molecule in her being, loosening her hold on gravity and reality; she collapses onto the cold stone floor, yet the sounds still erupt from her. She struggles to breathe between screams of laughter. Tears flow from her eyes. She is blind and deaf, and all she knows is she is finally insane.

Arms lift her off the floor and carry her to the bed. The cold towel presses against her face again. Starting to calm a little, she opens her eyes and stares at the woman, demon, god, tending to her. *God help me, I still love that face.*

Lilith seems to sense her thoughts. She slips an arm beneath Star and lies next to her. Her other hand wipes away Star's tears as they form.

Kissing Star's nose and eyes, she tells her how much she loves her. How the world is brighter each day they are together. How they can make it work between them whatever the barriers might be.

'I do love you,' Lilith says. 'I want to be with you, whatever mistakes we've made. You complete me.'

'I don't know,' Star says. Her lips tremble.

'Don't think about it,' Lilith tells her. 'Just feel.'

The towel goes from her face, and Lilith strokes Star's arm. Hairs rise to meet her fingers, begging to be touched. Star lets the thoughts melt from her mind and focuses on the feelings aroused in her body.

Her lips are brushed by Lilith's. When they kiss, Star's mind soars. She watches the scene from above, two bodies entwined, sharing their passion and their warmth. From here, she cannot feel her lover's hands against her skin or tongue inside her mouth.

She tries to dive back into her body, but she feels too light. Rising higher and higher, she pushes through the ceiling of the room, past shadowy shapes of furniture and boxes stored in the attic, and into the starlit night. Dwarfed by the limitless sky, she feels tiny and alone. Millions of stars pump out their light to the world below her. They shine so brightly and yet the woodland beneath and the mountains around her remain dark. No star shines bright enough to light her way in the world. She must find her own light.

This thought acknowledged, she is sucked back inside her body, moaning with the pleasure of Lilith's caresses. If she is alone in this world, let her enjoy the sensations of this bag of flesh, which separates her from others.

Her body rises and crashes with each heartbeat. She wonders whether Lilith's heart beats too, and she reaches toward the other's chest. Lilith takes Star's fingers in her mouth and kisses them.

'Take me again like you did that night,' Star says.

Lilith turns Star over onto all fours.

'No peeking,' Lilith whispers as Star strains her neck to see what's happening.

Lowering her head, she sees Lilith's eyes concentrate on her right hand. Star looks at it too and watches its shape change. Lilith clenches her fist, and it becomes a serpent's head, her arm the serpent's body. She strokes Star's buttocks, which are tense in anticipation. Star looks away, she has seen enough.

As the serpent enters her, she feels her world fall apart. Her head fills with stars. She tries to stay calm, but their white lights push behind her eyelids.

Oh my god, oh my god, oh my god. How can a feeling be so wonderful and so terrible all at once?

The serpent expands inside her, filling every groove, opening every gateway. It meets with the child in her womb. They communicate— parent and infant. The void within her is full of life and movement. The snake pulls back then forward and back again; its sensual rhythm works with the tribal beat of her heart to empty Star of anxiety.

This is real. This is love. It's what I need.

White light streams through her eyelids. In the light, she sees a man.

He is coming to save me, but do I want to be saved?

The pleasure lasts for hours. Star's body is consumed by exquisite agony. By the time she falls asleep with the serpent still between her legs, she feels sated and exhausted.

Her dreams, when they come, are gentle. Satori crouches before her, his eyes full of love. Smiling, she drifts into his arms.

CHAPTER FORTY

SATORI STANDS at the window, watching the sun paint the mountains. When he hears Douglas open the door, he turns and sees the bleary-eyed Scot head for the kitchen.

'Coffee?' Douglas asks him, pouring water into the kettle.

'Thanks,' Satori replies.

He hopes the man does not take too long to get ready but is worried he will appear ungrateful if he tries to hurry him. Sleep has left its mark on Douglas. His face is full of lines and creases Satori had not noticed the night before. His wild hair looks more peppered with grey than when it was brushed into submission. Together with his walking stick and awkward footsteps, Douglas seems fragile this morning. Satori wonders whether he should go alone.

He has already checked the map. Star and Lilith are still in the valley. He wonders what the women are doing, sleeping perhaps, although he doubts whether Lilith sleeps. At least Star is still alive, of that much he is certain.

'I can get a taxi if you're feeling tired,' Satori says. 'I am grateful for your kindness and hospitality, but it might be better if I finish my journey alone.'

'Ack, dinnae sound so dramatic lad. Anyone would think you was Romeo chasin' after yer Juliet. I guess that's what bein' young an' in love is all about, eh?'

Satori nods. 'I guess so.'

Douglas hands Satori a black coffee. 'Want milk or cream, or a touch of courage in that?' he asks, laughing to himself. 'When dae youse want to head over there?'

'It's perfect… thanks. I… I'd like to go as soon as we can. I don't want them moving on before I get there.'

'Dae they ken yer comin' for 'em?' Douglas leans forward, studying Satori's face in detail while sipping his mug of coffee.

'No, at least, I don't think they do.'

'Yer nae gonna dae nowt too stupid are youse?' Douglas looks afraid.

'Of course not,' he assures him. 'I love her.'

'That's why I'm worried,' Douglas says. 'Look, we all dae crazy things when we're in love. Comes with the territory.'

Satori nods slowly. He thinks back to the crazy thing which started it all: his attempt to invoke a demon to gain more power, to win back the girl who was already running from his power and magic.

She called it madness.

Maybe I was crazy, but I can make it right again. I can still save Star.

Of course, it's very likely she'll never want to see me again. It's all my fault, and I have to accept that it's… over between us.

I can accept that. I have to save her.

'Sure,' says Douglas, apparently satisfied. 'Let's go and deliver youse to yer Juliet. You want me to wait while youse speak to her?'

'No, I'll make it back, thanks,' Satori answers.

'But… okay, have it yer way. I've got better things to dae than hang about the mountains.'

Douglas retreats into the bedroom to get dressed. When he emerges, he is transformed as thoroughly as any glamour. They head out of the house and drive into the wild Cairngorms.

'We're here,' Satori says.

'I dinnae see anyone. There's nae e'en a barn here,' Douglas says. He doesn't stop the car but continues to drive around the next corner.

'Please, stop the car,' Satori asks. 'I know where the house is. I need to walk the rest of the way.'

'Okay,' Douglas says, coming to a halt against the grass verge. 'Youse be careful, though. It's easy to get lost, and if the mist comes doon, you'll freeze to death.'

'It's not far,' Satori assures him. 'Thank you.'

Douglas shrugs and shakes his head as Satori steps out of the car. Resting his bag on one shoulder, Satori waves the car away. He crosses the road and descends the steep bank to the rear of the cottage.

He would like to check whether Star and Lilith are still there, but he dares not look through a window.

He gathers stones and makes a circle in which to sit. Whispering words of blessing, he makes the space within the circle sacred, then takes off his clothes.

The mountain air is so cold he can hardly feel his hands as he reaches into his satchel for the book and dagger. The book is left open beside him. Even though he knows the ritual, it makes him feel safer having the words visible.

Calling on Isis to protect him while he leaves this realm, he promises to pay tribute to her should he return safely to his body. He clears his mind and sees the door.

His spirit walks through into Chaos.

The mad Arab described Chaos as a living, breathing void. Being here, within this shifting, transforming darkness, throws Satori's mind off-balance. He watches his fingers stretch and twist, his legs, too. He delights in the swelling and shrivelling of his penis like rolling waves on the shore. The darkness blossoms and ejaculates spores of deeper darkness around him. Glimpses of light weave around the horizon like shooting stars with purpose. He watches them for minutes or hours.

There is no time here, and his freezing body is forgotten in his amazement.

He sees the dagger in his right hand. The jewels along the shaft glow with a brightness to rival the dancing lights.

He twists his wrist and the metal bends and flexes, whipping the air. The dagger is important— he needs the dagger— he tries to remember why. A purpose niggles at the back of his mind. He tries to grasp it, but it is elusive, and the movements around him are hypnotic.

Star, her name is on his lips, and he remembers why he is here.

'Lilith, I evoke thee,' he whispers.

The words come back to him; they sing in his pulsing ears, stroke his body, and run fingers through his hair.

The tribute.

He summons her as before with his hand on his cock and her name on his lips. When he comes, the semen buzzes before him, glowing like fireflies. The droplets form a spiral, spinning faster and faster, and she appears.

He registers her look of shock and shields his ears from her angry scream. As he slices his exit door, she grows. Her body towers over him. Her face is an angry scar in the changing darkness, and her green eyes burn viciously.

When she laughs, he wants to rip out his ears. His heart is squeezed by his tightening rib cage. Paralysed by fear, he stares at her, cowering between her legs

Her sex is Cthulhu, a giant anemone; its tendrils reach for him, threatening to swallow him whole. Evil, knife-edged tongues lash at him from the coils. Serpents.

He ducks and parries in the darkness, trying to cover his head with his hands.

Her terrible laugh besieges him.

Pointing up with his blade, he slashes blindly at the snakes, which pull his hair and rip his skin. He looks up for a moment, and one darts at his face. Its tongue feels like fire. He screams as his cheek tears and burns. The tendril rips upward, launching him with the force of its blow. Green flashes across his right eye as he is thrown sideways through the door he created. Falling through the breach, he re-enters his naked body.

He lies, shivering, in his ring of stones. The intense burning of his wound does nothing to warm the rest of him. Sealing the door with his words, he tries to ignore the echo of her fury in his mind.

His fingers are blue and his eyelids frozen shut. He can sense his clothes nearby but is too numb to grasp them. He tries to stand but tumbles onto his face. Brittle grass breaks beneath his chest. Panic grips him as tightly as the icy air. He tries to open his eyes.

His thoughts fade and with it the panic. *Death. It is what I deserve. Let the coldness take me, but what of Star? Lilith is gone, but where is my love?* He hasn't saved her yet.

If he concentrates, he will know what to do.

Needles of frost prickle his hands and feet, but he pushes his fear away. He concentrates on two things. First, he imagines a warm sphere inside his stomach. The heat spreads, and with each second, his body feels warmer. Second, he calls to the salamanders.

Tiny red lizards push their way through the stone wall of the house, a dozen of them in total. Their pointed noses appear first, then toes and forelegs, followed by pale bellies, back legs and, finally, long tails. Free of the house, they drop onto his back. Their hot feet dance across his skin. One runs up his body and nuzzles into the back of his neck before curling itself in his hair. Others scamper to his toes and fingers. They lick his frozen digits with their fiery tongues and give life and movement back to him. They share their heat with him.

His eyes freed from the frost; he opens them. Sitting up, he thanks the salamanders and, as they run back into the warm house, he gets dressed.

As he pulls on his jacket, he realises he cannot see what his right hand is doing. Fear and panic rise through his chest. He touches the wound on his right cheek and winces with pain. *Why can't I see my fingers?*

He waves his hands in front of him. On his left, he can see his hand as he moves it to the side, on his right he cannot. Everything before him seems two-dimensional, like looking at a photograph. His depth perception has gone.

When he moves, his steps feel unreal, as though he is watching them on a cinema screen. Walking unsteadily to the front of the house, he feels emptiness in his hands. After weeks of wondering and waiting, plotting and planning, he is about to see Star. Will she thank him for sending her tormentor away or hate him for dispatching her lover? He brings her no gift other than Lilith's absence.

The coldness clings to him, and he wants to be held in her arms. Her welcoming embrace, though, is too much to expect. He does not even know what he will say.

Will you look the same? Will I?

He touches his face again and imagines the scarred skin. *A small price to pay*, he tries to tell himself, but it doesn't prevent tears from falling. Pushing back the fear and doubts, he opens the door.

The house feels warm. Salamanders curl up against radiators and hot water pipes. Satori is comforted by their presence.

Star is not in the living room. He turns toward the kitchen. A pot and a bowl sit upside down on the draining board. They are the only signs of recent occupation.

A door stands ajar at the end of the small living room. He walks to it. With every step he fights the urge to run away and not face her. He owes her more than that. He owes her so much more.

CHAPTER FORTY-ONE

STAR FEELS a hand stroke her hair. She turns over, eyes still closed.

'Lilith,' she whispers. 'You're insatiable. Let me sleep.'

The hand is withdrawn, and the bed dips near her feet. She hears breathing and knows it is not Lilith in the room. She opens her eyes. *Please, not another house owner wandering in while I sleep.*

The figure sits turned away from her. She opens her eyes and sees shoulder-length black hair and a black wool coat. She knows Satori's slouch too well to mistake him for another.

'Steve?' she asks keeping her voice as low as possible.

He faces her. As she sits up, the covers fall from her body; she grabs them to cover her nakedness.

'Star.' He smiles, but there are tears in his eyes.

'What are you doing here? How did you find me? What's happened to your face, your eye?'

'Magic.' He lifts shaking fingers to the vicious scar along his cheek then lets his hand fall. 'It's nothing.'

His face screams agony. Star wants to hold him, stroke his hair, and tell him everything will be okay. More than that, she wants to punch him, tell him how much she hates him, and expel him and his pain from the cottage and her life.

'Lilith will be back soon. You ought to leave. I don't know what she'll do if she finds you here,' Star says.

'She's gone,' Satori answers. He pauses, and they sit watching each other in silence for a few moments. 'Did she hurt you?'

'She loves me or, at least, I think she does. She mixes lies with truth so easily I forget which is which.'

He moves closer, his arms are open to hold her.

She shakes her head. 'What are you doing?'

'I'm trying to rescue you.' A tentative smile brightens his face. 'Usually, the fairy tale princesses don't give the hero as hard a time.'

'Hero,' she spits. 'I've killed two people and spent the last two weeks fucking a demon *you* brought here. My life is a train wreck. I don't see any heroes in this fairy tale, do you?'

His smile dissolves, and he hangs his head. 'No. We should go. Whose house is this?'

'I've no idea, we broke in.'

'We should leave,' he says, grasping her fingers.

She pulls her hand away.

'And go where, Steve? I'm wanted by the police.'

'I'll sort it,' he promises.

'With magic.' Her words drip venom. 'I'd rather you just left me here.'

'Well, I'm not going to leave you. So, you might as well get up and get dressed.'

He throws her clothes at her and marches out of the door. She hears him pacing across the living room and is shocked by his fury.

What did he expect? I'm with Lilith now, for better or worse, we belong together.

'Lilith's gone,' Satori shouts through the door. 'I sent her back to Hell.'

So, you can read minds now, can you? If he hears that thought, he does not answer.

She rushes after him. The desire to crush him, to silence his lies forever, gives strength to her limbs. When she reaches the door and hears him sobbing, the adrenaline falls from her fingers like water. Lilith is gone. She is alone. Killing Satori will not change that.

She picks her clothes off the bed and gets dressed.

'I wanted to kill you.' Her voice sounds mechanical, monotone, unreal, as she walks into the living room.

'But you didn't,' he answers.

'I don't know what I will do. I can't be trusted,' she says.

'I trust you.'

She shakes her head. 'There's evil inside me.'

'No, you were just brushed by evil. It's gone now. We're safe.' His forehead is heavy with lines. The worry of the past few weeks and lack of sleep have taken their toll on him.

She doubts they are safe. Lilith could return any moment. Whether they run and keep running, or stay here and wait, she will find them.

'It hasn't gone. Not completely. There's a piece of her left inside me.'

'Your memories will fade in time,' he says.

She laughs. Her laugh threatens to break into hysteria again.

'I'm not talking about memories,' she screams. 'I'm pregnant. Lilith's child is growing, squirming, and getting stronger every day. I can feel it inside me.'

Satori's face is a mirror of the horror and revulsion she felt when she first found out. She enjoys watching his expression crumple.

He runs to the bathroom door, sounds of his retching echo round the cottage. When he returns, his face has the pallor of bed sheets. He is not as strong as he pretends. He falls on his knees in front of her and rests a tentative hand on her belly.

'I am so sorry,' he says. 'I didn't know.'

Her own hands hover at her sides for a moment before she strokes his hair. The warmth of him wakens her nerves and mind out of their reverie.

'We should go,' she says. 'While there's daylight.'

'Can you walk?' he asks. 'It's mostly downhill from here, but it's about ten miles.'

'We've got a car,' she reminds him.

'Can you drive?' he asks.

She shakes her head. 'I'll pack my things.'

'And I'll carry them for you,' he assures her.

She does not feel the cold when they leave the cottage. Satori gives her the gift of warmth. He tells her it is a salamander and describes how it looks. Her brain cramps as she tries to see it, but she cannot. Still, she is thankful for its heat.

Standing outside the cottage, Star feels crushed by the density of the forest. 'I don't think I can do this.'

He touches her elbow and guides her away from the house and car. They pass the circle, and she bends to picks up a smooth stone then throws it into the wood. A bird breaks through the canopy of trees into the pale sky above them. Its lonely cry echoes inside her soul.

She places a hand on her stomach. *I'm not alone. I'll never be alone again.*

Satori's hand is at her elbow again. 'We've got to go.'

She steps away from the circle and walks with him.

Their progress is slow, and the mist descends around them long before they reach Aviemore. They sit by the roadside, Star waiting for a passing car, Satori using the time to let his mind wander. He is the first to bring good news.

'There's a cave just over there,' he points up a steep bank of earth.

They clamber up, grabbing at weeds and grasses for support. Star goes first; she keeps losing her footing, but he catches her. Eventually, they make it to the top. In front of them is a cave large enough for them to spend the night inside.

'I'll gather some wood,' he says. 'You rest a while.'

She sits in the cave, gentle sunlight kissing her toes, while her face is hidden in the shadows. Satori's bag lies beside her. She opens it and digs through the contents: a book, a crystal ball, a dagger, and some clean underwear.

She laughs. *Where's the food?*

She pulls her jacket around her. She is not cold, the salamander still nestles around her neck, but the pressure feels like a hug, and she misses being held.

She tries to visualise the life growing inside her. She sees its pin-head face turn to hers, and they share a moment of mourning for their mutual loss. Child, mother, and lover held in the circle of her mind. Only the crone is missing.

She picks up Satori's book. It is a modern-looking paperback edition so unlike the ancient-looking texts they read in his room. The cover is mottled purple and a jade-coloured crocodile or maybe an alligator— she can never remember the difference— stares at her from above the silver script.

She opens it. The words are mostly English.

Is this what you used to steal my lover from me?

Her tears fall on the page, and the words lift and dance in the air. Her fingers tingle. The black print from her index finger lifts too. The ornate letters join the text before her in a primitive dance. She shuts the book and looks at her finger again. For the first time in two weeks, it is clean.

Lilith is gone.

Satori scrambles into the cave. The mist is dense, and she marvels that he found his way back.

'I've got the wood,' he says. He arranges the firewood at the mouth of the cave then pats his pockets. 'Do you have a light?'

'No, can you rub sticks together?'

'Wait,' he says. 'I'll just need this for a moment.'

He reaches behind her and takes the warmth from her neck.

She stares at his hands but can see only air.

He holds his open palms near the wood and blows through them. A spark hits the twigs then fizzes and dies. He blows again, this time the fire catches.

'Thank you.' He places the salamander back on Star's neck.

She watches him intently. He has changed so much. Not only physically, although his ugly scar and blood-filled eye draw her attention, but emotionally.

He seems weak, resigned, and desperately sad. *Good! It serves you right.*

No, wait, I don't mean that. I'm sorry. I'm so sorry, Steve.

'I found some mushrooms and herbs, too. Are you hungry?' He pulls fists full of brown fungi and roots from his pocket.

'Are you sure they aren't poisonous?' she asks, eyeing them with suspicion.

'They're perfectly safe,' he says.

His left eye sparkles. She has missed seeing his childlike wonder.

'How do you know, city boy?' she teases.

'I asked them,' he says.

She laughs at him, but in a gentle, friendly way. He laughs back self-consciously; brittle, glass-like sounds erupt from his chest, as if he is relieved that the tension between them might be lifting and at the same time frightened that it will descend the moment the laughter stops.

'You seem different. This crazy magic, the salamander, the talking mushrooms, it's still insane but... I guess everything's relative,' she says more to herself than to him.

'I was an idiot, arrogant. I thought I was something special. I wanted your awe, and I thought if you saw what I could do, you would want me more. I'm sorry, Sarah.'

Her real name uttered for the first time in over a week, from the lips of Satori of all people, makes her smile.

The food is bland, but it takes the edge off her hunger.

He wants her to tell him about what has happened to her over the past weeks, but she refuses. The memories are too fresh, too painful to speak aloud. They live in her dreams. She has no desire to bring them into the cave. Her silence is an invisible wall between them.

The fire makes her sleepy. She rubs her head and feels the tender bump beneath her fingers. She sinks onto the cave floor, resting her head on her bag. Satori takes off his jacket and lays it over her.

Her dream takes her home. Donna holds three bowls of soup. The liquid is deep red, almost black.

'Thank you,' Star says. Her voice sounds strange, like two people speaking at the same time.

Donna picks up one of the bowls and sips; dark rivulets run down her chin.

Star sees movement to her right and knows who it will be before she turns. Raven sits on the velvet couch beside her. The woman's arms are pulled back as if bound. The shape of her body makes her large breasts jut forward and upward, wrapped in a black satin kimono which inches open each time she moves. Raven's thick hair covers her face entirely.

Star shudders. What does her face look like behind that black curtain? Reaching across, she pushes the hair back. A black scarf is coiled around Raven's mouth.

'I thought you'd like her better this way.' The voice might be Donna's, or Lilith's, or even her own.

Raven's eyes are full of fear. They dart toward Star then to the far corner of the room then back again. Star feels dizzy watching those eyes.

Star picks up a paintbrush and dips it into the hot soup. The thick liquid clings to the horsehairs. She paints Raven's throat and chest in bold strokes.

The memory of the paintbrush lingers in her hand when Star wakes. She pushes her body off the floor and shivers, shaking her head clear of the image of Raven— red, raw, and powerless.

She scratches her cheek. The pain makes her gasp; it stings, but it is not enough, so she moves her hand to her hair and tugs her curls. She pulls harder and harder while Satori stares at her.

'It's too much, too much,' she moans.

He shuffles toward her and puts his arm around her shoulders.

'Tell me,' he says. 'Tell me all that's happened to you.'

She stares at him. Her mouth twists into a snarl. 'I hate you.'

He nods but doesn't let go.

'You fucked Raven,' she yells. 'She told me, and I killed her.'

'It's okay,' he says calmly. 'We'll figure it out.'

'I don't want to think about it. Make it go away,' she says.

'You have to face what happened. It wasn't your fault. It was mine.'

He strokes her hair as she rocks herself back and forth like a pendulum, gaining momentum with each swing.

'You frighten me more than *she* ever did,' Star says.

'That's because I'm giving you space to feel and think, to heal,' he answers.

'I don't want to feel. I want to forget. Lilith made me forget.'

'Do you want me to be like Lilith?' he asks her. 'To fuck you and send those nasty memories away?'

'Fuck you!' she screams.

She tries to pull away, but the cave is small, and there is no room in which to move.

'I'm just trying to help,' he says.

'You're not. You're punishing me. You should know what I need. Not confuse me by asking questions.'

'It's your body and your emotions, Sarah,' he says. 'I wouldn't wish to presume. Not again.'

She slaps his face then punches him. He holds his nose. Blood falls through his fingers and splashes on the floor between them. She stares at him, punching him again and again, hitting his chest, shoulders, and face with a flurry of blows. When she is finished, she holds her head in her hands and resumes her rocking. Moments later, his arm is back around her shoulders.

'Fuck me,' she tells him. 'Make the pain go away.'

'It'll come back,' he says.

His body seems to melt as she stares at him through a storm of tears.

'I don't care,' she says. 'I don't want to feel it now.'

CHAPTER FORTY-TWO

HE HAS no idea whether making love to Star in this cold cave will help and he hesitates to touch her, but her face is full of longing. Whether longing for him or oblivion he does not know and as he studies her face, he feels his body respond.

What harm can it do?

He touches her cheek. Her tears make his fingers slip and slide against her skin. He kisses her lips, which feel warm and rough. She opens her mouth, but he doesn't push his tongue inside. He hovers around the edges. Kissing her softly, swallowing her exhaled breath.

She grabs for his jeans.

'Slow down, love,' he says.

She bites his lip. Shock and pain jolt him away, and he stares at her glazed eyes as she smiles. Her hair is too knotted to run his fingers through the strands. Instead, he strokes her crown as if trying to calm an aggressive kitten.

She pushes him against the rocks and kisses him, her tongue deep inside his mouth, not giving him space to move, determined to pin him there.

Unwilling to push back too hard and risk hurting her, he surrenders to her kiss.

She reaches for his jeans again, ignoring his protests. When she breaks for air, he holds her; pinning her arms to her sides so she can't push him away.

When he loosens his grip, she stays still. He puts a few more branches on the fire, takes his coat, and lays it beneath her. She does not move or speak and, when he kisses her, she is unresponsive. Only her shallow pants encourage him.

His lips return to hers, and she opens her mouth. He explores it with his tongue and the back of her neck with his fingers, tracing every curve with sensual slowness.

She clings to his neck as her tongue fills his mouth then sucks on his tongue as if trying to rip it from him. When one of her hands strays downward, stroking his chest and stomach as it descends, he luxuriates in the feeling.

She makes short work of his button and zip and slips her hand inside the denim. He shivers at the light touch of her fingertips as she traces the shape of him through his underwear. As she rubs harder, he swells beneath her touch. It excites him, this absolute power she has over his body. He is in the thrall of her sexuality. Whatever she wants him to do, he will do gladly. Just to be here with her again, nothing else matters.

Their lovemaking is furious, and the bliss ends too suddenly. Silence shrouds them as they dress. The mist has lifted. After Satori extinguishes the fire, they move on from the cave with no sense of direction, except away from where they were.

He carries his bag and her luggage, and she leans on him when the ground becomes difficult to negotiate. Their movements are slow, almost purposeless. Their feet feel heavy, and the ground drags them down, not wanting them to leave the mountains.

'Where are we going?' she asks.

He shakes his head. 'I never thought this far ahead. We could go to Paul's and hide there.'

'I hate Paul,' she says.

'He's dead. Lilith killed him, but his house could be a sanctuary.'

'I can't go back. People will recognise me.'

'I can make you look different. No one will recognise you.'

She shrugs. 'Wherever we go, I'm trapped, aren't I? If you want to go back, we'll go.'

'Or I could get a job here,' he offers. 'Would you prefer that?'

She sinks to the ground. 'Here looks good to me. Let the

frost take us, or the devil. I don't want to walk any further.'

He puts the luggage to one side and squats next to her, wrapping her icy hands in his to warm them.

'We have to keep moving.'

'We don't even know what we're moving toward.'

Laughter takes hold of her, and she pushes her nails deep into the skin of her stomach, struggling to breathe between stabs of hysteria. Falling to one side, she rubs her face in the earth, laughing.

Satori opens her luggage and stuffs as many of her clothes as possible into his satchel then slings it across his body. He bends down and lifts her up. Stumbling and tripping through the forest, he tries to find his way back to the cave or shelter before nightfall. Tears blur his vision. Star still chokes on her laughter and while the noise has grown softer, it is just as worrying.

By the time they reach the cave, it is too dark to find firewood. What little Satori had already collected quickly burns, and they huddle together for heat. Relief warms him when her laughter eventually stops, and she falls asleep.

It might be hours or minutes later when the violent shaking of her body wakes him. At first, he thinks she is having a fit, but it's a nightmare. She calls Raven's name, sobbing. He kisses her brow and holds her tighter. She seems to settle again, and they both fall back to sleep.

It is daylight when the frost nudges him into consciousness, and Star is no longer beside him. He rushes outside and scans the forest. Unable to see her, he shouts her name through the trees. He listens for laughter or crying but hears nothing as if the very air holds its breath. There are no sounds of animal or human life, and the wind is still.

He grabs the bag and walks downhill, cursing his lack of depth perception as he stumbles over the uneven ground. Five minutes later, he calls her name again. When the second attempt yields no success, he stops and closes his eyes. He clears his mind and her image forms. Opening his eyes, he walks toward her.

As he descends the steep, tree-covered slope, he sees remnants of her journey. Her jacket is caught in the branch of a tree, discarded like an old snakeskin. He untangles the garment and carries it. The ground evens out, and he spots a pile of black clothing. Light glints between the trees— a silver light that dances in his eye. He rushes to the loch.

Breaking the surface of the water is a black oval shape.

'Star,' he calls. 'Come back.'

She looks over her shoulder at him. 'I felt dirty.' There is the hint of hysteria in her tone.

'It's too cold, love,' he says. 'Please, come here. Let me dry you. We'll have breakfast.'

He dips his fingers into the water, and cold stabs his skin. He shakes his hand to stop the throbbing. She does not move; she just stands there in the freezing water, watching him.

'It's lovely,' she says. 'Why don't you join me?'

He closes his eyes and lays his palms on the water, willing it warm, but there is too much liquid, and each time he thinks his hands feel warmer, a new surge of icy aqua chills them again.

He gathers wood for a fire, aware that every moment could bring Star's final heartbeat. When the fire is lit, he strips, laying his clothes and hers beside the growing flames, then he steps into the water. The shock of it steals his breath, but he keeps moving toward her. When he can walk no further, he swims.

She tries to kiss him.

Grabbing her arm, knowing he is hurting her, he drags her back to the shore.

They sit beside the flames, shaking, unable to get warm or dry. She stares at him, but her eyes do not betray any emotion. He tries to dry her with his clothes as frost forms on her blue skin. Although she is still damp, he dresses her then dresses himself in his now wet shirt and trousers.

His teeth chatter so hard he fears they might shatter. Huddled in front of the flames, her face turns to him; her eyes judge him.

He is frightened to leave her to gather food, even though the sounds their stomachs make are now louder than the rushing of blood in his ears. He suggests she come with him, but she refuses.

So, he stays where he can see her and rummages. Although the leaves he finds taste bitter, they will sustain them for a while at least. He offers some to Star. She tastes the food and spits it into the fire. Trying to ignore the vicious flavour, he eats. He needs to stay strong for both of them.

'It's time to move, Star,' he says. 'We'll head for town. You can bathe in warm water, and we can go home.'

She nods. He fights back an urge to laugh. The relief is over-whelming. He throws earth on the flames and reaches for her hand. She stands up without his aid and walks away from him. He follows her.

The parade of two makes good time. When the mist falls, they are at the foot of the mountains in more varied woodland. Satori sees a cottage. Star walks past it, and he calls her back.

The roof is full of holes, and the door is ajar, but it is shelter for the night. The gelatinous darkness, smell of dust and damp seem to choke Star, and she coughs.

'We can go elsewhere if you prefer,' he tells her.

She does not answer. Already lying on the filthy floor, she turns away from him. He joins her, wrapping his limbs around her body and trying to keep them both warm.

CHAPTER FORTY-THREE

STAR LIES on the floor. Exhaustion overwhelms her. Hunger stabs at her belly. Her fingers and toes ache. She feels the weight of her leaden limbs dragging her body down, her mind follows, and sleep claims her.

She dreams of dancing in the nightclub. She whirls around the floor like a dervish, her hair and clothes whipping the air. She sees blurred faces as she spins. They seem familiar, but she doesn't want to stop moving to claim the image as a known. Her movements grow faster and faster until all is a swirl of darkness. She stops moving, but the darkness still moves around her.

Inside her womb, the child rotates. She watches it spin round and round. The umbilical cord connecting them never tangles. She holds her hand to the child. Despite its size, it seems perfectly formed. Not an embryo at all but a baby. Its eyelids and skin so translucent, she can see through them to the forming organs beneath. It opens its eyes and focuses on its mother. The green eyes are Lilith's. Star grasps its tiny reptilian fingers.

'Cut it out,' a voice whispers in her ear. She pulls back her hand and turns to see Raven beside her. Raven is remade, her face no longer smashed and torn but serene and peaceful.

'I'm sorry,' Star tells her.

Raven shakes her head. 'I'm happy now. Complete. You know what you must do,' she insists. 'That child cannot be born.'

'It's my baby,' Star says. 'I love it.'

'Cut it out,' another voice whispers.

She turns and sees the man she killed standing behind her.

'I thought you were going to kill me,' she says.

'No, you didnae,' he replies. 'But youse killed me anyway. I'm okay, though. I was lonely in life. I welcomed youse and the company youse offered, but I'm not lonely any longer. I'm free.'

'Cut it out,' says a third voice.

'Paul,' she says.

'Lilith is inside you. She will grow stronger. Cut out the evil while you still can.'

A chorus of voices rise to agree. A small, grey-haired man and three teenage boys join the throng.

'Cut it out. Cut it out. Cut it out.'

'Stop!' she screams.

She opens her eyes. Satori's limbs are still wrapped around her. She feels the weight of him and feels comforted.

Satori, no longer Steve to her. He has earned his name of power. *How many times has he saved me?*

She studies his face and the soft lashes that frame his dream-filled eyes, the gentle mouth that twitches in his sleep and the crop of hair on his chin. The scarlet scar along his cheek is already starting to heal. His is a face she has loved, maybe still does love.

He cannot save me.

They will not reach Paul's house.

Inching out from under his arm and leg, she moves slowly so as not to wake him. She hopes his are good dreams then wonders whether to leave him a note, but she is certain he will not understand. He thinks that forward is the only way to travel.

She heads out through the door. The full moon smiles at her. She feels approval in its silver rays. Gazing at Satori, she smiles, wishing there could be a way back for them.

She notices the bag next to his head and creeps across the room. The moon throws pools of light on the floor though the holes in the roof. She uses them to check her steps. Silently, she unbuckles his satchel. She leaves the clothes, his book and crystal ball, but takes the rest.

He doesn't need his map to find home from here.

She departs, blowing him a kiss from the doorway.

The wind has picked up. Trees whisper to her as she walks between them. They want to know what she will do. She feels lighter than air, dancing in the dark to the music, which fills her head. Her soundtrack has not deserted her.

The forest becomes darker as she heads toward the foot of the mountain. Trees jostle together for attention and pine needles scratch her face. A carpet of moss cushions her steps. The ground starts its incline. She throws back her head, hoping to see the mountain peak but perspective has hidden it, and her attempts just make her feel dizzy and nauseous.

'Are you here?' she asks.

'Yessss,' they answer.

'Is there no other way?' she whispers, her voice broken with tears.

'Noooo,' they reply.

They surround her, red eyes glowing in the dark. Their mouths, full of blood, gape at her. Twisted bodies struggle to stay upright. She knows she must pay for their suffering or risk causing more but she feels afraid— afraid of the night, of joining them forever, of being alone.

Tears sting her eyes. She nods and sits on the ground. Life weaves its way from the crushed moss beneath her and investigates her purpose. Spider legs and insects tickle across her skin.

Placing the atlas to one side, she looks at the other item. It is beautiful. Even in the dark, the jewels glow with colour. The object that released Lilith will release her as well.

The curves of the blade look like water. It will cleanse her.

It has been so long since she said a prayer. *Would it be right to say one now?*

Words struggle to form in her mind.

I have witnessed so many wonders. Who would listen? Who would care?

Music fills her head. She smiles and nods.

'Deliver me,' she whispers as she plunges the blade into her womb and twists it.

Hot blood covers her hands.

At first, she feels no pain then the burning of it rushes along nerve endings and neurons to overwhelm her. She falls backward onto the moss. Her body twists, and she stares at the jewelled hilt of the knife. She hears a voice and wonders whether her saviour is coming to deliver her.

'Star,' it shouts.

It is getting louder. *Maybe it's almost here.* It is hard to tell over the scream of her dying mind and the music, which fills it— her requiem.

A shadow eclipses the moon. She struggles to focus and sees Satori's face above her.

'Forgive me, Satori,' she whispers.

'The fault is mine, my love,' he answers. He wraps his hand around her numb fingers, but she cannot feel the pressure of his touch. 'There's nothing to forgive.'

'I should have believed you.'

'I should have protected you.'

'I love you, Satori,' she says. 'I always have.'

'I love you, too. I will see you again. I'll find you, and we can be together.'

She smiles at his words, believing them to be true and closes her eyes.

THE END

ABOUT THE AUTHOR

Carmilla Voiez is a British horror and fantasy writer living in Scotland. Her influences include Graham Masterton, Thomas Ligotti, and Clive Barker. She is pansexual and passionate about intersectional feminism and human rights.

Carmilla has a First-Class Bachelor's degree in Creative Writing and Linguistics.

Her work includes stories in horror anthologies published by Crystal Lake Publishing, Clash Books and Mocha Memoirs. She co-authored a Southern Gothic Horror novel with Faith Marlow and has self-published two graphic novels with art by Anna Prashkovich.

Graham Masterton described the second book in her Starblood Trilogy as a "compelling story in a hypnotic, distinctive voice that brings her eerie world vividly to life".

Her books are both extraordinarily personal and universally challenging. In the words of Jef Rouner (Houston Press): "You do not read her books, you survive them."
Carmilla is also a freelance editor and mentor who enjoys making language sing.

www.carmillavoiez.com